WAYWARD SON

ALSO BY STEVE GOBLE

Ed Runyon Mysteries

City Problems

Spider John Mysteries

The Bloody Black Flag

The Devil's Wind

A Bottle of Rum

Pieces of Eight

WAYWARD SON

AN ED RUNYON MYSTERY

STEVE GOBLE

OCEANVIEW PUBLISHING
SARASOTA, FLORIDA

This book is a work of fiction. Names, characters, businesses, organizations, places, and incidents either are the products of the author's imagination or are used fictitiously. Any resemblance to actual events, businesses, locales, or persons living or dead, is entirely coincidental.

ISBN 978-1-60809-445-5

Published in the United States of America by Oceanview Publishing

Sarasota, Florida

www.oceanviewpub.com

10 9 8 7 6 5 4 3 2 1

PRINTED IN THE UNITED STATES OF AMERICA

For Phil Huss,
and all the other cops who do the job the right way

CHAPTER ONE

THE PHONE BUZZED again, for the thirteenth time in the last hour.

The boy did not want to look. It would just be more of the same. More threats, more pressure, more demands.

He wanted to ignore it, as he had the last few. But they kept coming, and he knew they would keep coming. Relentless.

He'd blocked number after number, but that didn't stop the threats. The asshole just texted from a new number and started up again. Blocking was pointless.

Sticking the phone into his pocket, he peeked out into the hall and was relieved to find no one was around. He'd lost track of time, but Mom and Dad were still at work. *Thank God.*

He closed the door and put his head against it.

Stupid, stupid, stupid.

He was not accustomed to being stupid, and he hated it. He realized, on some level, that he wasn't stupid. His mind was simply numb with fear. He had too much to worry about. And he was not in control of the situation.

He was nowhere near being in control.

That was an unusual feeling, too. He was a rational person, accustomed to looking at things objectively and finding the best path forward.

That certainly is not what I'm doing now, he thought.

The boy shook. He paced. He wiped sweaty palms on his jeans. He wished he was a year older, so he could just get in the car and drive, drive, drive.

The phone buzzed yet again.

"Jesus," he muttered, then he pulled the phone from his pocket and screamed at it. "Leave me alone!" His own voice startled him. *What if one of the neighbors heard that? Get a grip!*

He paced some more, then stopped. He was standing in front of the bookshelf, looking at the Holy Bible. Eyes closed, head lowered, he began to pray. "Help me, Lord. What am I going to do?"

He steeled himself, then unlocked the phone with a touch of his finger.

Another message arrived before he could even look at the previous ones. He opened the messages—all from the same person, as he knew they would be—and decided to just delete them, unread.

But he did not do that. He looked at them.

ARE U HIDING? WHY U DON'T ANSWER?

"Jesus," the boy muttered, pacing again.

He read more.

"This is no game! You know that I am serious, do u not? You need to know I am no way playing games with you!!! I will absolutely ruin your life! I swear on my mother's breast I will destroy your entire life if you ignore me!!!!!"

That message included a picture. It was an image the boy had seen before and never wanted to see again.

It was a picture of himself. It was not a photo that would make his parents proud.

The boy stopped pacing, closed his eyes, and thought as hard as he could. His tormenter was right about one thing. This wasn't a game, he knew that. He wished it were a game. The boy was good at games, and wanted to think of this horrible situation as a game, because he was good at games and it was his move.

He glanced at the chessboard on his desk.

He needed a plan. He was good at plans, good at tactics, good at escaping traps. Ask anyone he'd ever played chess against. Or anyone he'd ever played Dungeons & Dragons with, for that matter.

He sat at his desk, staring at the board and the few scattered pieces and pawns. It was not a game in progress. It was a puzzle he'd found online. White to mate in three moves.

He'd been working on the puzzle before the new torrent of messages had started flying at him, and now he was trying to distract himself with it. The key, he was certain, was Black's knight. The entire defense depended on that well-positioned knight. He needed to force Black to move it. Then he could pounce.

It took him a few minutes, during which he stared at the black-and-white squares and ignored the rest of the world. Then, it all clicked into place.

The boy slid his rook to the right, but he stopped short of checking the king. It seemed counterintuitive, but chess was like that sometimes. The move that looks good is not always the move that is good, and a good move is not always the best move.

The boy nodded. He'd done it. Suddenly, the only piece Black could legally move was that pesky knight, because any other move would result in a check against Black's king. It did not matter where Black moved the knight. All that mattered was that he had to move it, or resign.

He popped Black's knight, which no longer guarded the crucial square, over to a new square. Then he knocked over a pawn with his own White queen.

Checkmate was now inevitable.

The phone buzzed again. Another text message:

ANSWER ME GODDAMN IT!

The boy shook. He felt trapped, just like Black's king. He needed a good move.

He dropped to his knees and prayed again, dropping the phone on the carpet beside him. It buzzed three more times before he was finished, but he fought hard to keep that from distracting him. Prayer was very important, and he had practiced setting other things aside while talking to God his entire life.

As always, prayer helped. By the time he stood up, he'd come to a decision.

He picked up the phone and deleted all the unwanted messages. Then he rose, quickly, and grabbed his ball cap.

The boy looked in the mirror and nodded. He had concocted a bold plan—and a risky one.

Sometimes, the move that looks bad is the best move.

"You can do this," he whispered to himself.

He glanced at the clock and realized his window of opportunity was very, very narrow.

"Shit!"

Planning time had ended. It was time to move.

He started tapping out a message of his own.

CHAPTER TWO

I DIDN'T PUNCH Tom Pickett in the face when I saw him, but it definitely crossed my mind. He had a punchable face. As he navigated his way through the crowded German Village deli, that face flashed miniature sneers and eye rolls whenever he spotted a nose ring or a heavily tattooed arm or foreign garb. He looked as though he was trying to avoid inhaling.

"Are you Runyon?"

No hello, no outstretched hand. He'd just meandered between the tables and walked right to me, and asked his question while my mouth was full of corned beef, slaw, and grilled pumpernickel. If you go to Katzinger's, get a sandwich on grilled pumpernickel. You can thank me later.

I'd told Pickett to look for a fairly big fellow wearing a black coat and a Willie Nelson ball cap. I hadn't thought to tell him to show some manners. You shouldn't have to tell people that, but . . . this is the world we live in.

I swallowed my bite of sandwich and took a swig of pop before speaking. "That's me. Ed Runyon, private investigator." I pointed to the empty seat opposite me. "You must be Tom Pickett." I did not extend a hand, either.

After he'd contacted me, I'd looked into his situation a little and I had already formed some tentative conclusions. I had a feeling Pickett was about to confirm them. That was no big deal for me. I had other things to accomplish on this trip to my favorite neighborhood in Columbus, so it was not going to be a wasted day even if this interview proved to be a bust.

The next few moments, though? Probably wasted. Oh, well. Private investigators waste a lot of time. I get calls from people who think their neighbors are aiming microwave beams at their brains. So . . .

Pickett didn't have a tray of food, but I figured that was his loss. I don't know how anyone walks into Katzinger's, sees that array of beef and pork and cheeses and chicken and salami and pastrami and desserts and all that, and does not place an order. The aromas of delicious food and spices just permeate the place. I'd picked this spot for the giant grilled sandwiches and the big garlic pickles. If the aromas didn't entice this guy to grab a bite to eat, well, there's no accounting for taste.

My opinion of Tom Pickett continued to nose-dive.

Anyway, I'd picked this spot for the food, not because I thought this was going to be a productive meeting.

I'd been a cop for a while, before going into the PI game, and I'd learned to sum people up quickly. Sometimes you just know. But I was going to be professional about this, because sometimes gut instinct is wrong. I'd learned that as a cop, too. So instead of telling him to go away, I decided to listen to his story.

I had not wanted to even talk to Pickett in the first place, but my fledgling private investigator business was not exactly taking wing. Maybe Linda was right, and trying to run a private investigation agency out of a rented trailer in the woods was a stupid idea. She seemed to have the notion that I was destined to wind up on the streets, begging for dimes and crumbs, if I didn't start drumming up paying clients.

I could see where she was coming from. I'd had plenty of prospects turn out to be shit, and I had a feeling this was going to be another one, but I needed to hear the guy out because I could use the work.

This visit to Columbus was about a missing wife case. So far, I'd only conversed with Pickett, the potential client, in a chat box on my agency website. I'd tried to discern some genuine concern from him among the misspelled words and atrocious grammatical errors in his messages, but damned if I could. Further investigation on my part had turned up nothing promising.

I'd decided to see him anyway, at Linda's urging. She wanted my new agency to prosper. And it gave me a good excuse to leave Mifflin County for a day and take care of another matter, one that interested me far more than Tom Pickett's problems. The side mission wasn't going to put any money in my pockets, either, but it was going to tilt the scales of justice a little bit in the direction I thought they should go. No need for Linda to know about that, though. A man has to have secrets, sometimes.

Pickett sat. "Yes. Thanks for meeting me," he said. He stared at me for a heartbeat. "You look like that guy in the movie."

I was sure he was referring to the late Heath Ledger. I'd heard that several times before, that I kind of look like him. I don't really think the comparison is apt. He was much better looking than me. But what the hell. "Yeah, the Joker, right?"

He sneered. "I mean the fucking gay cowboy." He rolled his eyes and did a little dance in his seat. I suppose it was meant to be a gay dance, whatever the fuck that is. His antics drew some stares from the people around us, and my opinion of Tom Pickett tunneled a little closer to the center of the Earth.

"Same guy," I said. I began thinking I could save a lot of time if I just started hating Pickett now.

Pickett was taller than me, but thinner, and his face was red from the early January air that frosted the deli windows and turned the few passers-by into sidewalk ghosts. He had a fat nose, and a perpetual air of distaste.

"You want to order a sandwich?" I hefted mine. "They're really good."

He looked around. "Not my kind of food."

"Well, that's up to you, I guess. I'm going to finish mine."

He nodded. "So, do you think you can find my wife?"

I swallowed, then answered him. "Maybe. Tell me again how she vanished?" I took a sip of Mountain Dew.

"Just up and gone. Been two goddamn weeks."

"I know you contacted the police."

"Yeah, lazy fuckers. Didn't do a damned thing."

I nodded. I'd talked to a cop about Pickett's situation already, but I wanted to hear what this guy had to say. I was willing to wait and see if the data confirmed my preconceived notions about him. "Did the police say why they weren't interested in your case?"

"Said she's an adult, she can do what she wants, some shit like that." Pickett laughed bitterly. "Adult. My Jackie, an adult. Anyway, they shuffled some papers around and sent out some bulletins or whatnot, but I'm pretty damned sure that's about all they did. That's why I contacted you."

I looked at him, trying to find some sign that he was actually worried about his Jackie, but not seeing one. "Were there signs of foul play? Broken lock, scattered furniture, bloodstains, anything like that?"

"No."

"Was she having an affair? Or maybe, someone wanted to fool around with her?"

"No, man," he said. "I never left her enough daylight to fuck around on me, you know? She just up and left, like I said."

"She took her clothes?"

"Yeah, some of them."

I considered that. "Cellphone, personal items, etcetera?"

"Yeah, all gone."

"But she doesn't answer when you call her."

He sneered. "Hell, no."

"Is she active on social media? Chatting with people there?"

"I ain't got time for that shit. I don't know what she does on there."

I could empathize with that, at least. I tried to avoid that shit, too. But if I was looking for someone, or worried about them, I'd have been checking that out. "Does Jackie have a car?"

"No, she don't drive."

I nodded. "Have any of her friends or family been calling you, looking for her?"

He shook his head, and frowned as though I'd asked him to calculate the amount of dark matter in the universe. "No one called me at all."

That was another data point. The picture was starting to coalesce in my mind.

I asked: "I assume you've called them? Her friends and family, I mean."

He smirked. "Of course, I did! Do you think I'm an idiot?"

I did, to be honest, but it seemed the wrong moment to tell him, so I kept my mouth shut.

He continued. "They don't tell me shit."

I nodded. "She ever do this before? Disappear like this?"

"Hell, no." He stared at me. "She stayed home, like she was supposed to."

"Until she didn't," I replied.

"Exactly."

I stopped looking into his eyes and took another bite of my sandwich. Once I'd swallowed that, I looked into his eyes again. Still no worry there. No hint that he feared his Jackie might be stretched out dead in an alley somewhere, or locked away in a rapist's basement, or selling her body to strangers, or wrapped in chains at the bottom of the Olentangy River. Nothing like that at all.

"So, Mr. Pickett, I have to say, you do not seem to be too concerned about her welfare. Don't you think maybe she's in some sort of trouble?"

He shook his head, and glanced away, sneering just a little, peering outside at the pedestrians. "I think the bitch just got up and left."

"Can't say as I blame her."

His head snapped back toward me, like a turret on a tank, so hard I thought it might cause swelling. His angry eyes stared at me. "What?"

"I'm not surprised she left. You aren't worried about her; you're just pissed off that she defied you. Go find her yourself, if you can. I'm not interested."

He shook his head. "Jesus. Just like the cops. Can't a man look for his wife if she runs out?"

"Sure, you can," I said. "But I don't have to help you."

He stared at me. I stared at him. It was not a bonding moment.

"You can go now," I said, then took a bite of pickle. I made sure my eyes looked their meanest when I took that bite.

"Look, man, I've got money and I can pay you. You're a detective, right? So work for me."

I shook my head. "I don't know how long you've been married, but I haven't known you five minutes yet and I'm already sick of you. I imagine it was way worse for her." I realized my attitude was not going to help Whiskey River Investigations become a going concern, but I at least had a good sandwich thanks to my own foresight. So that was something. And I still had that other chore, the one I had not mentioned to Linda because she'd have tried to talk me out of it.

I continued my impromptu dissertation. "I talked to local cops about you already, and they have been to your place a time or two."

"Cops," he snorted. "Lazy asses, never listen to me. She's not the angel, you know."

I waved a hand to shut him up. "I'm going to side with the cops on this one. You just strike me as the kind of guy a woman would get tired of, and a smart woman would not tell you where she was going." I'd been a sheriff's detective for a few years, and a New York cop before that, before deciding to chase potential clients away from my own private detective agency. I'd met hundreds of "that kind of guy."

"You don't know shit, Runyon. Fuck you."

"Say that again and I'll make you eat a chair." I winked. I wasn't really going to do that, of course. I couldn't afford to pay Katzinger's for any damages at the moment. But I did my best to make him believe it.

I must have succeeded. Tom Pickett did not say it again. He got up and left.

I grinned between bites. The little interview was not going to put money into my coffers, but it had me primed for my next task, the one that was, frankly, more important to me. I was going to need a little belligerent attitude for that job, and the slight dose of adrenaline from pissing off Tom Pickett wasn't going to hurt, either.

I finished my meal, got a pastrami-and-salami concoction without slaw to go for Linda, and stepped out into the chilly morning air. My new truck, well, new to me, that is, was parked a couple of blocks away on a brick-paved side street because that's just how German Village is. You go there, you park in the first spot you find, and expect to walk a bit.

I walked past a couple of art galleries, a lawyer's office, at least three BMWs, and even a PT Cruiser. I wished I had time to dash into the Book Loft, an amazing store with a labyrinth of small rooms full of books, but I was on a mission.

A few people on the sidewalks nodded or said hi before passing me by, and everyone's breath sent little ghosts of steam lifting into the air. We all were walking briskly, to combat the cold, but German Village is a fun place to be so we all were in good, friendly moods, hence the greetings to strangers.

I turned down a narrow side street toward the used, gray F-150 I'd bought to replace my older model that had been shot up pretty bad last fall when I was still a public servant. I liked the new truck, but I missed the old one. In the old one, I knew right where my CDs were stored and could get at them and pop them into the player without looking. I was still developing that muscle memory with this vehicle. Oh, well. Things change.

I told my phone to call Hippie Angel. After a few rings, Linda picked up.

"How did it go?" She sounded way too perky for someone who knew how badly my business efforts were going. She'd seen projections of my bottom line. I suspected she was trying to sound more upbeat than she felt.

"The potential client was an asshole," I said.

"Was?"

"Yeah. Well, he's still an asshole, but he's not a client."

"Ed."

I sighed. I could see her cute scowl in my mind, framed by long and curly red hair and probably accompanied by a middle finger. "Yeah, I know. But he's not looking for his wife because she got into some bad shit or because he thinks she was abducted by terrorists or aliens or anything. He's just pissed at her for leaving and he wants a chance to put her in her place."

"Are you sure?"

"I was a cop, remember? Yeah, I'm sure. I've met worried men. He's not one of them. My guess is he wants her back so he can whop her with a belt, and I am not going to help him do that."

"OK," she said. There was an audible sigh. "But you need to generate some real business."

"I know. Just not with assholes."

"Asshole money spends as well as any other money."

"I'm doing OK. Haven't depleted all my unused vacation money from the sheriff's office."

"You will one day, Ed. Probably soon."

"Yeah," I answered. "So, I'll find me a couple of non-asshole clients who don't want to beat their wives and then I'll have income. How is your day going?"

"Grading essays," she said. She did not sound excited about it. "The one I'm reading now is an analysis of *Babbit*."

"Why the fuck does a high school kid read Sinclair Lewis?"

"Hell if I know." She sighed. "Probably recommended by Miss Deal in the library. She likes that stuff. I mean, it's a great book, I guess, but not when you're a sixteen-year-old alive now and not way back then."

"No explosions, either, I'll bet."

She chuckled. "Not that I recall. But . . . anyway. I've been reading these papers and looking at the news. Did you know there is a blogger in China who says some damned virus is going to kill us all?"

"Uh, no. I have not heard that at all."

"A friend told me about it and I've been reading it between papers. It's a potential pandemic, this blogger says—I mean global. Nothing the world has seen before. We're all gonna die. I keep going back and forth, reading a student paper then checking this blog, then another paper, then back to the blog. Ugh. I am not sure which is more depressing, to be honest, this oncoming world disaster or the apparent illiteracy of most of my students. It is not doing my attitude any good, I tell you."

"Well, if we can set aside gloom and doom for the moment, your day is going to get better. I'm bringing you a sandwich. From Katzinger's."

"Ooooooh, yummy! Bring it to my place."

"I was hoping you'd come to mine," I said. My place, a pond-side trailer in the remote woods, had all my Willie Nelson and Waylon Jennings and New Grass Revival tunes, and I had a damn fine set of speakers. At Linda's, it's mostly hard rock and progressive stuff. She has good speakers, too, but what the hell good is that if you use them to play King Crimson? I'd suggested more than once we could stream some of my music at her place, but she seemed to think it would melt her speakers. And there was no way I was allowing her stuff at my little hideaway. No no no. It would scare the wildlife. So we ended up listening to the Grateful Dead and the Beatles a lot, because we both liked that stuff. But sometimes, I just need to hear a mandolin or Willie's voice.

"I'm not coming over there until you get a vacuum cleaner that works, Ed. Too much dust. And your bathroom is too small. Can't sit down properly. Also, disinfectant wipes. They're a thing. You should check into that."

"I'm out in the woods. Just go outside and squat if you need to pee."

"Um, no. I am not a raccoon, or a squirrel, or whatever. Bring me my sandwich."

I sighed. "On my way. It's going to be a little while, though. I have a stop to make."

I knew at once that was a tactical error, because Linda is not stupid.

She was silent for a moment before continuing. "What stop? You are not going to . . ."

She knew damned well what stop.

"Just something I gotta do. I'm at the truck now. I'm going to drive instead of talk."

"Ed, damn it, Tuck asked you to mind your own business. Don't even think about it. Just come on back."

"These little brick streets are really narrow, Linda. I need two hands to navigate the truck. Talk to you soon."

"Dial down the testosterone, you dumbass."

She hung up.

I slid into the truck and popped her sandwich into the cooler on the seat next to me, then fired up the engine. I turned on some Bocephus at low volume while I navigated my rusty, trusty new-to-me truck out of German Village, thankful that the chill had kept most people indoors. German Village's brick-paved streets are narrow enough without having to deal with other drivers.

Once I was headed north on asphalt, I contemplated my arrival back in Mifflin County. It would likely be a cold welcome. I should not have mentioned my errand to Linda, and I realized now the sandwich was not going to mollify her. Simply put, she did not approve of my planned stop.

I was going to beat the shit out of a guy.

CHAPTER THREE

ABOUT FORTY MINUTES later, I was halfway between the state capital and my home in Mifflin County, working slowly down a meandering two-lane road bordered by skeletal trees frosted with a thin layer of snow. I slowed down once for a doe who stared at me from a vacant field, but she made no sudden moves.

I'd found my quarry's home and knocked on the door, but no one was there. He had one of those fancy doorbells with a camera and microphone, but I'd decided not to leave a message. The only words I had for the son of a bitch were going to be delivered face-to-face. And probably would be preceded by my fist.

The house, a simple ranch with a barn serving as a garage, was in the middle of nowhere, so surveillance was not a real option for me. There is a very limited number of reasons to park on a country road. I thought about the old "my truck is having problems" gambit, but there was really no good place within sight of the house where I could do that without also impeding traffic. I didn't need someone rounding the bend and swerving to avoid my truck while it was mostly off the road, and mostly was about as far off the road as it was possible to get here. There were no neighbors around, so I couldn't park in someone's driveway and then knock on nearby doors and pretend I wanted to tell people about Jesus or sell raffle tickets as an excuse to stay within sight of my quarry's place.

I'd thought about just waiting in his driveway, but had decided against it. His high-tech doorbell may have notified him when I'd knocked, so he'd possibly already seen my face on his smartphone. If I waited around after finding no one about, it might spook him and put him on edge. I didn't want him having time to think.

Donnor Brogan was likely to be the suspicious type.

Donnor Brogan was a cop.

So, my plan was to make a couple of trips up and down the road and hope to be passing by once Deputy Brogan got home. If that happened, the next steps were crystal clear. I'd pull in, walk up to him slowly with a big smile, and tell him I was a detective with a few questions about a guy he'd pulled over a week ago.

Then I'd sucker punch him, grab him by the collar, and smash his fucking face against any handy hard object—a vehicle, that barn, the driveway gravel, whatever. Improvising can be fun.

After gaining his full and undivided attention, I would deliver a little lecture about not roughing up a guy during a traffic stop. I'd ask a few pointed questions, too. Did it make you feel like a man when you smacked his head against his car? Did you really think speeding was probable cause for a frisk? Did the gentle soul you'd pulled over give you any goddamned reason at all to rough him up?

And, of course, I'd ask one more question: Did you enjoy beating on him because he's black?

I had not been there when Brogan had pulled Tuck over, of course, but I knew my friend. By his account, he'd complied with everything the deputy ordered, including getting out of the car. I've been pulled over for speeding a few times in my life. I've never once been told to exit the vehicle. Maybe that's because I'm white.

Tuck said he had complied, but he had also asked why he'd been told to get out. Brogan didn't like that, apparently. Some cops don't like anything that resembles questioning their authority. That's the moment the deputy turned Tuck around roughly and shoved him against the car. That had busted Tuck's nose. He'd had to drive himself to the ER, one hand on the steering wheel and another holding a handkerchief to his face to stop the blood. That image had filled my mind many times ever since he'd told me about it, and it made me want to break things inside Donnor Brogan.

A therapist once told me I do not deal with anger well. She probably was right. I did not care at the moment.

Tuck said he had offered no resistance, and had done everything he was supposed to do. I believe him. I've seen my friend around law enforcement officers a few times, and he's described his strategy for such encounters at length many times. We have long talks, Tuck and I. Tuck goes automatically polite around cops, deferential as hell, and says life trained him to be that way. I had no doubt at all that Tuck had said and done nothing, absolutely nothing, to prompt the busted nose Brogan had given him. It just wasn't Tuck's way to provoke anyone, and it sure as hell was not his way to provoke a cop.

My truck's speakers were blaring New Grass Revival singing "this ain't police business up on White Oak Hill tonight." The guys in the song were hunting a fellow named Colly Davis, to avenge their dead cousin. I nodded, feeling a common bond with the guys depicted in the lyrics. I wasn't engaged in police business, either. I didn't plan to go as far as Sally Jean's avenging cousins—I wouldn't need to dig a shallow grave—but I might break a bone or two.

I turned off the music as I rounded the bend and approached Brogan's house again. The barn was no longer empty. A bright, shiny black-and-red Ram truck was just backing into it. It had to be a new model. It was a massive Texas wet dream of a truck, with custom everything—giant wheels, huge fog lamps, even a set of longhorns mounted up front, across the hood, ready to take down any matador who happened to be standing in the road.

My truck has a CD player.

Brogan stopped and climbed out of his vehicle, then went to get something out of the bed. I recognized him from my online research. He'd been Deputy of the Year three years ago, after finding a lot of weed growing between cornfields. He had a shaved head and weightlifter's shoulders, and a lower jaw that jutted enough to make a tempting target.

I made a mental note to avoid slamming his head on the truck's horns. I wasn't out to kill him, after all. I was just going to make sure he hurt. A lot.

I was slowing down when my phone buzzed.

It was Tuck.

I answered and tried to sound like I was doing something boring. "Hey, buddy."

"Don't 'hey buddy' me, Ed. Linda told me what you are doing. I thought we agreed you would keep your nose out of it?"

"You and Linda agreed. I sort of grunted noncommittally."

"I don't need you doing this white knight shit, Ed. I never should've even told you about it."

"I'd have pieced things together once I saw your busted nose," I said. "I'm a detective."

Tuck started yelling, a torrent too hot and fast for my phone speaker to handle. He's polite to everyone, but sometimes he vents at me. To be fair, I usually deserve it.

I pulled my truck, rust and all, into Brogan's driveway. My quarry stepped away from his much nicer and newer truck with two plastic bags of groceries dangling from his hands. He looked at me, and his face automatically went to that default "don't fuck with me" law officer face. He seemed the type to practice that in the mirror.

"I gotta get go, Tuck."

"Look, Ed, I don't want you hurting this guy or him hurting you because of me, damn it. Understand?"

I shut off my engine. "I won't get hurt. You've seen me fight."

"Damn it, Ed. This is not a good thing, man. Think about it."

"Thinking slows me down. Bye." I put my phone in my pocket and got out of the truck.

Brogan stepped out of the barn. His jacket was open, despite the chill. I could not tell from a distance whether he wore a shoulder holster, but it was a pretty good bet that he did. Cops who rough up black guys on traffic stops for no good reason probably don't ever get too far away from their guns. I was glad his hands were full.

"Can I help you?" Those were his actual words. The tone said, "Who the hell are you and what do you want? And I'll shoot you if I don't like the answer."

The passenger door of his truck opened. A blonde girl, maybe seven or eight years old, hopped out. She was paying attention to her phone, and smiling big.

"Fuck." I'd muttered that under my breath. Then, louder, I added, "Colly Davis live here?"

Brogan shook his head. "No. Never heard of him."

"No? Is this White Oak Hill Road?" I looked around as though I was confused. It was easy, because I was confused. I had all this adrenaline built up so I could smack this asshole around as payback for roughing up my friend, and now I had Tuck's anger swirling in my head and this cute little girl bouncing around laughing because she apparently was winning some sort of game on her phone. None of this was going according to plan.

I wasn't going to beat up the man in front of his kid. Was I?

Nah. I didn't want to traumatize a child. She probably had no idea what a racist asshole her dad was. At least, I hoped that was the case. Maybe he was teaching her to be a racist asshole, too. I don't know. It's a weird planet we live on.

"I never heard of White Oak Hill Road," Brogan said, sternly. "You're lost."

I laughed. "Yeah, I guess I am." I dug my phone out of my pocket and pretended to poke around on a map. Instead, I snapped a picture of his truck and license plate. "Let me see where I went wrong. Yeah, I took a wrong turn."

"OK. It happens." He still sounded pretty pissed off, but he wasn't dropping groceries and reaching for a gun, so, that was good.

The little girl waved at me. "Hi!"

I waved. "Sorry." She seemed nice. I hoped her dad would not teach her to be a racist asshole.

I went back to my truck.

CHAPTER FOUR

LINDA WAS SCOWLING. "You didn't, did you?"

"I didn't."

She sighed. "Good. That would have been stupid. I know the guy is an ass, but I'm glad you didn't go all hothead and pick a fight."

"Oh, I was fully prepared to leave some permanent scars, but the son of a bitch was saved by a little girl."

"What?"

I closed the door behind me and left the chill out there with the broad lawn, the twin oaks, the stacked firewood under the porch roof, and the white picket fence. Linda Scott had the small farm all to herself now, because her parents were seeing America in a Winnebago. "He had a kid with him, probably a daughter. I decided not to bust dad's face while his kid was watching, because I'm trying to be a role model for the youth of America."

"My hero," Linda said, shaking her head. Her tone did not make me feel like Superman.

I stepped over to the fireplace, enjoying the warmth. "I'm sure the girl goes to school sometimes or her bastard dad goes to bars or someplace else. Justice can still be done; punches can still be thrown. I'll just have to be patient and pick my moment."

"Or," she said, stretching the word out like a trombone slide, "you could do what Tuck asks and not get involved. The world will go on spinning just the same whether you go playing avenger or not."

I hoisted the sandwich. "For you."

She clapped her hands and almost jumped out of the recliner, but she toppled some kid's essay onto the floor. "Shit. Can you put it in the fridge? And bring back a couple of beers, please."

"Absolutely."

"And don't go thinking a sandwich gets you out of trouble."

"Of course not."

She leaned down to pick up the spilled papers, and I got a peek down inside her Led Zeppelin T-shirt before a curtain of long red hair blocked the view. I sighed, because my impatience with Linda's many helpful questions and suggestions concerning my fledgling PI business—and regarding some dark mental places I'd only recently climbed out of—meant our on-and-off relationship was currently off, and that meant the T-shirt was going to stay on. I was going to need that beer.

I hung my jacket in the closet, steered clear of the Christmas tree that was still up because it had not yet started shedding needles, and headed toward the kitchen. "Should you drink when you are grading papers?"

"I should always drink when grading papers. They should instruct every teacher to drink heavily when grading papers. Especially a teacher dumb enough to assign papers she'd have to grade over the weekend. And I am so far behind, thanks to the Distraction Demon from Hell." She pointed at her phone on the side table.

"Picking fights on Twitter again?" I pushed at the kitchen door.

"No," she yelled. "Lesson learned on that! Been reading a blog, though, the one I told you about, with the virus thing. Woman says she works in medical research and there is some damned virus coming that's gonna wipe us all out."

I popped her sandwich into the fridge and grabbed beers while she continued her account. "The world is not ready for it, this blogger says."

"We'll cope." I returned to the front room.

She looked up at me. "Thank you for not picking a fight with a cop. Even on Tuck's behalf. Ever since that poor PI got killed . . ."

That "poor PI" was a guy named Parker, who'd been in the Ohio news for a while after he was found dead in an abandoned grain silo, gnawed by feral cats. That had happened far from here, but it was a gory tale and it had spread across the state, probably farther. Linda had read those horrific accounts, so her well-wishes for my fledgling detective agency were mingled with fears that I'd be eaten by cats and desires that I'd learn to sell insurance instead. Linda worries a lot.

"Parker didn't get killed because he was a PI," I answered. "He got killed because he pissed off the wrong people trying to make money on the side. If he had a brain, he'd still be alive, and not so cat-chewed."

She shook her head. "Sometimes, Ed . . ."

Linda had organized her stuff by the time I handed her a Commodore Perry IPA. We clinked our bottles together. "Here's to another banner day for Whiskey River Investigations," I said.

She took a swig of beer. "At least you didn't put that cop in a hospital. Don't go looking for him again, either. I mean, he deserves it, don't get me wrong, anyone who would slam Tuck into a car deserves an ass-whooping, but, well, you know what I mean."

I didn't know what she meant, but I nodded as though I did. I plunked my ass onto the sofa and took a long drink.

"If you are going to be a PI, you ought to be in Columbus, or Cleveland," she said, reiterating something she'd said a few times before. "I don't want you to move away or anything, believe me, but I don't know why you think you can run a private investigator business from your little rented trailer in the woods. There is zero money coming in, Ed."

"I like my little rented trailer in the woods. I like my pond. I like eating fish from my pond. I like watching Cooper's hawks swooping low among the bushes trying to catch a rabbit off guard."

She sighed. "Do you like paying the bills?"

"No. I hate bills. But I don't need to move. I am only an hour away from two big cities full of clogged highways and murderers. I can go there when I need to and relax in my hideaway when I can afford it."

She got up, and began pacing. "I know you hate the city. New York was a nightmare. I get it."

Nightmare is right. I'd gone to New York City because the woman I was dating at the time had taken a legal internship there. A few years later, I was a junior detective earning next to nothing and she was screwing some rich lawyer. I hated the city, especially the way cases and calls piled up faster than we could really handle them. There are other things I hate about New York, but I try not to think of those things. Those things give me nightmares.

Now, I rent a trailer from an older couple who used to let their kids use it when they visited. When I step out of it in the morning, I see clear pond water, tall trees, soaring hawks, and not much of anything else. Everything smells like woods. It's bliss.

And I was not going to move to the city. "I have a website, and that works whether I am in the city or not. I get calls."

She laughed. "Whiskey River Investigations. Dumb name."

"It's named for a Willie song."

"Yeah. I know. Makes you sound like a drinker."

We raised our bottles and took big swigs.

"How many papers do you have to grade?"

She sighed. "A lot. I'm not at peak efficiency."

I sighed, too, and rose from the sofa. "OK. I'll let you get back to it. Tomorrow is Saturday. How about a night out? Somewhere nice. We can run up to Cleveland, maybe catch some music somewhere. Live music is the best. I don't mind going to the city if I can get out right away and go back home, you know."

Linda started pacing again, then stopped and flashed the beautiful green eyes at me. "I have a date, Ed."

It took me seven or eight seconds to come up with my brilliant rejoinder. "Oh."

"Yeah." She extended her arms and spun around slowly. "I don't want to sound conceited or anything, but take a look, will ya?"

I took a look. I enjoyed it quite a bit.

"I get noticed, Ed. And I notice back, sometimes."

"Absolutely, sure. I understand."

"And if I'm lucky I might even find someone who doesn't clam up and run away anytime the conversation turns to anything important."

I closed my eyes. "Now, wait a minute."

"Maybe that was uncalled for, I guess."

I looked at her and sighed. "No. It's fair. Enjoy your date. Anyone I know?"

She shook her head. "Sam Briggs. New history teacher. Started this year."

I nodded. "I hope you have a good time."

She looked forlorn, so I turned toward the closet to get my jacket. I saw my bowling ball bag in there, too, and pulled it out. "So, my weekend won't have to be a complete loss. I'll go bowling."

"Ed . . ."

"It's OK. Look, I'm sorry if I seem—"

My phone dinged, the special tone indicating someone had made an inquiry at my website. I gave it a look.

After several seconds, Linda could no longer stand the suspense. "Well?"

"It's a case."

"Good! What kind?"

I gulped. "Missing kid."

Linda forgot for a moment that we were not an item, and wrapped me up in her arms. "Oh, Ed. This is what you wanted, right?"

I kissed the top of her head. When I'd established my private detective business, I'd decided to specialize in finding missing kids. "Yeah. This is what I wanted."

She pulled back. I could see a weird parade of emotions in her eyes. Excitement that I might just have a case that would bring in some money, mingled with fear that I might just descend again into depression, as I had last fall. Missing kid cases hit me hard, and Linda knew that.

I knew it, too.

"I'm going to find this one," I said.

"I know you will," she said.

Neither of us, of course, could justify such confidence, but you cling to what you can. It's how we get through the day, right?

CHAPTER FIVE

So, ABOUT THOSE things in New York I do not want to remember. The one thing I most want to forget, but never will, is the search for Brianna Marston. She was a teen, a beautiful girl with brains and a million do-gooder causes and a thing for kittens and a family who loved her. But she was one of hundreds of missing kids in my NYPD precinct, and we detectives had murders and rapes and drug rings to cope with. We sent out the proper notices, notified other precincts and neighboring departments, entered all the info into all the databases, told everyone to keep an eye out, asked around and found nothing to indicate her case had been anything more than a typical runaway. We figured she'd gone off with a boyfriend, as teen girls often do, and would turn up somewhere.

We went and dealt with murders and rapes and drug rings. We were busy.

When she turned up, Brianna Marston was dead. Some bastard had stripped her and flayed her and nailed her to a wall. He'd used her blood for ink to write his own goddamned version of what he called his New Revelation on the walls. She'd been killed by some autodidact theologian and philosopher who'd sacrificed her to whatever demented god he'd decided to worship.

One look at her froze that image in my mind, and it's still there. I decided that night that I did not want to be part of a universe where something like that could happen. I grabbed a bottle of bourbon and I drove west. I called my boss and told him I was done. I barely recall that phone conversation, because I was drunk.

The best proof of God I can personally attest to is the fact that I made it to Ohio without killing myself or anyone else. I wasn't purposefully choosing to go to Ohio, mind you, although I'd been born there. Ohio is just where I happened to stop.

I woke up the next morning, with my car stuck in the mud a few inches from a creek. I wandered around aimlessly for a while and eventually learned I was in Mifflin County, in the Buckeye State where I'd been born. It wasn't the part of Ohio I'd grown up in, but it was close enough to feel kind of like home.

That next Sunday, I went to a little white church in Jodyville. Church is not my kind of thing, really. I'm pretty sure the people who are most certain they have a clue about God are the ones furthest from any kind of real truth. But I was messed up, and I knew nobody in the area, so I went to a church. And I told my story, and people listened.

I met people, good people like the Langstroms, who rented me their trailer. I called my former boss, and he helped me get a job at the Mifflin County Sheriff's Office. I went to therapy, took lots of prescribed pills, learned to meditate, and made friends with Tuck at his bar and grill in Jodyville. I met Linda while I was working security at the county fair. Eventually, things got better. I was healing. The demons were at least fading, and on good days they were out of sight.

Then, just last year, the demons returned.

A Columbus cop came to Mifflin County looking for a missing girl named Megan Beemer. I was assigned to help, and all the ghosts came rushing back.

Rural cops get busy, too, of course. I devoted as much time to the Megan Beemer case as I could, but I got diverted by a SWAT call—I was a sniper—and by all the other things a detective has to handle.

A farmer found Megan Beemer in Black Powder Creek, and by the time we'd tracked down the local football hero who, along with teammates, had raped and killed her, I was in a murderous mood. I almost killed the son of a bitch, and most days now I am still surprised I didn't. The trial was still in the future, and I was going to have to testify, and the boy's dad is a right-wing fellow with a lot of friends who have a lot of guns, so, yeah, sometimes I worry. The crime was horrific, though, and dad seemed shaken to the core, so I think he is spending his time on his knees and asking God a lot of questions instead of loading up an AR-15 and sneaking up on my trailer at night. At least, I hope that's what he's doing.

Anyway, missing kid cases get to me, and once the arrests in the Megan Beemer case were made, I went to Sheriff Daltry and turned in my badge and gun. I opened Whiskey River Investigations, with an intent to specialize in finding missing kids. I figured once I tossed off all the red tape and distractions that come with being a civil servant, I could focus on one case at a time and make a difference.

Business had not been good, though, and I'd stooped to taking infidelity cases and doing boring background checks on new hires in an attempt to pay my bills. This missing kid case would be my first since going private, which was what sparked Linda's emotional embrace.

Her eyes in that moment revealed what I already knew. I had slipped into depression before, and lost my way a bit. That meant I had the capacity to descend again, and Linda knew it. She was worried another missing kid case would be the catalyst.

To be honest, I worried about that, too. But I'd made one big change since the last time. I was my own boss now. There was no one to tell me I had to go on a SWAT call or talk to a burglary victim or try to find somebody's fucking stolen tractor. I could concentrate all my time and energy on any case I chose, and I could ignore distractions.

That was an important difference. That was going to pull me through.

I could do this.

I looked at the message from my potential client again, and called the number. A woman answered, and I could hear the tension and weariness and fear in her voice, even though all she said was hello.

"Mrs. Zachman?"

"Yes."

"This is Ed Runyon, the private investigator. I got your message. I'm pretty close by and can be there in about ten minutes."

"Oh, thank God. Yes, please. It's about our boy, Jimmy."

"On my way."

I aimed the truck toward Ambletown and popped a Willie Nelson CD into the player. "On the Road Again" started playing.

It's one of my feel-good songs, and I smiled.

I was going to find this boy.

CHAPTER SIX

I ROLLED UP in front of the Zachman house, one of many similar ranch houses on Poplar Street in Ambletown, and flipped my middle finger at the political sign in the front yard. I checked the house number on the mailbox, 501, to make sure I had the right address. OK, then. I tossed my Willie Nelson cap onto the seat beside me because I wasn't sure how that would go over with Jimmy's obviously conservative parents, and I needed the business. I also reminded myself that Trump voters love their kids, and that politics was not the big concern here. I did flip off the sign again, though. I have my opinions.

I stepped out of the truck and into the mild sleet, having replaced my hat with a decent ski cap, and headed for the front door. Salt on the walkway crunched beneath my feet. The home was well cared for, with plots awaiting spring gardens flanking the porch and a sign on the door: "As for me and my household, we shall serve the Lord."

I glanced back at the sign and wondered exactly how that math was supposed to work, but shook it off. I wasn't here to discuss politics or theology. I was here to find Jimmy Zachman.

The door opened before I knocked. A woman looked at me with an odd mix of apprehension and hope. She looked to be in her late thirties, and her dark hair hung loose. It hadn't been combed recently. She wore jeans and a blue wool sweater, and obviously had not slept well for a while.

"Are you Ed Runyon?"

"Yes. Tammy Zachman?"

"I am. Come in." She could not get me into the house fast enough. "Bob is in his study. Bob? Bob! He's here. The detective."

I wiped off my boots on the front porch mat and stepped inside. The living room was built around comfort, and the wall next to the fake fireplace was a shrine to their boy. I saw Jimmy through the years. Dark curly hair, peeking out from beneath a Reds cap in one photo, full of Silly String in another, finally tamed in a formal family portrait in the largest frame. Jimmy, apparently, was their only child.

Tammy Zachman had crossed the living room and stood by a door to the right. She looked at me as though I was the answer to a prayer. I hoped she was right.

"This way, Mr. Runyon."

"Ed, please." I followed her into a small home office, paneled with dark faux mahogany in a way that assured no amount of light would ever be truly sufficient and sporting numerous bookshelves. At a small desk in the back, a man typed furiously at a keyboard. "Just a second. OK."

Bob Zachman swiveled his chair, faced me, and stood up. A very brief smile flashed in the midst of brown beard, and he ran a hand across his bald scalp. "Bob Zachman." He wore jeans and a button-up short-sleeved shirt, tucked in tightly.

"Ed Runyon." We shook hands, and Bob glanced at his wife. "I emailed Becky. She hasn't heard from Jimmy," he said.

Tammy seemed uncertain as to how to respond. Eventually, she nodded.

"May I ask, who is Becky?"

Bob looked at me. "She's my sister. We don't really talk much, she and I, really. Not these days. Politics. She's a liberal, and I'm, well, I'm not, so things get testy. I need to work on that, I guess."

His wife inhaled sharply, then turned away, but Bob did not seem to notice.

He continued. "But Jimmy is fond of her, and she is fond of him, so I'd hoped, well, you know. I thought maybe he'd said something to her, told her where he was going, I don't know. Something like that." He indicated a loveseat against the wall opposite his desk, and I sat.

"You are sure he ran away?"

"Yes," Bob answered. "But I have no idea why."

"Let's start at the beginning," I said. "Your son, Jimmy, he's how old?" I decided not to start with the list of things that might happen with a missing kid, ranging from prostitution to drugs to kidnap and rape and murder. I could tell from his parents' faces that they had already thought of such horrors.

"Fifteen," Tammy said.

"And when did he disappear?"

"He left the house sometime yesterday," Bob said. "We don't know exactly when. He did not have any plans that we knew of. He did not come back last night."

"No phone calls, no messages, no notes?"

"Nothing," Bob said. "Nothing at all. He just vanished."

"It is not like him," Tammy said, crossing her arms nervously. "He's a good kid. He never gets in trouble. Very smart. Very mature for his age."

"You said he left the house. He wasn't in school?"

Tammy answered this one. "He attends a Christian school, and we had an extended Christmas break this year. Teachers are training this week, I think, or something like that."

I nodded. "I presume you called the police?"

"Of course," Bob said. "We called last night when we got worried. They came out right away, asked a lot of questions."

His wife jumped in. "I was worried they would not do anything. I thought we had to wait forty-eight hours before they would do anything. At least, that's what I heard."

I gave her a smile intended to be reassuring, one I'd practiced a million times as a cop. "When it's a kid, especially one who has no history of running away or anything like that, you don't have to worry. They'll get going right away. They're not going to let parents worry."

Bob nodded. "They sent his photo and information all over the state, they said. Every unit that they have will keep an eye out for him. Still, I want to do everything. We want to do everything, I mean, to find him. That's why we called you. There is so much trouble out there in the world for a kid. No safe place out there. Full of crime, and apostates, and the gays . . . it's just not safe."

Tammy gave him a look that seemed to beg him to shut up. "I think Jesus has room in his heart to forgive gay people, Bob."

He scoffed. "Forgiveness if they stop their ways, sure," he said. He looked at me. "This is why women don't lead the church, bless them." He smiled. "They have their wonders, but theological thinking is not their thing."

I waited for Tammy to tell him to fuck off, but she didn't. "I'm not into theology or church politics," I answered. "Let's just focus on finding your son."

"Of course," Bob said. "Just so much trouble out there in the world," he continued. "Boys who think they're girls, girls who think they're boys. Insanity."

I kept a poker face and did not respond to what he said. I'd had plenty of practice doing that as a cop.

Tammy Zachman gulped and wiped away a tear. "Mr. Runyon, your website says you specialize in finding missing children?"

"I do," I said. "The police will do what they can, and that's more than you might think. An awful lot of runaway cases get solved because of that network the cops have. A car gets pulled over a hundred miles from here, and the driver turns out to be someone's missing kid. Or the kid shows up at a church seeking shelter for the night, or someone reports a kid trying to get a motel room, things like that, and the network does what it does and word gets back to you."

Or a body is found in a river. Or in a drug house. Or a girl is caught offering herself to strangers with warm cars. Or a boy does the same, for that matter. I did not mention those possibilities.

I went on. "One issue with the police, though, is they have a big job to do, actually a lot of big jobs to do, and a lot of people to protect and serve. So their attention is somewhat divided at times. I can work on this full-time, as my single priority. I have no other cases at present, and if you hire me, I am not going to take any other cases until I find Jimmy."

They glanced at each other. "That sounds expensive. We're not rich."

I told them my rates. "As for expenses, if I have to travel on your behalf, I stay at the cheapest hotels you can imagine or I'll sleep in my truck, and I'll live on coffee and peanut butter sandwiches. I won't bilk you. I didn't get into this to become rich."

It hit me hard in that moment. I really wanted to find their boy. I needed this.

Bob glanced at the floor. "That sounds reasonable, and I appreciate that. I have another question."

"Sure."

He looked me in the eyes. "You shot Jeff Cotton last year."

News gets around, especially when you shoot a local high school football star being scouted by Ohio State.

"I did. He was trying to shoot me."

"I asked the police about you, whether I should hire you. They said you made some bad decisions, could have gotten some officers killed."

I sighed. "Yes, Mr. Zachman. That is true. I went charging into the woods after that boy, knowing he had a very powerful weapon, knowing I should have waited on backup, and we had plenty of backup nearby because we knew it could get dicey, but I ignored that because I wanted to get my hands on him. And when he turned his rifle on me, a gun that could have put a dozen holes in me in a couple of eye blinks, I shot him in the leg. I should have shot him in the chest, several times, because I had brother and sister officers combing the woods for that boy and he could have killed them if he got past me. But I shot him in the leg. That was my bad decision."

Linda, of course, had called it a good decision. Me? I kept replaying that day in my mind and still could not tell you if my call was right or wrong. I just know my head was too messed up at the time to be clear on anything.

I didn't tell the Zachmans I'd been so zealous because Jeff Cotton had killed a missing girl, and the case had sent me skittering sideways, mentally. The newspeople had done some digging, and reported on my experiences with missing kid cases, so I was pretty sure they'd heard that part of the story, too. I figured they didn't need to hear that part now.

"Why did you shoot him in the leg?" Tammy placed her hands before her face, as though praying, and her big brown eyes widened.

I shook my head slowly. "I don't really know. It was a snap decision. I was worried about my own motives, I guess. I was in a vengeful mood. But I'm not supposed to be the cop and the judge. Not supposed to play God."

"Do you believe in God, Mr. Runyon?"

I turned to look at Bob. "On good days, yeah, I suppose."

"Do you think God stayed your hand, and made you decide not to kill Jeff?"

"I don't know."

We stared at one another for an uncomfortable amount of time, and I wondered if I was going to lose this job because I hadn't been enthusiastic enough about Jesus.

"I want you to find our boy," he finally said.

Tammy nodded frantically. "Yes. Yes. Yes."

"I'll do my best."

CHAPTER SEVEN

Tammy went to make coffee. I stood up and began pacing and peppering Bob with questions.

"So you said no signs of foul play, nothing like that. You talked to his friends, and their parents?"

He nodded. "No one has seen him. No one has heard from him. They will call if they do."

"Did any of them notice anything unusual about his behavior lately? Has he seemed worried? Scared?"

He shook his head. "Not that anyone said."

"Does Jimmy drive?"

"He's fifteen. Learner permit, no license."

"Does he drive, though? I mean, he knows how, right? If he got his hands on a car, he could drive it?"

"Yes."

"Does he have a passport?"

"No."

"Girlfriend?"

"No, none so far. He's not old enough to date. We don't need that kind of trouble."

"So he's not allowed to date."

Bob's jaws tightened. "It's our job to raise him right. To make sure he's fully prepared before he takes on—"

"I'm not judging," I said. "I'm just trying to figure out why Jimmy might have left. Teens don't usually do that unless there is a reason. Fifteen-year-old boy, the reason might be a fifteen-year-old girl. It happens."

He planted his face in his hands. "I know. No girlfriend, though. Not that we know of, anyway, and I don't know how he'd have arranged anything like that."

"He's shy," Tammy said, entering with a tray of coffees with sugar packets and a carafe of milk. "He's always been shy."

She passed out cups. The coffee was strong and dark, the way I like it. "Thanks. This is good. Jimmy took his phone, you said, but he's not answering. Does he have a laptop, or an iPad, anything like that?"

"No, just his phone and the family computer." Bob pointed his thumb over his shoulder at the older-model Mac on the desk behind him. "We all use the same one."

"Jimmy uses that a lot?"

"Yes."

"Does he have his own private log-in?"

"Yes, but we know the password. That was a condition for him using the computer." Tammy sipped her coffee, which she'd loaded with milk. "We try to keep things focused on Jesus in our family. No outside distractions, like those games and those movies. So we know his password, so we can check on him."

I nodded. I'd had time to scan the bookshelves in Bob's study while we talked. A dozen versions of the Bible, and the titles of almost every other book contained the words *God*, or *Jesus*, or *Christianity*, or *faith*. A few were devoted to debunking atheism, and several offered junk science, especially the variety that tries to pretend humans aren't just apes that learned to wear clothes and copy sitcom plots from one another.

"The police had a girl log on, she hooked up a machine, they made a clone of the computer," Bob said. "Copied everything that's on it, they said. They are going to comb through that for any messages Jimmy sent that might give us a clue. They didn't see anything right away, though."

"I'm going to want to look, too, if you don't mind, before I go." There was no way I could be as thorough as the police in examining the computer, but I could get lucky. "Who does Jimmy hang out with?"

"Church friends, mostly. Church, school, it's all the same for us and other families we're close with. We're all pretty tight-knit."

But none of you know why Jimmy left, or where he went, I thought.

I heard a phone go "ding" nearby. Tammy was looking at it. "The police are talking to all of those people. Anne just texted me—the police left there a little while ago."

Bob nodded emphatically. "Good."

I interrupted. "Who is Anne?"

"Family friend, from church," Bob said. "I know all those people very well, and they know us. If any of them knew anything, I know they'd give an arm or a leg to help us. Good people, all of them."

"OK. Any influences outside the church? Boy Scouts, library book clubs, anything like that?"

"Chess club," Tammy said.

"He plays chess?"

Bob's eyebrows lifted. "Yes. He's pretty good at it. Plays online with people all over the world. It's fine, though. Chess, you know? Develops the mind instead of rotting it, like all those shooter games full of aliens and monsters and who knows what."

I nodded. "I try to play, but I stink at it. Does Jimmy play actual people, too, face-to-face, I mean?"

"There's the local club. They play at the middle school on Saturdays. I wasn't sure about letting him do that, you know."

"It's not affiliated with the church," his wife said, almost whispering. "Kids from the secular high schools play, too."

That sounded promising to me. Maybe somebody outside the family's circle would know something Jimmy's parents didn't know.

"Jimmy wanted to play against an opponent he could see, not just someone online," Bob interjected. "He said that was part of the game, to be able to play your opponent, and intimidate him." Despite being worried about his son, Bob's pride showed through. "So, even though it's not church-oriented, we thought, why not? He's really very good. I can't beat him anymore, and I taught him to play. I can't even come close to winning anymore."

"When does this chess club meet?"

"Saturday mornings. Ten. Middle school library."

"I'll be there. Maybe one of his chess friends will know something that will help."

I asked more questions, then asked if I could sit down at the computer to see what Jimmy had been up to online.

"Go ahead," Bob said.

"We don't have his email credentials," Tammy said, almost apologetically. "We wanted to show we trust him." She began weeping.

I thought maybe they'd go to the living room while I poked around on the Mac, but they sat on the loveseat and supplied random facts as they came up. From them, I learned Jimmy preferred Batman to Superman, which I understood but Bob didn't. I also learned Jimmy is a picky eater and Mom wondered what he'd eat wherever he was. And I heard several times that Jimmy would not ever use drugs. No no no no no.

Jimmy's browser history was scant. Clearly, his online time was limited mostly to homework for Doan Road Christian School. I went way back in his browser history, but found no chat sites, no porn, no image searches for Hollywood hotties or anything like that. And he had not cleared the history recently. It went back for more than a year. If he was looking at things he shouldn't, he was doing it in private mode to avoid leaving tracks. The cops could probably find that out when they went through the forensic image they'd made, but I wasn't able to check that out myself.

One thing seemed conspicuously absent. "I don't see a chess site on here," I said.

"He plays that on his phone," Tammy answered. "I don't know the app he uses."

"His chess club friends will know, probably," I said. "I'm sure they talk about such things, probably play one another outside club meetings. Do you all monitor his phone use, too?"

"Well, some," Bob said. "But we've eased up the last couple of years. We used to do random spot checks, you know, hand it over and we'll take a look. He always handed it right over, never an argument, and we never found anything objectionable."

"Those atheist videos, Bob."

He shrugged. "He was watching those to learn what they had to say, to sharpen his apologetics. Know thine enemy."

"They're not the enemy, they're lost," Tammy muttered.

I changed the subject. "I'll keep looking. Never know what's going to prove useful."

I spent an hour searching for phone backups or chats or photos that might be relevant, but found nothing. I hadn't really expected anything different. If I had been Jimmy, I'd have made goddamned sure my parents wouldn't find anything, too.

"Do you mind if I see his room?"

"Not at all," Bob said.

"It's a mess," Tammy added.

"My room's a mess, too. I won't judge."

They led me out of the study, around a corner, and down the hall that ended in three bedrooms and a bathroom. "That's Jimmy's room," Tammy said. "Police already looked in there."

"It'll save me time if I can see for myself, and not have to go combing through the police reports. I'll do that, too, of course."

I stepped into the room and flipped on the light. There were no immediate revelations. There was a bed, a small computer table without a computer on it, and a shelf full of minor league baseball caps, including a Carolina Mudcats cap I thought about stealing. I opened drawers in the desk, but I did not expect to find anything. If Jimmy was a chess wizard, he was smart enough to know Mom and Dad search his room.

There was a chessboard on the desk. White had mated Black. "Does he have friends over to play chess?"

"No," Jimmy's dad said. "Well, not very often. He plays on his phone. But he uses the board here to do puzzles and things like that, or to visualize a position. He says he can see it better on a real board."

"Smart kid," I said. I looked in the closet. "Did he take clothes?"

"Just what he was wearing," Jimmy's dad said. "Reds T-shirt, jeans, sneakers, Buckeyes jacket, a Reds cap. He doesn't go anywhere without that cap."

I lifted the mattress, just to be thorough, even though I doubted I'd discover anything. I saw Jimmy's reading material, then shifted my position to block dad's view.

I used to hide *Playboy* under my mattress. Jimmy had hidden *The Demon-Haunted World* by Carl Sagan, a book that pretty much eviscerates the notion that evolution and science are bunk and treats religion as so much superstition. I wondered whether Jimmy's parents might prefer him to be reading *Playboy*.

Tammy Zachman entered the room. "Bob . . . did you take money from my purse?" She was carrying a large bag, and digging around in it.

"No, I never do that. Why?"

"I went to get cash to pay Mr. Runyon. I had an envelope in my purse, almost seven hundred dollars."

"I didn't take it," Bob said.

"Then maybe Jimmy did," she muttered. The tears started again. "What kind of trouble is he in?"

"Hey," I said, "that might not be a bad thing. If he took money, that indicates he left on his own, and had a plan, as opposed to any kind of abduction or something like that."

She blinked. "You think?"

"Could be, yeah. Any credit cards missing? Debit cards?"

"No," she said. "I checked that as soon as I noticed the money missing."

"So, he has a lot of ready cash but no cards. He'll be able to buy food or pay for a hotel room, at least for a little while." It occurred to me he might have grabbed the money to pay for some extravagance, like a pair of fancy basketball shoes or a collectible comic or some other dumb thing a fifteen-year-old might spend his mom's money on. It also occurred to me he might have taken the money to buy something for a girlfriend. Maybe jewelry. Maybe an abortion. Who knows? But I did not mention that to the parents, of course. "Anyway, if he has money then he most likely isn't starving somewhere."

"Well, that is some hope, right?" She sighed heavily. "Thank you. I'll write you a check."

CHAPTER EIGHT

By the time I had parked in front of Tucker's Bar and Grill in Jodyville, I really wanted a drink. My initial assessment was that highly intelligent young chess master Jimmy Zachman probably had finally gotten tired of his parents and pastor telling him Adam and Eve rode dinosaurs that never ate meat before things went awry in the Garden of Eden. The kid probably had holed up somewhere with a like-minded friend reading science fiction, watching Christopher Hitchens videos, and indulging in other dangerous shit. Maybe the smart friend was a cute girlfriend with a car, and they were spending Mom's money on a hotel room and, one can hope, condoms.

There was no indication he'd run off with the circus, been kidnapped by aliens, or moved into an opium den. I figured I had time for a beer or two, and I needed to eat something, anyway. Might as well be one of Tuck's cheeseburgers.

Tuck waved as soon as I walked in and started pouring me a beer. The place was crowded, despite being in a one-red-light town off all the main traffic routes, because it was Friday night. I found a seat at the bar. Luke Bryan—I knew the voice because the dispatchers at the Mifflin County Sheriff's Office played that shit at every holiday party—was singing some godawful country song about a really horny woman. I think that's what it was about, anyway. I was trying not to listen.

I pleaded with Tuck as he placed my beer in front of me. "Can you put on some Waylon?"

"Sorry, friend. That's the old stuff, and the crowd likes the new stuff."

For Tuck, this was purely a business decision. If it had been up to him, the speakers would be blasting Thin Lizzy or AC/DC or Deep Purple or something else fast and loud. But Tuck had a business to run, and he knew his customers.

"This beer is not Commodore Perry," I said, pointing to my glass. "This is darker."

"Just try it," he said, whipping his long, braided hair behind him. He no longer wore a bandage across his nose, but the bruising was still impressive. A darker stain across his dark face.

"Not another IPA. Jesus, Tuck." I grimaced. Tuck is a beer nerd, a rather annoying subspecies of human. Such beings can't be satisfied to see you drink the good old reliable beer you know you like. No. They have to evangelize and try to sway you from the known path into the wide world of beers. "They all taste different; I never know what I am going to get. I know I like the Commodore Perry."

"Is Tuck pushing another beer on you, honey?"

I looked over my shoulder and caught a fleeting glimpse of tattooed shoulder and multi-colored hair. Shirley, the new waitress, was always in motion. She was behind the bar and in the kitchen before I could answer.

"I'm buying this round, so you are not risking anything but your taste buds," Tuck said. "Drink up. If you don't like it, I'll finish it for you."

"Fuck, man."

"C'mon, drink up for daddy like a big boy." He even scratched at my chin like a dad trying to get a baby to eat.

"Someday, I am going to forget I like you and hang you from the deer antlers over there."

"No, you won't, because if that happens the cheeseburgers stop."

"You got me there, I guess." I took a swig.

Tuck's eyes widened, and so did his smile. "And?"

"Damn you."

"And?"

"Fuck you."

"And?"

"It's really good. What does it cost, fifty bucks a bottle?"

"No. It's 90 Minute IPA from a brewery called Dogfish Head. They don't hyphenate that, the ninety-minute part, but they are brewers, not grammarians. I forgive them. It only costs you a little bit more than your beloved Commodore Perry."

"If I finish this glass, will you stop pushing new beers on me?"

"Probably not." He shook his head so hard the beads rattled. "When a man learns the truth, he wants to tell the world, you know?"

"Tell me about it. My new client is an armchair preacher."

He stepped away to pour a couple of bourbons for two women who probably should have been showing ID. I wasn't a cop anymore, and Tuck seemed to know them, so I decided not to get involved.

"The blonde thinks you're cute," Tuck said when he came back. "Her friend says you look kind of mean."

"They are both too young," I muttered.

"Totally legal," he said, smiling.

"Still too young."

He took my empty glass. "More of the same?"

"Yes, damn you."

He brought back another. "This is on the house, too. Thanks."

I nodded. "Thanks for the beer. How did I earn it?"

A huge shadow occulted the overhead lamp and Tuck turned to fill a pitcher. Ollie Southard, a very large, very gay local biker who hates guns and probably grows pot in season, filled the space next to me. "Hey, Ed."

"Hey, Ollie."

Tuck set the pitcher down. "Don't drink all of that by yourself, Ollie."

"You are no fun, Tuck."

I laughed as Ollie moved away. Tuck and I both knew he was going to drink the whole pitcher. The real question was whether he'd pour beer into a glass first, or just upturn the whole damned thing. "So, how did I earn this beer?"

"You did not beat up that cop."

"Oh," I said. "Right. Yeah, about that. My new case is going to delay justice on that son of a bitch for a while. He's got a nice truck, though." I showed him the picture.

"I absolve you of any need to be my avenging angel, Ed."

"He smacked your face against your car because you are black."

"Yes, he did." Tuck wiped down the bar, then turned when the bell rang. He grabbed two cheeseburgers from the window behind the bar, and I got really hungry. Tuck handed the tray to a guy I did not know, then came back to talk to me.

"I want a cheeseburger and fries. To go, though. I have work to do."

He laughed. "Yeah." He gave my order to the kitchen and returned. "Hey, Shirl, can you mind the bar for a bit?"

"Hell, yeah, hon."

Tuck led me to a small table and indicated I should sit. I did.

He leaned across the table so he would not have to shout above the jukebox twang. "Ed, I know you just want to do me a favor and all, but I don't think violence should beget violence and I do not want you to go after that man. I don't want you getting hurt."

"So you are just going to let it go?"

"Yeah."

"Not even going to file charges?"

"He'll just say I resisted arrest. His cop buddies will all agree. Jury will, too, probably."

"Probably, but . . ."

Tuck shook his head. "No, Ed. Let it go."

I scratched my head. "I don't have to do it for you. Hell. I'll do it for me, you know? Cops like him make all cops look bad." I'd been a cop, and I'd met some like Donnor Brogan. But I'd known plenty who were damned good people, too. A young patrolman who organized outings for kids without dads. A dispatcher who oversees Girl Scouts. An older guy, retired now, who still puts on his clown costume to entertain kids in hospitals. His hands could crush yours if you shook, but he preferred using them to make balloon animals. I'd be willing to kick the shit out of a Donnor Brogan on behalf of all of them.

Tuck wasn't buying it. "Cops who beat up other cops make cops look bad, too, right? And probably beget other cops beating on cops out of revenge."

"Nobody says 'beget' in everyday conversation, Tuck." I shrugged. "Fine. OK. You win."

"I'm going to need you to look me in the eye when you say that and promise me you'll stay away from the dude."

I looked at him, and refused to blink. "I, Ed Runyon, being of sound mind and not too many beers in, do hereby solemnly swear that I will not beat, thrash, kick, bite, shoot, stab, punch, or otherwise do violence upon the person of one Donnor Brogan, though he be fully deserving of having such violence done upon him for crimes committed against Jodyville's most esteemed barkeeper, poet, metalhead, and beer nerd, one—"

"Do not say my full name out loud," Tuck said, leaning forward.

I grinned, and used the name he signs checks with instead of the full name his parents gave him. Tuck was of the opinion that Tiberius was a ridiculous middle name, no matter how much his father loved *Star Trek*, and he hated explaining the name to people who didn't love *Star Trek*. "One James Tucker."

He smiled. "Thank you. Now you can concentrate on your paying client. Tell me more."

"Missing boy, fifteen." I filled him in on the interview with the Zachmans.

"Yikes."

I shrugged. "Yeah, the parents have some goofy ideas, maybe, but so what? You can believe all kinds of silly things and still be a good person. They love their kid, even if he's been reading some naughty Carl Sagan atheist stuff, and they are worried about him. I'm going to find him."

Shirley brought my food. "Here ya go, hon."

She dropped a bill on the table, but Tuck tore it up. "On the house."

"I'm starting to like this place."

"Go find the kid, Ed. Probably found a friend with a lot of science books or something."

"I sure hope so. I'll find out."

I got up to go, then paused. "You talked to Linda."

"Yeah," he said. "She was going on about some damn virus that's coming, saw it on a blog or something."

I nodded. "Skimming blogs is an avoidance technique when she doesn't want to grade papers. Did you know she has a date?"

"No, but I am not surprised. You two kind of cooled off, looks like, and she is just not designed for sitting on the sidelines, you know?"

"Yeah, I know."

"You should not leave her on the sidelines, in my opinion."

I ignored that. "Do you know who she's going out with? Some guy named Sam Briggs."

Tuck's eyebrows did the Spock thing, except it looks less Spockish when they both go up. "Sam Briggs?"

"Yeah."

He shook his head. "Oh, boy. Sam Briggs. New history teacher. Smart as hell, really good-looking dude."

I am not sure how long I stared at Tuck before I asked, "Do you think I could beat him up?"

He laughed. "I'm pretty sure you can beat most men up, but I don't think that would win Linda back, man."

"I was kidding. Probably."

"I know. Anyway, don't beat him up."

CHAPTER NINE

I GOT OUT of the bar before Tuck could hit me with his full micro-analysis of my relationship with Linda. It usually goes like this: "You were pretty messed up when you came here, Ed. Linda was part of the cure. She's good for you, and you know it, but whenever she worries about you, which is always, it reminds you of how messed up you were, so you don't like that. And that's why you scoot away."

Tuck's analysis always pisses me off, because I know he's right. I went to a dark place once, and now I always know that it could conceivably happen again. That's not a good feeling. Linda knows it, too. So when she worries, I worry, and . . . well. I end up not talking much, and she ends up dating another guy. A smart, good-looking guy, and Tuck says I shouldn't beat him up.

I felt like beating up somebody, that's for damned sure.

I turned off of Big Black Dog Road and down the narrow lane that leads to my pond-side trailer. The pines scraped a little more rust and paint off my truck, because I had not gotten around to trimming the branches. I parked and stepped out, and took a few moments to gaze across the fog capping the water, almost glowing in the moonlight. A whitetail doe lifted her head on the opposite shore, water dripping from her snout. It was a nice little moment, and for just a second, I was aware of nothing but the water, the deer, and my own misty exhalation.

The doe ran off.

"Well, then," I said. "Time to get back to work."

Had this been August, I'd have sat at the picnic table outside. But this was January in Ohio, so that wasn't happening. Inside the trailer, I got the space heaters going, grabbed a Commodore Perry, and sat down to eat my burger and fries. I had to move a stack of books—Wilkie Collins, John D. MacDonald, Mark Pryor, James W. Ziskin, and Lawrence Block—off of the table so I'd have room for the laptop. I had not yet decided which to read next, and it was going to be a while before I got time for reading, anyway. I had a kid to find.

I ate while I played digital detective. I started by sending Jimmy an email. Subject line: "Please tell me you're safe." The body of the email reiterated that, and explained that I was a private detective working for his parents. I added that I was willing to keep anything he told me completely confidential as long as I could establish that he was safe. I just wanted the kid to reply to me and tell me what was going on. If I got a response, I could decide later whether I needed to keep my promise of confidentiality or not. I'm not a saint. I'm a detective trying to find a kid who may be in trouble.

I had no reason to expect he'd answer my email when he wouldn't answer his own parents, but you try everything.

I counted to ten and then checked for an answer.

Nope.

I spent the next few hours poking around online, checking the databases. I found very little on Jimmy, not even much of a social media presence, just a Facebook account he seldom touched. Dad had worked at Ambletown Thrift Bank for seven years and had no criminal record. He apparently spent a lot of his leisure time on various blogs trying to convince people that the ontological argument for God was foolproof. God is defined as the most perfect being imaginable, a being who actually exists in reality is more perfect than one who exists only in the mind, therefore God exists in reality, checkmate. Bob did not convince many people, including me. But to be fair, I skipped over a lot of that.

Bob also had many, many deep discussions concerning how homosexuality is a sin and that's why gay people should not get married or teach in school or, apparently, exist. He did not convince me of that, either. But he had convinced me he loved his kid and wanted him back home safe and sound. That was enough for me.

I hoped I'd be able to find Jimmy before I had to spend much more time with his dad. That was, perhaps, selfish of me, but then again, I'm only a collection of atoms with a few opinions unless I embrace Bob's theology, according to Bob, anyway. But I wanted to find his kid fast so I could stop caring what his dad thought or said.

Mom was a receptionist for a dentist, and, if you took a straw poll of her Facebook friends, she was simply the most loving and awesome person ever. She belonged to a couple of garden clubs. She did not spend time on blogs arguing about religion, but she posted a lot of things on Facebook about how much she loved and trusted God, and it looked like she had access to a deep library of platitude memes. Her most recent Facebook post, though, was about Jimmy, begging friends to keep an eye out for him. I read all sixty-two comments, looking for clues. It was not productive.

I checked for news accounts mentioning injury crashes or unidentifiable bodies. Nothing nearby, and nothing involving a teenage kid.

I kept plugging away for a couple of hours, without success, then realized there was something odd about the comments on Tammy Zachman's Facebook post. Bob Zachman had a sister, Becky, but she had not responded. That seemed out of kilter. Family members don't generally stay quiet about such things. So, why hadn't Jimmy's aunt weighed in?

Bob kept his profile private, but I was able to check Tammy's Facebook friends list. Jimmy's aunt wasn't on it.

I looked up Becky Zachman. She had a Facebook account, but hadn't done more than change her profile pic a few times for the last couple of years. She was dark-haired and attractive, even though she looked rather like Bob. I call it Mira Sorvino Syndrome. When you see her in a movie or on TV, you can't help but think she is drop-dead gorgeous, but she looks just like her actor daddy, Paul Sorvino. Tuck and I had discussed it, and whether I'd actually make a move on Mira if I had a chance, or whether I'd just freak out because she looks like her dad. Tuck was sure I'd crash and burn. I kind of thought I'd get past the issue. It's not a theory I was ever going to get to test, of course, but that's the kind of nonsense we talk about when Tuck's not trying to expand my beer horizons or straighten out my commitment issues.

Becky Zachman's background image on Facebook featured a big red letter "A."

"A" for "atheist."

That, I figured, explained why Bob's sister wasn't on good terms with Jimmy's parents. I'd seen a lot of that stuff as a cop. Everybody's got reasons for not talking, and not listening, to everybody else.

The aunt's atheism, though, gave me an idea. Jimmy had been reading Sagan and checking out atheist YouTube channels. Had Jimmy run to his atheist aunt? Had she been covering up for the kid when she'd told Bob that Jimmy had not contacted her? Maybe she thought she was doing Jimmy a favor, rescuing him from his own family.

It was a place to start, anyway. A glance at the clock told me it was late, but what the hell. I found her number in my notes and called.

She answered on the first ring. "Hello?"

"Hi, my name is Ed Runyon. I am a private investigator looking for Jimmy Zachman. I understand you are his aunt?"

"Yes," she said. "He has not shown up?" I could hear the fear in her voice. It sounded real, but it's difficult to discern such things when you can't look a person in the eyes. Jimmy preferred playing chess opponents face-to-face, and I felt the same way about conducting interviews. But for now, I was stuck with a phone call.

"No, he hasn't," I said. "I was hoping you might know something."

She sighed. "I wish I did. I talked to the police when they called. I can't believe Jimmy ran off—it makes no sense. It's not like him. And he's just not really, what am I trying to say, worldly, you know? I mean, he's extremely intelligent, very smart, very kind, but he's led kind of an isolated, no, I mean, a sheltered life. You know?"

"Jimmy's parents are very religious," I said. "I see by your Facebook that you are not."

Her guard went up quickly. "I'm not sure how that is your concern."

"It's not, really. Theology is not my thing and I'm pretty sure we're not ever going to figure all that out, anyway. But I found a copy of a book by Carl Sagan that Jimmy had hidden in his room. I read that book years ago, and it doesn't treat religion kindly. So, I wonder if Jimmy was having doubts, maybe, and if so, did he maybe reach out to his atheist aunt?"

There was a pause of a few seconds. "You work for Bob and Tammy, right?" She was still guarded.

"Yes."

"I will need to be assured that you won't tell them some of what I can tell you. Bob and I already hardly speak at all, and it hurts. I don't want it to get worse. and I don't want anything Jimmy told me in confidence to get back to Bob."

"I totally understand. My big concern is finding Jimmy safe and sound. The more I know about him, the better my chances are. I don't need to spread discord or anything like that."

Another pause. "Well, OK. First, I gave Jimmy that book. A couple of summers ago. They stopped by here, his family did, and Jimmy asked me a couple of questions when we had a moment alone. He'd seen my bookshelves—I think Bob had mentioned my non-belief a few times. Anyway, he knew I was not on the same page as his dad where religion is concerned. And Jimmy is a smart kid and he was doubting a lot of what his dad and mom were teaching him. Especially when it comes to science. Jimmy's into astronomy, in particular, and he's damned well aware the universe is more than six thousand years old like his dad says."

"OK."

She continued. "Jimmy was mad. He wanted to go to a real school, he said. Wanted to learn about science. I raided my bookshelf and tucked Sagan and Dawkins and, I think, Jerry Coyne into his backpack before they left. It was our secret, just between me and Jimmy."

"Was Jimmy an atheist?"

"No," she said, with a bit of a laugh. "No. He and I have talked a few times, on the phone, since then. He is quite convinced his dad and mom need to open some science books, but he is definitely still on Team Jesus. Jimmy can do quite the dissertation on the existence of God and the Gospels and all that. He thinks Jesus is real. He just thinks the Bible gets a lot of things wrong, or maybe he thinks people get the Bible wrong. He's still working on that, I think. But he's a believer. Absolutely."

"OK."

"Tell Bob I never tried to steer Jimmy away from God," Becky said, with an audible gulp. "Never once. I mean, I applaud Jimmy's explorations, you know? And I always answered his questions as honestly as I could. But I never, ever once tried to convince him to abandon his belief, you know?"

I believed her. "Is that why you and Bob don't talk, though? Because of Jimmy?"

"Not really. Bob and I stopped having civil discussions because of religion and Trump and a lot of other bullshit, but I don't think he knows Jimmy and I talked about anything like that. I never told him, and I doubt Jimmy would have told him."

I thought about that. "Do you think Jimmy would be afraid of his parents finding out about him questioning things?"

She paused a long, long time. "I don't know. I really don't. And I don't know how Bob would react. I mean, he makes a big show of having what he calls civil discussions with the other side, as he calls anyone not in his camp, and he says questions are good and discussions are good, but . . ."

"But what?"

"He never really behaves as though discussion is good," she said, sighing. "He doesn't listen, he just jumps from one talking point to another, and I'd swear he'd miss a point even if he had a fucking catcher's mitt. You know? Just so convinced he knows what he's talking about that nothing else can get in there—there's just no room in his gray matter to absorb anything new. If it was his own son, though . . . I don't know. Maybe he'd be different. Maybe he'd listen. I know he loves Jimmy, and he's very proud of him."

"OK. Do you know of any places Jimmy might have gone?"

"No. I live in Columbus. I don't see him often. We just talk on the phone now and then."

"Did he ever mention a girlfriend, or an, I don't know, atheist club, or anything of the sort?"

"Not that I can recall, no. There are several atheist groups in Ohio, easy to find online. I suppose he might have contacted people at one of those. Maybe."

I gave her my number and urged her to call me if any news turned up or if she remembered Jimmy ever saying anything that might give me a clue where he might have gone.

"I will do that. I hope you find him. Please let me know if you do."

"I promise. Thanks for your help. Bye."

I slipped on a jacket and walked down to the pond to get some fresh air. A small trailer with space heaters gets a bit close and, frankly, what's the point of living in a pond-side trailer in the woods if you don't step outside and enjoy it? Cold air be damned.

I stared at the stars and thought about the case. No sign of foul play, and Jimmy apparently had taken some money. No clothes, though, indicating he'd left in a hurry. A spur-of-the-moment decision seemed out of character for a smart chess wizard who liked to parse theological arguments, but it seemed on par for a fifteen-year-old boy. I know I was pretty goddamned stupid when I was fifteen.

The moon was lower now, behind the sycamores, oaks, maples, and pines, and it was very dark. I could hear an owl in the distance, and there was just enough wind sweeping through the trees to give the owl's call a supporting chorus. And Linda thought I should move to Columbus or Cleveland. Ha!

Lungs full of chilly night air, I went back inside to grab some sleep. I wasn't going to find Jimmy tonight. I'd hit the trail early tomorrow, though. Maybe one of Jimmy's chess club friends would know more than the parents.

I did not sleep much that night.

CHAPTER TEN

I DID A morning lap around the pond. It's not a course for running fast, because you have to duck beneath branches or step over the occasional root, and you have to be wary of muddy spots and goose crap. But that's one reason I like it, because I like working on reflexes along with building endurance. Another reason to like it? I'm in the middle of nowhere and no one is going to see if I slip in the mud. No one but the geese, or maybe a doe or a squirrel.

Also, running on flat roads bores the hell out of me.

After a quick shower, I drank a pot of black coffee and headed to the school to meet the chess club kids. The few moments of sleep I'd managed before the alarm went off were dominated by dreams, mostly featuring me asking people questions, then them shaking their heads sadly and saying they didn't know anything. I recalled Carl Sagan once describing dreams as some evolutionary development leftover from the days when humans were living in trees or caves, something our brains did to wake us up now and then so we could make sure something wasn't sneaking up to eat us while we slept. I have no idea whether Sagan was right about that or not, but I was pretty sure my dreams were stupid.

Breakfast was a leftover donut and a Thermos with more coffee, to be consumed on the road. I patted myself on the back for remembering to turn off the space heaters before leaving the trailer. Space heaters and piles of paperback detective novels are a bad combination.

I stepped back outside and took in a deep breath of fresh, cold air. I'll be honest. If I could spend way more time doing that, I'd be a much happier man. I ignored the fluffy snowflakes falling and waved at a turkey vulture circling above the pond. I climbed into the truck and fired it up. I fumbled through the country music CDs, but decided not to play one. I was too keyed up for music. I had a kid to find.

Fifteen minutes later, I was walking into Ambletown Middle School's library. A sign on the door said the library was open until noon on Saturdays so kids could study, clubs could meet, and community groups could use the conference room.

Even though school wasn't in session, it was a busy place. I saw eight tables with chessboards, and more than a dozen teenagers staring at those boards. None of them paid me the slightest attention, but a middle-aged guy with a pot belly, bald head, and wire-frame glasses looked up from his phone and saw me right away. I went straight to him.

"Are you in charge of this bunch?" I used a thumb to point toward the teenage Magnus Carlsens.

The man smiled. "You could say that, I suppose."

"Hi. I'm Ed Runyon, a private investigator. I'm looking for Jimmy Zachman."

"He's not here," the man said. Now he looked a little worried.

"I know. He left home the other day and did not come back. His parents hired me to find him."

"Oh," he said. "Oh. Well, I hope you find him. Is he in some kind of trouble?"

"I don't really know yet."

"I hope everything is OK. I'm Jerry Furniss. I teach math. I'm no chess player myself, but they wanted a club and needed a faculty member to supervise, so here I am."

"Good of you to do that. I hope the kids appreciate it. Mind if I ask you a few questions?"

"Go right ahead." He looked more worried now.

I sat down. "Is it unusual for Jimmy to miss a meeting?"

He frowned. "Very, now that you mention it. We always have one or two no-shows, of course, but Jimmy is always here. Except for today. He likes to play face-to-face as much as he can, and there are some kids in this club who challenge him."

"Did he send you a text or anything to apologize for his absence, or let you know he would not be here?" Based on what Jimmy's parents had told me, such a thing would be expected.

"No, he didn't."

"In your opinion, do you think he would have contacted you about that?"

The teacher's face screwed up in thought. "Yeah, I think that would be in keeping with Jimmy's character. Very polite boy. Please, sir, I'm sorry, but do you think something has happened to him?"

"I don't know. I hope not. I'm told Jimmy plays online chess, too?"

He nodded. "All the kids do. There are numerous apps, and they play people all over the world."

"Do you know which apps Jimmy used?"

"I don't, but I'll bet the kids do. They play each other online, too. They like coming here, though, and playing across a real board. There is an advantage in being able to see the fear in your opponent's eyes, or so I am told."

"I know the kids might be in the middle of a tourney or something, but this is important. I'm going to interrupt their games and ask a few questions."

"Oh, it's just a general game day," Furniss said, "not a tourney day. But even if it was a tourney, I mean, hell. Ask away. Chess is only a game, right?"

"Yeah, exactly. Thanks. Which of these kids knows Jimmy best, do you think?"

He pointed toward a heavyset redheaded boy with an impish grin. "That's Eric Murray. He and Jimmy play a lot. They are fairly evenly matched, the two best players in our club, really. Judging by Eric's little smile, he's about to win his game."

"Maybe I'll play him next," I said. "Thanks."

"Good luck. Eric favors flank openings, I hear, and he's actually tougher when playing Black."

"I'll keep that in mind." I had no goddamned idea what a flank opening was, but damned if I was going to let this guy know that. And I'm not a patient player, anyway, so it probably didn't matter what opening we played.

I walked over to Eric's table. He was playing White against a skinny brunette girl, and it seemed at first glance that he had placed both a knight and a bishop under attack. She could save one, but not both, as far as I could tell. She wasn't paying attention to the threatened pieces, though. Her eyes were locked on her queen, and I could almost see the gears rolling in her head.

"Oh!" She grabbed her queen and moved it on the long diagonal, all the way across the board. "Check!" She punched the chess clock with a dash of authority.

Now Eric's clock was ticking away, but he did not seem concerned. He still had several minutes to go. He scoffed. "My pawn will just take her, Marci."

"I know," she said, beaming. "Your pawn absolutely has to take her. It's that, or resign. And tell me what happens then, genius." She tended to talk fast.

Eric scanned the board for twelve seconds, by my count. He saw the trap before I did. To be honest, I wasn't sure I had spotted it. I only had a vague suspicion that her bishop was well placed to swoop in.

"Son of a bitch," he muttered.

"Pawn takes queen, my bishop slides in, check, you have to move the king, and—"

"Yeah, yeah," he said, toppling his king. "You win."

She raised her arms in triumph. "Yes! I win! That's what you get for peeking down my blouse instead of paying attention to the board!"

"Is that why you wore that shirt?" His eyebrows went up and down in a way he probably thought was devastatingly cool. It wasn't.

"I'll use every tool at my disposal," Marci said. "Cope."

"Fair," he said, extending a hand.

She shook it, then jumped up. "I beat Eric!"

That drew a round of applause. I half expected the librarian to tell them to keep quiet, but she clapped, too. The times, they are a-changing.

I took Marci's seat. "Mind playing a grown-up?"

The boy looked at me like I was a smudge on his shoe. "I don't have anyone waiting, so sure. Mind losing to a kid?"

"I might win," I said.

"Nah. You don't have distracting boobs."

I wasn't sure the girl who had just beat him was old enough to have distracting boobs, but I let that slide. I scooped up two pawns, Black in my right hand, White in my left. I put my hands behind my back, did no shuffling whatsoever, and extended my closed fists to Eric. He tapped my right hand, meaning he would play Black.

He reset the clock. I pointed at it. "Mind if we skip that? I'm rusty, and I don't need the extra pressure."

He shrugged. "Whatever, dude."

Once we had all the pieces swept up and arranged on the board, I moved my king's pawn forward two squares. If it's good enough for Bobby Fischer, it's good enough for me. I had now pretty much exhausted my knowledge of chess openings. The only other thing I knew for sure was that whenever I open with the queen's pawn, Tuck absolutely kicks my ass.

Eric moved his queen's bishop's pawn up two squares, and I already felt like I was in trouble. Tuck had never done that in response to my king's pawn opening. I stared at the board in confusion.

"Jesus," Eric said. "Really? It's a standard defense."

I ignored that. "I'm a private detective, looking for Jimmy Zachman. He seems to have run away from home. You play Jimmy a lot, I hear."

"Yeah, I do. He's pretty good."

"Would you call him a friend?"

"I guess."

"You guess?"

He shrugged. "We play chess, he usually wins but not so much lately."

"Do you and Jimmy play online, too?"

"Yeah, it's good practice."

"Do you play on a website?"

He shook his head. "An app." He tapped his phone a few times, then showed me. There was a home screen, with a list of games in progress, a bunch of chess puzzles, a challenge board, and more. Eric's profile picture was a medieval knight mounted on a rearing horse. A lance pointed right at me, and the steed snorted flames.

"You are King Eric? Who is Jimmy?"

He drew a finger across the screen and showed me a list of his recent games. "GodsPawn64."

Jimmy's profile picture was a cross, looming over a chessboard. I looked at Eric. "You can chat while playing, I guess? Send messages back and forth?"

"Of course."

"Do you know if Jimmy uses any other chess apps?"

"I don't think so," Eric answered. "We all kind of like this one best."

"I'm going to download it," I said. "Thanks. Did it surprise you when Jimmy did not show up here today?"

Eric grinned. "He's ducking me! And he should! I got his game figured out."

"No," I said. "He disappeared. Left home, did not come back."

"Shit," Eric said. He blinked three times.

Once I had the app downloaded, I moved a knight on the real board in front of me. Eric moved another pawn before my hand even left the piece. He had that weird smile going again, too, the one the teacher said was a bad sign for Eric's opponent.

"That's not good," I said, mentally patting myself on the shoulder for not saying "fuck" in a room full of kids.

"You don't play much, do you?"

I stared at the board. "Not much. I am going to add you as a friend on the app, OK? Will I be able to see your recent games? And Jimmy's?"

"Yeah. And yes, you can see the games."

"Great. Please accept my friend request. I won't bug you much, but if I can see who Jimmy has played recently, and maybe reach out to ask you questions, like have you played this person or chatted with them, or whatever, maybe that will help me find Jimmy. Maybe one of his online friends might know something." It was a long shot, but sometimes long shots pay off. "And can you give me your phone number, please? I may have more questions."

"Sure." He gave me the number.

"Thanks. Did Jimmy ever say anything to you about running away?"

"No. Why would he do that?"

"I don't know. Did he ever mention any kind of trouble?"

"No."

I advanced a knight. Eric smiled.

"I said I was rusty, kid."

"Yeah," he said. "You are." He slid a bishop across the board, taking my idiot knight.

"Fuck," I said.

"You shouldn't say that to a kid," he said, grinning widely.

"I know." I advanced another pawn to what I assumed was certain doom.

"Look," he said. "Jimmy and I only know each other here, across these sixty-four squares. We don't hang out, or talk online, or anything else." He moved his other knight. "He's OK. A good guy. Not sure Marci's tactic would work against him, though." He shot a glance away from the table, and I turned to see what he was looking at. He was looking at her rear end.

"What do you mean?" I moved my remaining knight.

He grinned. "I think maybe he likes dick better than tits."

"OK, well, I guess you can stop clutching pearls at my language, kid. You think Jimmy's gay?"

He grinned again. "Marci would do him right now, I swear, but Jimmy never even realizes it. He's gay as hell. I'd be all over Marci, you know."

Yeah. I knew.

Eric moved his knight, and I realized my position was hopeless. I stared at the board for thirty seconds to confirm that, but yeah, hopeless. "Well, you are pretty good at this."

"And you aren't."

I tipped my king over. "I'll let you play a more worthy opponent. But here's my card. If you hear from Jimmy or think of anything that might give me a clue as to where he's gone or who he's talking to, please contact me, anytime, day or night. Even if it's just a hunch, even if you think it's just a silly notion, if there is any chance at all it might help, you call me. OK?"

He picked up the card. "Yeah. OK. I'll do that."

I processed what my chessboard conqueror had told me. If Jimmy was gay, running away started to make sense. Assuming the boy had an inkling of Dad's thoughts concerning homosexuality, and given Dad's blogging and such Jimmy almost certainly did have a clue, then home might not have been a very pleasant place for him. He'd have to watch every word he said, everything he did, and he'd have to be constantly worried his parents might find out. He might even be dealing with shame, brought on by growing up in a house where gay people were believed to be abominations. Maybe he wasn't just worried about Mom and Dad finding out. Maybe he was worried about his eternal soul.

Jesus Christ.

I shook my head, unable to imagine what that might do to a kid. I had not grown up in a particularly religious home. As a cop, I'd occasionally run into adults who suppressed their sexuality, sometimes because it clashed with their religion, sometimes for other reasons. But I'd never encountered that with a kid, as far as I knew.

Bob Zachman had said there was no safe place for a kid. No safe place, indeed. Not even home.

His parents loved him, though, I told myself. I could see that. I could hear it in their voices even when they didn't say it. Whatever they thought about Jesus and homosexuality, they loved their boy, and that, I hoped, would be enough to get the family through.

"Hang on, Jimmy," I muttered under my breath. "I will find you."

I looked around and saw Marci, watching a couple of guys playing a game that seemed to involve more talking than analysis. She was trying not to kibitz, which involved a great deal of biting her own tongue, holding her breath, and rolling her eyes.

If she had a crush on Jimmy, there was a good chance she might know something, or perhaps she had spotted something out of the ordinary in his recent behavior.

I took up a position next to her. "Hi. My name is Ed Runyon. I'm a detective. I'm looking for Jimmy Zachman. Can I talk to you for a few minutes?"

"Ohmygodyes," she said, making it all one word. "Follow me!"

She ran off toward the science fiction section, and I followed. We ended up in front of some novels by Octavia Butler. Linda had recommended those to me more than once, but I had not gotten around to reading them yet.

"IsJimmyOK?" Again, all one word.

"I don't know," I said. "He left home the other day, and has not been seen or heard from since."

"Oh, no," she said. "OhmyGodIhopeJimmy'sOK."

I hoped for her sake that speed talking would someday become an Olympic event, because she was a surefire medalist. "Take a deep breath, please, and slow down for me, OK?"

"Sorry." She inhaled deeply, her eyes widened, and then she released the breath very slowly. It was all very deliberate, like something she'd practiced. "I said I hope he's OK."

"So do I. Have you heard anything from him?"

"No."

"Do you have any clue where he might go if he was in trouble?"

"What kind of trouble?"

"Any kind of trouble."

She frowned. "That's not a very helpful answer."

I nodded. "I realize that, and I'm not trying to be evasive. I know you're worried about him. But I don't have any idea yet what kind of trouble he's in, or if he's really in trouble at all, so I can't say much. He might be perfectly safe at a friend's house, for all I know. And I hope that is all that is going on. But his parents are worried, he's not answering his phone, and his parents want me to find him. And, to be honest, he might well be in some sort of trouble. So I want to find him as soon as I can."

Marci's forehead scrunched up. "He has an aunt he likes," she said.

"That one's on my list," I said. "Anyone else?"

"Not that I know of."

"OK," I replied. "So he's mentioned his aunt to you?"

She nodded, not quite as rapidly as she tended to talk. "A few times, yeah. Jimmy says she is really smart. He likes talking with her, says she challenges him."

I pondered that. If Jimmy had mentioned his aunt to Marci, then it seemed even more likely he might run to her if he needed help. How often do kids mention their aunts to other kids? She had told Bob that she had not heard from Jimmy, but maybe Becky Zachman thought she was protecting the kid. I don't know. It was a working hypothesis, anyway, which was more than I'd had when I'd woken up.

I smiled at Marci. "You like Jimmy, right?"

She shrugged. "Jimmy is a gentleman, you know? He's basically Darcy." Then she looked at me apologetically. "You probably don't read Jane Austen."

"Not all of them," I replied. "But I have read that one."

She grinned. "Everyone should read that one. So, Jimmy reminds me of Darcy. Smarter than everyone, or thinks he is, anyway, and kind of impatient about it sometimes, and full of honor and all that. Cute as hell, too. Yeah. I like him."

I nodded. "Does he like you?"

She stared at me a while. Tears started, but she got them under control before they streamed down her face. "Not that I can tell. I mean, we're friends, but, we're not . . . I think, maybe, he's . . ."

I stared at her. "He's what?"

"He's not into girls." That time, sobs interposed themselves between the syllables.

I didn't have a handle on my own love life, so I didn't feel qualified to comment or try to help this girl with hers. I gave her my card. "If you hear from him, or remember anything that might give me a clue where he's gone . . ."

"I will call you, day or night, hellhounds at my heels, the Dark Lord's agents surrounding me, no matter what," she said, snapping to attention. "If I can help you find him, I will."

I spent about three seconds wondering how I could inspire that kind of devotion in someone before deciding it probably was a hopeless cause. If Jimmy was not gay, or was at least open to a relationship with a girl, I hoped he would soon realize how much Marci adored him. "Thank you," I said. "It will help."

"You'll tell me if you find him, right?"

I nodded. "Give me your number."

We emerged from the science fiction section to see kids stuffing folded or rolled-up chessboards into backpacks. Most of the backpacks featured anime. A couple sported Marvel movie characters. One had a Hello Kitty theme.

"Can I have your attention, please?" I said it loudly, and I felt a little like all the high school teachers I loathed when I said it. "My name is Ed Runyon, I'm a private investigator, and I am trying to find a member of your club, Jimmy Zachman. He's disappeared, and his parents are worried sick. These are my business cards."

I took a few from my wallet and placed them on a table. "Please take one. If you think of anything, and I mean anything, that might help me find Jimmy, please, give me a call. Anytime. Day, night, I don't care. It is very important."

Mr. Furniss jumped in. "We all like Jimmy, right? And a couple of you think you are ready to beat him. So, if you know anything, please, speak up."

Heads nodded, and kids took cards. A few typed notes on their phones or jotted my number down in their notebooks.

"I sure hope you find him," Mr. Furniss said. "He's a good kid."

"I'll do my best."

Kids started filing out of the library as Mr. Furniss provided me a chess club membership list. It included addresses and phone numbers. I thanked him and headed out to my truck.

I did not get far before I heard a somewhat timid voice behind me. "Mr. Runyon?"

I turned and looked at a brown-headed, big-nosed kid wearing a "Black Lives Matter" T-shirt and jeans with big rips in them. Not at all appropriate for the weather, but Ohio kids learn to endure the cold. And it's Ohio, so things could warm up in a hurry anyway. As we always say in the Buckeye State, if you don't like the weather, just wait a minute, and it'll change.

The boy did not speak up when I faced him, and his eyes were shifting around. So I nudged. "Yeah?"

The kid looked over his shoulder, then came closer and gave me a stage whisper. "Can I talk to you for a second? I think Jimmy's in some deep shit."

CHAPTER ELEVEN

"GET IN THE truck, and I'll give you a ride home. We can talk privately. What's your name?"

"Ross," he said. "Ross Mason. I live on Blanche."

We both got in the truck, and he scoffed at the CDs piled up on the seat between us. "Dude. Sirius XM."

"I've owned these for years and they're already paid for," I said. "And I like deciding exactly what song to listen to instead of delegating such an important thing to some deejay. Now, what kind of trouble is Jimmy in?"

"He's got some dude sending weird messages."

"Like what?"

"Pictures."

"What kind of pictures?"

He shook his head. "I don't want to say."

"Look," I said, my patience thinner than my investment portfolio, "if Jimmy's in trouble, I need to know what's going on so I can get him out of it. And, by the way, you chased me down to talk, right? So talk."

"You won't tell his dad?"

"Not a word unless I really have to." I wondered why that was the big concern here.

Ross sighed as I rolled the truck out of the parking lot. "Well. You were a sheriff's deputy, right?"

"Yeah. Detective."

"I guess I can trust you. I got a weird message on Facebook Messenger yesterday. From someone I don't know. They wanted to know if I was a friend of Jimmy's."

He paused, as though I was supposed to extrapolate the truth of the universe from that small bit of data, so I nudged again. "Yeah?"

"Yeah. I did not answer the message, because it had a weird picture."

"What do you mean, a weird picture?" I aimed the truck for Blanche Avenue.

"It was a picture of Jimmy. A selfie. He wasn't wearing a shirt. His face was all . . . twisted up. Kind of gross, mouth wide open, eyes closed. I saved a screenshot."

I pulled over to the curb and parked. "So, you still have that message?"

"Yeah," he said. "I was going to show it to Jimmy. If I could do it away from anyone else, that is. I don't think he'd want anyone to see this."

"Show it to me."

He dragged fingers across the Android phone screen and handed me his phone.

Jesus.

Jimmy's face was as described, but despite the distortions, this was definitely the same nice young man I'd seen staring back at me from photos at the Zachman home. This photo was a vertical shot, taken in front of a bathroom mirror, with the bottom half blacked out. Jimmy's left hand was holding the phone. Judging by Jimmy's contorted fifteen-year-old face, the right hand was busy doing something else.

"Son of a bitch," I said. "Son of a bitch." There were no words with the message beyond what Ross had mentioned: "Do you know Jimmy Zachman?" The message was from an account under the name Darius Happninbooey.

I shook my head and looked at Ross. "Did you tell Jimmy about this?"

"No. We don't really know each other, except for chess club. I was going to show him today, like I said, if I could, you know, without anyone else around to see or hear. But he did not show up to play, and then you came looking for him, and, well, I thought I better show you."

I grabbed my own phone and tried to check out Darius Happninbooey's account on Facebook. It was gone.

I looked at Ross. "Did this guy contact you again?"

"Before that message, yeah, a couple of times. First time he just said he was interested in the chess club. Just saying hi, wanted to ask when we played and where. Said he wanted to join."

"You answered him back, even though he has this weird name and a cartoon character for a profile pic?"

Ross shrugged. "Lots of people have vague Facebook profiles. I have friends who have fake accounts just so they can talk to each other without their parents knowing about it. Cartoon pics and weirdo names are actually kind of normal. I just thought it was someone who wanted to play chess."

I considered that. "Did you give this person any details? I mean, about where the club meets or any of the members, especially Jimmy?"

"No," Ross said. "I just told him about the chess club website. He said that's where he found me."

"OK."

Ross pointed at his phone. "Then he sent me that. I ignored that. He never sent me anything after that."

"Did he explain why he sent you this, or try to?"

"No."

I realized I was holding my breath, so I let it out in a gush. So. Jimmy probably had gotten himself roped into an extortion scheme. He'd shared this photo, and now someone was hitting him up for money. That probably explained the cash missing from Mom's purse. And now the guy was sending cryptic messages to people Jimmy knew, probably in hopes they'd ask Jimmy about it. That would turn up the heat on Jimmy, maybe compel him to pay up.

I shook my head in disbelief.

I remembered an extortion victim in New York, a guy we'd called Bible Bill. He was a self-published writer of Christian-oriented books, and a deacon in a local church. Married, two kids, successful, well thought of. He'd gotten involved with a gay prostitute, and the relationship endured for several months while Bible Bill vacillated between giving up his sinful ways and running back for more sex with the hooker, named Salvador, believe it or not. Eventually, Bill attempted to part ways with Sal, but Sal wasn't ready to part ways with steady money, so the extortion started.

Salvador threatened, Bible Bill paid, and then Salvador threatened again. Rinse, lather, repeat.

By the time Bible Bill had come to NYPD for help, he'd already paid Salvador more than $10,000 to prevent his wife, church friends, and the Christian reading public from finding out what he'd been doing.

I'd never had a single ounce of sympathy for Bible Bill. He'd created all of his own problems, as far as I was concerned. Some cops defended him, saying he'd turned to a hooker because his religiosity had compelled him to try to live a lie, that he was actually more afraid of being gay than of getting caught, etcetera. Maybe there was something to all that. I'm not a psychologist. All I know is he'd lied to his wife and kids and spent a huge part of the family's income trying to hide his dirty little secrets.

Bible Bill never filed formal charges, not even after coming to us a dozen times begging us to "do something, please!" Us doing something would have meant arrests, which would have meant public records and, considering Bill's solid book sales, probable news coverage. That is one of the things blackmailers count on, of course. Nobody wants to see his deep, dark secrets broadcast on the nightly news or shared a million times on Twitter. So, Bill wasn't going to file charges, and he wasn't ever going to testify.

A couple of my colleagues went around to put a scare in Salvador, busted him on prostitution charges, told him to back off. And he did, for a while. Eventually, though, Salvador wanted more cash, so he leaned on Bible Bill again.

And Bible Bill kept paying and begging us to do something.

It all came to light eventually, anyway. Not because of anything we did, and not because Salvador made good on his threats to expose Bill's extracurricular activities. It all blew up in Bible Bill's face because he'd gone to answer the door for a visiting Jehovah's Witness, and left his phone unattended for a few crucial minutes. Bill's wife, Connie, was already suspicious that Bill was up to no good, and she snatched that thing up before the screen locked. She found the latest threatening text messages from Salvador, which included photos of her husband in a silky black bra-and-panty set and some spiky heels. Bill did not have the legs for those.

There were some photos of Salvador and Bible Bill together, too. I'll spare you descriptions.

Anyway, I hate blackmailers. At least muggers and armed robbers take some risks. They have to get up close and personal, giving you a chance to whip out a gun or a knife and defend yourself. Blackmailers just hide behind the scenes and play on people's fears. When blackmailers go to hell, I'll bet the other people who are roasting away for eternity piss on them. Nobody likes blackmailers.

And now, it looked as though Jimmy Zachman had gotten himself involved with one.

I doubted Jimmy had met someone local, though. His parents seemed to keep a pretty tight net around him, and it takes time to get out of the house and meet a guy and then do things you don't want the world to know about. I doubted Jimmy could get out of his parents' sight long enough to manage all that.

But an internet fling? Love and sex via video chat? He could arrange that from home, no problem. And that meant the perpetrator could be anywhere in the world.

Jimmy had probably met someone online, they did a video chat, things got explicit, and then, boom, here come the threats. Send money, or everyone sees you in all your glory.

And Jimmy, terrified, had bolted from home hoping to keep his churchy parents from finding out.

I spent a couple of moments wondering how humankind had ever managed to master the arts of making fire or inventing toilet paper. If people were callous enough to set such traps, and other people were dumb enough to fall for them, well, how the hell did we become the dominant life form on this earth?

Maybe we weren't the dominant species. Maybe the cockroaches, or the tardigrades, would be laughing at us and drinking toasts to our memories in a few billion years. Who really knows?

Anyway, Jimmy was a fifteen-year-old boy and that meant hormones, which no amount of chess know-how and book learning could ever defeat. Boys will be boys, and this one was in trouble.

I blew out a gust of air and tried to focus on the present day, where I'd been hired to find a missing kid. I suddenly remembered there was a boy sitting next to me. "How did this guy know you knew Jimmy?"

"Scroll back. I took other screenshots."

I did so, and saw the previous message. It said: *I play at the chess and I see you do it too!* It included an image, a screen capture of the chess club roster from the website, with Ross's name circled.

So the blackmailer had poked around online, found some of Jimmy's friends, and now was trying to turn up the heat.

I read the message again. *I play at the chess* did not sound like proper grammar to me. Granted, proper grammar seems to be going the way of *Ankylosaurus* these days, especially in online messaging, but even considering that, this message seemed distinctly foreign. I pictured someone in a third-world country, laughing out loud because he'd tricked another dumb American into dropping his pants on video.

I looked at the kid next to me. "Have you told anyone else about this?"

Ross shook his head violently. "No way. What Jimmy does is his business."

"That's good of you. Don't tell anyone. Do you know Jimmy's parents?"

"Seen them, don't really know them. Very religious, though. I've read his dad's blog. If Jimmy showed his thing to someone online, his dad's gonna kill him."

"No," I said. "His dad won't kill him."

The kid laughed. "Have you met his dad?"

"Yes. His dad won't kill him."

But did Jimmy know that?

Maybe not. Maybe that's why he ran.

CHAPTER TWELVE

I dropped Ross off at home, after forwarding the damnable messages to my own phone, then drove toward the Ambletown Police Department. I called ahead, using the non-emergency line because I'm not a dick.

"Ambletown Police." A woman's voice. She did not sound as hot as Debbie, the weekday dispatcher at the Mifflin County Sheriff's Office. I didn't miss the SO much, but I missed flirting with Debbie. I wondered if she missed flirting with me? Probably not. There were plenty of men willing to flirt with Debbie.

"Hi. This is Ed Runyon, used to be with Mifflin County, now I'm a PI."

After a slight pause, she answered. "How can I help you, Mr. Runyon?" I could hear the chill in her voice. Most local cops are not happy with me since the Jeff Cotton incident. The general populace was somewhat divided. If you don't believe me, just go on Facebook or Twitter. Some of them believed anything a cop did was OK because of law and order blah blah blah, while others blamed me for ruining the boy's football career. Some cops hated me for that, too, of course, but most had a better reason. I'd gone off half-cocked, then put a lot of other cops at risk when I'd taken a low-percentage knee shot instead of killing the boy who was carrying a big bad rapid-fire gun with a bump stock. My decision could have cost other officers their lives.

I understand their anger. I'm still angry about it myself. But I'm managing that better these days.

Well, I had been managing it better. Now Linda's dating another guy. So, I don't know what the hell is going on, I guess.

I stopped ruminating and spoke to the woman on the phone. "I have information for the lead detective in the Jimmy Zachman case."

"The runaway?"

"Yes." That was one big difference between policing in rural Ohio and doing the same in New York. What were the odds the dispatcher at NYPD would know what case I was talking about off the top of her head? A trillion-zillion to one, probably.

"Detective Dillon Spears is investigating that," she said.

I sighed with relief. "He's a new guy, right?"

"Started last week."

Good, I thought. *Maybe he doesn't hate me yet.*

"Please connect me to him. Thanks."

"One moment. I'm going to put you on hold. I'll see if he is in."

After five rings, a man picked up. "Detective Spears. I hear you have information about Jimmy Zachman?"

"I do. It looks like he's being blackmailed."

"What?"

I explained how I knew that, which included telling him who I was and who I was working for and how I'd obtained the extortion information.

"I wanted to go talk to those chess kids myself this morning, goddamn it. Got called away on something else."

He couldn't see me, but I was nodding. Getting called away on something else had fucked up too many missing kid cases when I was a cop, because there is always something else to get called away to. This is why I left the sheriff's office and struck out on my own. "I know you guys are swamped. Listen, I'm close. Can I pop in and get a copy of your report? I can show you these images Jimmy's friend got."

"Yeah," he said. "That'll work, I guess, unless you'd like some coffee? We could meet up somewhere?"

I wasn't going to dilly-dally. "No, thanks. I have a couple of other things I'm going to run down."

"Like what?"

"Long shots," I said. "The kid loves chess. I play a little. I'm going to try to find him on the app he's using, see if he's still playing, maybe message him that way. He won't answer when his parents call, but I'm thinking he's probably still playing chess. It's a game people obsess over, and his dad says he is really good at it. I figure I'll try to get him to play me, if I can, and establish contact that way."

Spears replied, "Yeah, he's not answering phone calls or going on his Facebook lately. OK, good idea, actually. Might work. You'll keep me posted?"

"Sure. I hope you'll do the same for me."

"Yeah, I can do that. I'll have copies of our reports for you when you get here."

"Ten minutes."

Nine minutes later, I was walking into the Ambletown PD lobby. A broad-shouldered man in uniform was awaiting me. He did not look glad to see me, and I knew why. Officer Peter Burns blamed me because he'd been denied some off-duty overtime pay during the county fair a couple of years ago. I'd mentioned to one of the fair board members that Officer Burns seemed to follow some of the younger girls in really short shorts a little too closely for comfort. They'd asked me and some others to keep an eye on him after that. None of us saw him touch any of the girls, but he sure did flirt with them. A lot. And more than one girl had complained to me about things he'd said.

I'd talked to the fair board again and they'd kicked Burns out.

"Runyon. I heard you were coming. Smelled you in the parking lot. I read about a PI got found murdered dead in an old corn silo. Bunch a wild feral cat felines had chewed him up pretty good, made it hard to ID the remains. I was hoping it was you."

I looked past the ugly, warty nose and into the dull gray eyes. "Sorry, Burns. Different PI. Guy named Parker. But congratulations on learning to read. I had bet against that."

He sneered. That did not stop me from continuing. "By the way, cat felines is redundant, and wild feral cat felines is ridiculously redundant, but I suppose you don't know what redundancy is." I suppose I could have riffed on his name—Peter Burns? Really? Did your parents hate you at birth?—but that was low-hanging fruit and to be honest, every cop in Mifflin County had already mined that fertile field to death. We were collectively all out of STD jokes where this guy was concerned.

He took a step toward me. I stopped in my tracks and let him do it. We stood close to one another. He'd been eating bacon.

"I'd like to pound you," he whispered. "I really, really, really want to beat the shit out of you. You put our SWAT guys at risk."

I stared into his eyes. Mine were about an inch higher than his, and I leaned forward just a bit to make sure he realized that. "If we keep standing close and whispering like this, the lady behind the glass will think we're kissing. I hope people know I could do way better than you."

He shook his head slowly, and I watched his face turn red. "You shouldn't be allowed in here."

"I pay taxes, though, which means I help pay your salary, so go fuck yourself."

His face scrunched up in a way that seemed to indicate a punch was coming my way. I have no idea whether he'd have really taken a swing at me or not, because a side door opened and Burns stepped back. A voice came from the open door. "Runyon?"

A slender, bald man in his forties emerged into the lobby, holding a folder and proffering a hand. "I'm Detective Dillon Spears."

Burns stepped aside. I took the detective's hand and shook it. "Ed Runyon."

The detective casually pulled me away from Officer Burns. For a slender guy, he was strong. "Everything OK here, Officer?"

"Will be when this piece of shit leaves." Burns looked proud of himself, as though *piece of shit* was the height of witty insults.

Spears stepped between me and Burns. "Runyon's here on official business and he's already done more useful police work this morning than I've seen you do since we met," Spears said. "Go eat a fucking donut."

The officer squared his shoulders. "Now, listen, Detective, I don't have to take this shit from you just because you wear a tie."

Spears glanced at the wall clock. "What time was your patrol supposed to start, Burns?"

"I'm going." Burns glared at me as he walked out the front door.

The detective faced me and held out the information I'd come for. "Here you go."

I took the folder from Spears. "Man, I think I love you."

He grinned. "That's why I suggested coffee somewhere else. You are not very popular around here. I wanted to avoid that kind of scene."

"No need. I gotta live around here, you know? And there are people who are not cops who don't think highly of me, either. I've learned to live with the shame and condemnation."

He nodded. "Well, that's a philosophical approach, I guess."

"Why don't you hate me?"

Spears shrugged. "I wait until I actually meet someone before I make such an important decision."

"Damn," I said. "I'm going to try that approach myself. But it's too late for Burns. I already started hating him a while back. What's your take on the boy's father?"

"Zachman? Seems a solid guy to me."

"Jimmy's chess pals think he, Jimmy, not the dad, is gay. Jimmy's dad is really not the approving sort. I think he's a loving father, though. I could hear it in his voice when he was telling me what a good chess player his boy is. I think maybe Jimmy got into trouble, and now there is a man threatening to show Jimmy's dad a picture of his pride and joy playing with his you-know-what. A guy Jimmy plays chess with got these messages, via Facebook."

I brought it up on my phone and showed it to Spears. "Oh, shit," he said. "Teen boys are stupid. Glad that got cropped."

"Me, too," I said. "Give me an email address, I'll forward these."

He did, and I sent him the pictures.

I looked Spears in the eyes. "Jimmy might be more worried about the gay angle than the extortion angle, if he reads his dad's blog."

Spears sighed. "I read some of that, but gave up very quickly. But you could be right."

"Could be." I nodded. "I'm hoping Jimmy ran off to stay with a friend. He apparently took some money from mom's purse, by the way. She discovered that when I was there, so you may or may not be aware of that fact—about seven-hundred bucks. Anyway, I'm hoping Jimmy left because he's terrified Dad will find out he's gay. Not that that's a good thing, of course, but it beats the shit out of a kidnapping or a murder or whatnot. I am hoping Jimmy called a friend, holed up safe somewhere, everything is really fine, family can be reunited, and dad and son can work things out, but . . ."

Spears looked at me. "But?"

"But . . . I can't rule out the idea that Dad maybe already found out his pride and joy is a homosexual, and Jimmy's in a hole somewhere."

"Jesus Christ, I doubt that," Spears said, eyes rolling. "I really, really, really doubt that."

"Yeah, I doubt it, too. Have to consider all the angles, though, right? Dad's blog is kind of tough on gay folks."

He looked at me with intense skepticism. "Do you know a lot of child murderers who hire private detectives to come and investigate their crimes?"

I laughed. "Not a one, but I tend to think out loud, and weird things happen in this world. I mean, someone married Burns."

Spears tried not to chuckle at that, but failed. "Yeah. Damn. I'm going to look closer at Dad's movements, his car, and all that. I really don't expect to find anything, though."

"I don't think you will, either. Gotta check, though."

"Yeah, Dad seemed a decent guy, but . . . gotta check. Well, nice to meet you, Runyon. You should know not everyone around here hates you, but some of the ones who don't aren't as loud as the ones who do."

"Yes. Ever the way in the court of public opinion."

"Coffee sometime?"

"Yeah, sounds good." I hoisted the folder. "Thanks for this. Coffee, or beer. After we find Jimmy."

CHAPTER THIRTEEN

I GOT BACK to the trailer and made a three-egg omelet with cheddar cheese, then slathered it in hot sauce and put it between two slices of toasted sourdough bread. Most of it went into the sandwich, anyway. Lots of it fell out onto my plate, so I grabbed a fork. I have a tendency to overstuff egg sandwiches.

I thought about eating outside on the picnic table because the sun was shining, but the sun wasn't really making things warmer. So I opened a can of Mountain Dew, sat down to eat in the trailer, and looked through the case folder Spears had given me. It was far too scant to give me much hope. The Zachmans had told the police all the same things they'd told me. Officers had scoured the neighborhood, but no one had seen Jimmy leave or noticed anyone visiting the Zachman house.

One new thing the report told me was that nothing useful had turned up on neighbors' security cameras so far. That did not surprise me. Those things were fine for snapping photos of people standing right in front of the doorbell, but mostly useless when it came to identifying cars in the street or people far away from your porch. Definitely useless when it came to identifying someone across the street.

The report was encouraging in one sense, though. The police were taking the case seriously. They would continue exploring the Zachmans' computer and the neighbors' security footage, things they were much better equipped to handle than I was.

My advantage? I was a free agent, and I wasn't going to let myself get distracted. Not this time.

I put the folder down and sighed. I needed to know more about this extortion scheme, so I called my favorite Columbus cop, Detective Michelle Beckworth. She worked for an agency much bigger than the little old Mifflin County Sheriff's Office I'd previously worked for, and it was a good bet her department had heard a lot more about this kind of extortion shit than I had. And because Shelly is blessed with dark curly hair, a great smile, and a curvy, athletic body, I decided FaceTime would be better than just a call. Shelly is a lesbian, but she's nice to look at all the same, and I was spending nights alone these days, so what the hell.

She answered right away. "Ed Runyon, how are you, cowboy?"

"I'm living the dream, Shelly. You?"

"Enjoying a day off, unless you're calling to drag me into some gruesome crime. I gotta tell you up front, I am not in the mood for a gruesome murder today." She was in a living room, apparently, and from the camera angle it looked as though she'd answered on an iPad, not her phone.

"Looks like you are working already," I said.

"Well," she said, and she ducked her head. Was she blushing? "I'm working on my own thing. I'm writing a novel."

"No shit," I said. "Well, that's awesome. Cops?"

"Horror, actually. Blood and gore, but funny, sort of Stephen King meets Monty Python."

"Nice. Sounds like exactly the kind of thing this world needs. I'll tell Linda to make it required reading for her classes."

"I'd appreciate that! How is that cutie?"

I sighed. "Working on her own horror novel, tired of me, branching out in new directions, exploring relationships that do not include me."

Shelly paused for a second. "I'm sorry, man. I thought you two crazy kids were going to make it."

"Not tonight," I said. "Anyway, none of this has anything to do with why I called. I'm working on a missing kid case, and it has taken sort of a masturbatory turn."

Shelly did a facepalm. "I'm going to need you to explain that, but I kind of wish I didn't have to ask you to explain that."

I told her about the disappearance, and about the extortion scheme Jimmy had fallen prey to. "I figured you see more of that kind of thing than we do in the sticks."

"Oh, it happens everywhere," she said, shaking her head. "Country boys, city boys, teenagers, old married guys, anyone with a penis. Y'all are stupid. We get plenty of calls. You would not believe."

"I knew it happened, but not how often. Is there much that can be done about it?"

"Not really, Ed. I've read up on this stuff, because someone has to read all the department bulletins, right? The FBI has some data and information about this, but it's usually a jurisdictional mess, you know? The internet is everywhere, of course, so these perps are almost always in the Philippines, or Nigeria, or somewhere else where the cops don't care if someone is ripping off Americans who can't keep their dicks in their pants. Sometimes the perps are in the U.S., but that's a bigger gamble because law enforcement can maybe get hold of them. Those guys tend to be idiots, or kids, who don't think about consequences."

"Gotcha," I said. "I kind of get the feeling Jimmy's blackmailer is a foreigner. The messages I saw had some odd grammar. It's a small sample size, so I can't really assume, but what you're telling me jibes with what I've seen."

Shelly nodded. "What they do is this. They get a hottie, and she goes on Instagram or Facebook or dating sites and she just makes friends, you know? Hi, how are you? Let's talk. She is usually flirty, with a super-hot profile pic that'll make you look twice. They might do the same damned thing for a dozen guys a night, just hoping one of them will bite. And, since guys are fucking stupid, one of them always bites. When they do, she'll start talking to the guy, get kind of flirty, talk about how the internet is a chance for people to connect for some safe sexy fun and all that shit, and then she'll move them to a video platform, Google Hangouts or something like that."

I nodded. "Yeah. Everything you are telling me is confirming my conviction that the internet was a bad idea."

"Too late to rethink it, cowboy."

"I guess."

Shelly continued. "They chat for a while, flirt for a while, turns out she likes all the same music and movies he does, blah blah blah, yadda yadda yadda. Then she starts taking off her clothes . . ." Shelly lifted her T-shirt as though she were about to take it off, then dropped it and laughed. "Sorry."

"Don't do this shit to me, you tease."

"Couldn't help it." She reached for something out of the frame and then showed me a glass of red wine. "I'm a little drunk. Write drunk, edit sober. Hemingway!" She took a drink.

"I think that quote is misattributed or taken out of context," I said. "I know it's controversial, anyway. And I know he never said 'write drunk, tease your horny detective friend drunk.'"

Shelly laughed. "Oh, yeah, OK. Not fair of me. I know you think I'm hot. And you are right!" She took another sip and gave me some side-eye.

"Jesus, Shelly, you're killing me here."

She bowed. "Sorry. So, the Filipino hottie takes it all off and starts touching herself in a lot of exciting and interesting places, then she urges the idiot on the other end of the video call to show what he's got and do the same. Only fair, right?"

"What a trap. Do women even really want to see that kind of thing?"

Shelley shook her head. "The answer to that is an unequivocal no," she said. "Even straight women have told me that. Nobody wants to see that."

"But guys fall for it."

She nodded. "Yes, but it's a trap. After watching her do her thing for a few minutes, the average dude seems to whip it out in record time. I mean, seriously, y'all just whip it out. Anyway, the dude does his thing, then, bam! The hottie says hey, I recorded that! Won't your mommy be so proud to see it? Or your wife? Or your boss? Or, hell, the whole damned internet?"

"Yikes."

"Yeah. They hit some of these guys with the threat before they even get a chance to, you know, um, finish what they are doing, shall we say. After that, the hotties usually turn the poor son of a bitch over to a collector, some tough-talking dude, so he can continue making the threats and collecting the money and the hottie can go rope in some other poor dumb bastard. Time is money, you know."

"And this happens a lot?"

"Fuck, yeah. It's a cottage industry. Easy money. I think they have goddamned call centers in Nigeria."

"How do they get paid?"

"Lots of ways. Western Union, but I think the wire transfer companies are making some moves to prevent that. But these guys get creative. They have the victim buy gift cards, and then the victim scratches them off and takes a picture of the code and sends that to the perps. The bad guys just get the code from the picture and, *voila*."

Damn, I thought. *What a fucking racket.* I told her Jimmy had apparently taken a wad of cash from his mother's purse, and I figured he'd used it to pay off an extortionist. But I knew from my police experience that blackmailers never, ever let go once they've got you. "Do they send shit to parents or wives if the victim doesn't pay?"

She nodded. "Sometimes, yeah. Not always, though. The FBI says they usually have a lot of victims and they spend most of their time and effort on the ones who get scared out of their wits and cough up some money. They send pics around to people if you piss them off or something, though. Or if you ignore them."

"Fuck." *Poor Jimmy*. "I suppose the perpetrators can't be traced?"

"There are some ways to do it, technically, that can work," she said, "but why bother? You can't get cops or judges in these foreign countries to do anything. Those people think it is hilarious when Americans fall for this shit, and the people in the U.S. with the know-how to track them down have much more important demands on their precious time, you know?"

"Yeah. Somebody needs to track these bastards down, fly to their hideout, and do some serious ass kicking."

She shrugged. "Can't disagree. I'd send Iron Man. He'd fuck them up, for sure." She laughed. "But Iron Man is fictional. But . . ."

I waited for her to finish the thought, then nudged her. "But?"

"Sorry," she said. "Got distracted for a moment. Please continue."

"The kid I'm looking for is fifteen, Shelly. And he may have whipped it out for a dude, not a woman, which may be why he ran off, because his dad is very religiously not in favor of anyone being gay. People the kid plays chess with say this boy is gay. One of those kids got a Facebook message from a Darius something or other, asking if he knew Jimmy. That was accompanied by a picture that indicated that Jimmy was, you know . . ."

Her eyes rolled. "I know."

"Yeah." I sighed. "Look, Jimmy's dad is very Christian and kind of loud about homosexual sin and all that."

Shelly grew suddenly stern. "You don't say. Maybe Jimmy ought to be out of that house."

I shook my head. "I'm not defending the dad's attitude, understand, but I talked with the parents a long time. They're good people, and they are worried sick about their son. I want very, very much to look them in the eye and tell them Jimmy is safe."

"Yeah, Ed. I get it." She took another sip of wine. "But if the dad beats that boy . . ."

"I do not think that'll happen, and there is absolutely no indication anything like that has ever happened, but if it does, I'll see to it dad regrets that very much."

"OK. So, Darius?"

"Yeah." I checked my notes. "Darius Happninbooey."

"I can pretty much guarantee that's a fake account."

"Yeah, and it no longer exists."

Shelly sighed. "It is so easy to set up fake accounts."

I nodded. "Yeah."

Shelly took another sip of wine, then returned her gaze to the camera. "They really apply the pressure, Ed. Relentless. One fake account after another will just keep hammering at the boy. I mean, they scare the shit out of people. The collectors are almost always dudes, no matter who the victim showed his cock to."

A voice came from somewhere out of view. "Are we getting a cockatoo?"

Shelly laughed. "No, baby."

An absolutely stellar California blonde walked into view and planted a kiss on Shelly's lips. It was a long kiss. "You've been drinking," California Girl said when they finally parted.

"Yeah, and writing." Shelly pointed at the screen. "Lana, meet Ed. Ed, this is Lana."

"Hello, Lana." I tried to say it without sounding creepy or horny, but . . . it was a hell of a kiss and Lana was movie star material, somewhere between Charlize Theron and Margot Robbie—which, you have to admit, would be a nice place to be. Anyway, I'm pretty sure I sounded both creepy and horny. But the women were too polite to comment on that.

Lana looked at the screen.

"Oh, hi, Ed! Nice to meet you! Shelly says you're a book guy and she's going to have you read this monster book she's writing when she's done, says she wants your opinion and all that."

"I'd be honored. And, well, yeah, I like a good brain-melting horror book now and then."

Shelly patted Lana on the ass. "Ed's consulting with me on a case. I'll be done soon."

Lana leaned in for another kiss. The maneuver offered me a peek down the neck of Lana's blouse, so I averted my eyes. I admit I was a little slow about it. I'm only mortal.

Their lips parted, and they stared into one another's eyes for three seconds. Finally, Lana said, "I'm going to go shower."

"I'm going to finish this paragraph as fast as I can," Shelly answered.

Lana disappeared.

I probably turned red. "I'm going to, um, hell, I don't know."

Shelly laughed again. "Sorry, Ed. So, anyway, in my professional opinion, the big thing for your case, I think, is to concentrate on finding the kid. You can deal with the extortion shit later. It honestly may be best if your boy tells the perps to fuck off and stops worrying about everyone seeing his dick. His real friends will get over it, and no one else, frankly, is going to give a shit. There are dicks all over the internet."

I sighed. "Yeah, maybe, but I have a feeling his parents might feel otherwise. OK. Well, thanks, Shelly. Send me a copy of your book when you are done. I'd love to read it."

"I'll do that. Even if you love Dumas. I hate Dumas. He's so wordy."

"But shit happens in his books. Swords, guns, affairs, spies. Shit happens."

"Shit happens in my book, too. I guarantee! Mostly gruesome, splattery, gory shit!"

"Can't wait to read it. See ya later, Shelly. Kiss Lana for me."

"I'm going to kiss her for me, cowboy. Sorry."

I signed off, then finished my lunch. Next time, I'll remember to finish my egg sandwich before I call the hot, distracting lesbians. Cold omelet sandwiches suck.

CHAPTER FOURTEEN

I OPENED THE chess app and got to work.

I created my own profile after spending way too much time trying to come up with a username that I thought would sound like a teenage boy. I am not a teenage boy, and what the fuck do I know about teenage boys, anyway? I settled on GodzillaStomp. Would a teenage boy even know about Godzilla? Hell if I know. I only know that sometimes teen boys masturbate for strangers on the internet and then run away from home.

Once I was logged in to the chess app, I looked up Jimmy's profile, GodsPawn64. His profile was open to challenges, so I went ahead and issued one. I chose the option to let him choose White or Black, and left him the choices of how much time to allow between moves and whether the game would count toward ratings or not. I wanted to make things as easy as possible for him, in hope that he would take up my challenge and thus open a line of communication. Jimmy's rating on the app was 1999, while mine as a newbie was set at 1200, indicating he was going to kick my ass no matter which pieces I got or how long he let me think about my next move. None of that was important. Finding him was. Still, my ego was somewhat bruised.

I could see Jimmy's recent games, but the list stopped at twenty. Fourteen of those games were against someone named Wunderkind. The most recent game against Wunderkind had ended just four days ago. Jimmy had won. As near as I could tell from the limited data, Jimmy and Wunderkind habitually started a new game as soon as one ended. But they had no current game in progress. That, as they say, was an anomaly.

Jimmy had, however, started two games with other people since last playing Wunderkind.

I sighed with relief. If Jimmy was playing chess online, he was alive. And he wasn't tied up in some blackmailer's sex dungeon, either. Probably.

I had another thought, too. If Jimmy and Wunderkind played a lot, odds were good that they had chatted a bit online. At least, that's what I told myself. I was, admittedly, grasping.

I tapped on Wunderkind's profile. It featured an Ohio State logo.

My head started spinning at this point. If Wunderkind was a Buckeyes fan, then he or she might not be too far away. Jimmy might well have called Wunderkind for help.

Wunderkind was currently playing someone named Foucho and Wunderkind was winning. I looked at recent games. Along with all the games against GodsPawn64—Jimmy—I saw Wunderkind had played against KingEric, the young man in Ambletown who had lost a game because he had paid too much attention to Marci's anatomy. That reminded me I had only moments earlier been peeking down a lesbian's T-shirt, and I realized I was probably never going to grow up and didn't really want to, anyway. Eric and I were kindred spirits, of a sort. Denizens of Neverland. But he was a kid and thus was expected to do crass things, whereas I was, allegedly, an adult.

Sorry, not sorry, as the kids say.

It looked as though players could converse with one another, but the app would not let me see whether Wunderkind routinely chatted with his opponents or not. Such things, apparently, remained private between participants.

Well, then. I would participate. I issued a challenge to Wunderkind, then checked my notes and called Eric Murray.

He answered right away. "Hey, detective guy, did you find Jimmy?"

"No, but I noticed something on the chess app. He was playing a guy named Wunderkind, a lot. Stopped playing him, or her, a few days ago. I noticed you played Wunderkind, too."

"Yeah, kicked his ass. He attacks waaaaaaaaay too soon."

I'm not a chess nerd, so I had no idea what that meant and I did not care to figure it out. "Do you know who Wunderkind is?"

"Um, sort of. I mean, I never met them or anything, but I played them because Jimmy thought they'd give me a good game."

I felt like a hound who'd picked up a scent. "I can see games between people, but I can't see any of their chats. It looks like the app lets you do that, though?"

"Oh, yeah," Eric said. "You can send messages to people while you play them, do some smack talk, beg some guy who can't possibly win to just resign already, whatever."

"Did you chat with Wunderkind? Do you know anything about him? Her?"

"Them," Eric said. "Wunderkind prefers *them*. I don't know a lot more than that, but I know they and Jimmy are friends."

I was grinning. Maybe Jimmy had stopped playing online chess with Wunderkind because he was now able to play Wunderkind in person. Maybe Jimmy had fled from home and rushed to Wunderkind, a friend who used gender-neutral pronouns and thus might be totally open to Jimmy's sexuality. It was an idea, anyway. "OK, then. Did you chat with them?"

"Yeah," Eric said. "Of course I chatted with them. Psychology is a big part of the game, you know? I always chat with them. If I can't look at the other player across the board and see fear in his eyes, I want to at least chat at him. You know? Use some smack talk, some misdirection, some psychology, learn whatever I can about him. Or, in the case of Wunderkind, them."

I took a deep breath. "And what did you learn about Wunderkind?"

"They live in Columbus, but I don't know where. And they play Jimmy. A lot. An awful lot."

Columbus was about an hour south of Mifflin County. Not at all too far away to serve as a haven for an Ambletown kid who was scared to death.

"Does Wunderkind drive?"

"Um, yeah, actually. At least, I think. They were complaining one time about their car being in the shop, anyway, so I guess they drive. I guess you would not complain about that unless you were a driver, right?"

"Right." I crossed my fingers. "Did you get anything else from them? Even just a first name, or a last name, or anything?"

"Let me look at the chat. Hang on."

I paced while I waited. The trailer is pretty damned small, so pacing is more like step, step, turn, step, step, turn, try not to overturn a pile of books, step, step, turn. Rather frustrating, when you get right down to it. But having a spot to hide away from the rest of the human race? Priceless.

Eric returned. "Yeah, they told me a first name."

"Awesome. What is it?"

"Kyuuketsuki."

"What? Can you spell that?"

He spelled it. "I looked it up," Eric said. "It's a Japanese term for vampire. They go by *Suki* for short."

“Oh,” I said, because it was the most rational thing I could come up with at that very moment.

“Yeah,” Eric said. “Cool name.”

“But probably not the name his, or her, I mean their parents gave them.”

“Well, no,” Eric said. “But a person can pick their own name, right?”

“Right. Sure. Thanks, Eric. If that is your real name.”

“I’m thinking of going with King Crusher, actually,” he answered. “What do you think?”

“I think I need a drink. Anything else, like an address for Suki?”

“No, sorry. Only dumbasses share their addresses with random people online.”

I said thanks, hung up and headed to the fridge.

I sat down with a beer and looked at my phone again.

My challenge to GodsPawn64 had been declined.

CHAPTER FIFTEEN

I TRIED TO imagine myself in Jimmy's situation. I'm fifteen and smart as hell, but full of hormones so I do dumb stuff sometimes. I'm on the run because some foreign bad guy wants to show the whole goddamned internet my naked pictures and tell everyone I'm gay. I do not want to be around when mom and dad find out I'm gay, because that might not go over well, and I am fifteen so, what the fuck? I run off to stay with a chess friend named Suki, and then get a chess challenge from a random stranger.

Yeah, I'd decline that challenge.

I tried to issue a new one, but the app was frozen. I refreshed, and suddenly GodsPawn64's profile was gone. When I searched for it, I got zip. Zero. Nada. Nothing but an uncaring universe laughing at me.

I had no idea whether Jimmy had deleted it or just gone into some kind of private mode, but I couldn't blame him in either case. Assuming Jimmy was in control of his own phone, he had probably gone private to avoid any more contacts from his tormentors. Shelly had called them relentless, masters at inducing panic. Who wouldn't just go private to avoid that, right?

I said a little prayer, despite my uncertainties where theology was concerned. All theology is amateur theology, and we're all basically just swimming in mystery, but I prayed anyway because what the fuck else could I do? I didn't really think it would work, but I had to try.

Jimmy's parents believed, I told myself, and his aunt said Jimmy believed despite reading that radical Carl Sagan stuff, so I figured what the hell. If somebody out there in the universe could command some guardian angels, I'd call in the cosmic air support. Couldn't hurt.

I looked to see if Wunderkind had accepted my challenge. There had been no response.

I opened up my laptop so I could check some online databases. I didn't have much to go on. A chess app username, Wunderkind, for someone Jimmy played a lot of chess with. A self-chosen name, Kyuuketsuki. Suki for short. A location, Columbus, Ohio, about an hour away and close enough for Jimmy to seek sanctuary there if a ride could be arranged. Wunderkind was a driver, Eric Murray had said. If I could get the kid's real name or address, I could, maybe, find out if Jimmy was there. It was a thin thread, admittedly, but it was the only thread I had, so I was going to follow it. Detectives who decide a thread won't pay off before actually checking it out never get lucky. Detectives who pursue every goddamned lead sometimes hit pay dirt. So sayeth Ed Runyon, private detective.

The main thing working for me, along with any guardian angels that might have been summoned by my plea, was the fact that kids pretty much live online these days. If Jimmy's friend used the same nicknames on other websites—Wunderkind, Suki, Kyuuketsuki—then I might be able to find some other avenue of communication. Hell, if I could find an online chat somewhere that Suki had participated in, I might even find an address or a phone number. I know kids are told "once it's online, it is online forever" and all that, but hey, the kid I was looking for had shown his dick to a stranger, so I could hope Suki had maybe dropped an address or something online somewhere.

I input the information I had into the databases I use for this kind of stuff, now that I don't have brainy people at the sheriff's office to delegate it to, and waited thirty seconds or so while wheels spun around on my computer screen. Then I almost shouted with glee. Suki had quite the online presence.

There was an Instagram account. All the pictures were anime. No addresses or anything.

There was a Twitter account. It had not been touched in three years. Twitter bores kids, I hear. According to the bio, Suki preferred the pronouns "they/them." This was consistent with what I knew so far, so I counted it as a plus.

There was a Facebook account. Thank God for Facebook.

Suki's Facebook page did not use whatever name the parents had bestowed upon their child, but it definitely confirmed the kid was in Ohio. One recent post warned friends about an impending snowstorm, and it included a map showing a big red and yellow blob bearing down on Columbus. The edge of that blob had skirted past my trailer. I remembered it very well, because it is a gigantic pain in the ass to lose power in my trailer.

Suki's previous posts exalted in the glory that is Ohio State football. Suki was a big fan of Skyline Chili, an Ohio-based chain. In a selfie, Suki looked like a boy with long hair, colored bright red and yellow. In another, they looked more like a she.

Two posts within the last month warned people about the evils of drugs. Three mentioned support for LGBTQ people. One urged people to adopt dogs from shelters instead of buying them from puppy mills. In another, Suki wished that they had a dog.

Suki seemed to be a good kid, open-minded and not judgmental, maybe the kind of person Jimmy would seek out for help in a tight spot.

I clicked on Suki's friend list. Jimmy was there. A quick click told me Jimmy had made his Facebook profile private since the last time I'd looked. Good move, but probably too late. I figured the extortionists probably had grabbed Jimmy's friend list before ever issuing a threat. That's what I would have done, if I were black-hearted enough to prey on people's fears of exposure. It's kind of sad how much a detective's job depends on learning how to think like very bad people, but it's true.

I scanned Suki's friend list for other names, hoping to find parents or siblings or anybody else who might be able to lead me to Suki's home, on the off chance that I might find Jimmy there. That was a fruitless search, though. All of Suki's friends seemed to be anime characters or cosplay stars. A few played Dungeons and Dragons. I recognized one profile image, a bizarre eye-shaped monster, as a beholder.

I got up and paced. I felt like I was close to a breakthrough. I poured myself some water.

Thus refreshed, I sat down and continued scrolling. I saw more of the same. Anime posts. Dumb jokes. Puppy wishes.

Then I found wishes of another kind. Birthday wishes.

Suki's birthday was August 2, 2005. Another data point.

I flew through the birthday wish comments, hoping someone had dropped a birth name or some other clue.

Bingo.

"Happy birthday, son! I love you, and miss you."

That came from a woman named Molly Mingus.

More data.

A background check revealed Molly Mingus had died almost a year ago, in a car crash. She had been divorced at the time from her husband, Charlie Boone.

I did another background check, and thanked my lucky stars I'd remembered to pay for the database access. Charlie Boone was still alive, and lived on Indianola Avenue in Columbus, not far from the Ohio State campus.

Charlie and Molly had one child. Thomas. Born August 2, 2005. Currently going by the name of Suki, and living with dad.

Bingo.

CHAPTER SIXTEEN

I CALLED THE number I had found for Suki's father. No answer.

I called the one I had found for Suki. No answer.

I texted both numbers, with short notes explaining I was a detective, looking for Jimmy and interested in nothing but assuring he was safe.

Then I paced.

It would be dark soon, but it was not too late for me to drive to Columbus. I thought about just calling the cops there, or calling Shelly, but decided against that. I wasn't sure Jimmy was with Suki. It was a hunch, really. And I wasn't sure what kind of situation Jimmy might be facing at home. The cops might go to the house on Indianola at my request, but if they found Jimmy there, they most likely would contact the parents immediately and have them come get the kid. Based on dad's blog posts, that might be ugly, even dangerous.

If I found Jimmy myself, on the other hand, I might be able to smooth things over. Play the go-between. The reasonable, open-minded guy who smoothed everything over. That's what I told myself, anyway. The truth is, I needed this. I really wanted to be the one to find Jimmy.

I paced for another two seconds and then decided to be impetuous. I could be at the house on Indianola in a little over an hour. If my hunch paid off, I could talk to Jimmy, scope out the situation between him and his father, find out what was going on with the extortion, maybe even offer a little friendly advice. And if I called the cops? They might check right away, if possible, or they might get diverted to a homicide or a drug bust or a traffic accident or God knows what because the world never runs out of reasons to call a cop.

That's the main reason I'd left the Mifflin County Sheriff's Department, right? So I could focus on finding kids instead of being at the beck and call of every damned taxpaying citizen or superior officer. This was my moment. Time to mount the white steed, take up my lance, and charge forth against a sea of troubles and by opposing end them.

I realized I had just tossed Malory and Shakespeare together into a mental word salad, which Linda no doubt would find amusing if she ever took time away from dating her new boyfriend to talk to me again, but I blamed my literary infraction on adrenaline. I was going to find Jimmy.

I called Tuck. "I need a perch sandwich to go, ASAP. And a Mountain Dew."

"You got it, man."

"Thanks."

My order was ready when I got there. "Can I owe you? I'm in a rush."

"Yeah, no problem," Tuck said. He looked like there was a problem, though. "Not to slow you down, but . . ."

He pointed toward a corner table. Linda and a devilishly handsome fellow, presumably Sam Briggs, sat in a corner. They were laughing over a pitcher of beer. Sam, from a distance, looked animated and attentive. Linda looked her best, all red hair framing green eyes and bright smile. I could not tell what they were talking about because of the general hubbub and the goddamned faux country song playing at an ungodly volume.

But I could tell they were very into each other. Their hands were touching across the table, and their eyes were locked on one another.

"Fuck, Tuck."

"You had your chance, man. Chances, actually, when you get right down to it."

"Yeah." I grabbed the bag of food. "Thanks, man."

"What's the rush?"

"Gonna go find a kid," I said.

He offered a fist bump. "All right, man! You got a clue?"

"I put some pieces together. It might be like trying for an inside straight, but it's the hand I've been dealt so I'm going to play it. I think I tracked down one of Jimmy's friends, a kid he plays chess with online. A lot. They had been playing almost every day online, but now they've stopped. Maybe that's because they can play face-to-face now."

"Could be," Tuck said. "Damn, that's actually kind of smart. You might actually make this detective thing pay off."

"I have my moments. I'm headed to Columbus. The friend lives on Indianola, not far from the campus." There actually are several campuses in Columbus, but everyone in Ohio knows which one you mean when you say "the campus." The Ohio State University, home of the Buckeyes. Sure, they'd lost to Clemson in the Fiesta Bowl in December, but we love them all the same. And there was at least one bloody goddamned bad ref call in that game. An epically bad ref call. I was pretty sure I was never going to get over it.

Tuck and I had mutually agreed to stop talking about that loss, and it wasn't relevant to the current situation, anyway, so I decided to focus on the task at hand. But it was a monumentally bad call. It was a catch and a fumble, goddamn it.

Tuck grinned. “Good luck, Ed.”

“Thanks, man.” I bumped Tuck’s fist again and headed toward the door. I tried not to pay attention to Linda and Sam, but I could not help sneaking a peek. They were now holding hands.

No big deal, I told myself. I have a kid to find.

CHAPTER SEVENTEEN

I FINISHED MY sandwich and reminded myself to convey my appreciation to Tuck. The perch was perfectly crispy on the outside and perfectly tender on the inside, as God intended. Fast-food places often call their fish crispy, but apparently, they use some alternative definition of the word. All I know is that it is a serious disappointment to order crispy fish and then receive something about as crisp as a wet dish towel. I considered that a sin worthy of hell. Maybe I could discuss that with Bob Zachman one day.

I called Dillon Spears en route to tell him what I'd found out.

"I have news for you, too," the Ambletown detective said, once I'd finished.

"What's that?"

"The day Jimmy disappeared? His dad was absent from work all afternoon."

My mind started racing. "No kidding?"

"No kidding. His manager told me this. Bob had gone home sick, he said. This is a fact Bob had not disclosed when we talked to him previously. And Tammy did not mention it, either."

"He didn't mention that to me, either," I said. "He sure seemed healthy to me."

"Same. I just found this out, talking to Brent Walters, the guy's manager at the bank. I was just about to go talk to Bob about it."

I sighed. "Yeah, need to do that." Several possible scenarios popped into my head because I'm a pessimist with little faith in humanity, but I went with the one that gave Bob the benefit of the doubt. "Hopefully, he's just boinking a church secretary or something, and wasn't out arranging his kid's disappearance."

I'm not sure how I envisioned this, because Spears gave no sign, but I could imagine him rolling his eyes and wishing I'd not think such deep and dark thoughts. "I hope so, Ed. I really hope so. I hate secrets, man. I fucking hate secrets."

"Me, too. I doubt Bob would hurt his kid. I really do." I really did not want to live in a universe where parents hurt their kids. I'd been a cop long enough to know I could not discount that possibility, though. I'd seen such things more than a few times. That stuff is as good a reason to have a hell as any. There ought to be a hell for parents who hurt their kids.

Spears sighed. "Agreed. Have to check it out, though. Let me know what you find in Columbus."

"With any luck, it'll be a couple of kids playing an intense game of chess on a real board, not an app, while hiding from a foreign extortionist and keeping their dicks in their pants."

"I hate depending on luck."

"Me, too. Talk to you later."

I continued down the highway, alternating between calls to Charlie Boone and the kid, Thomas a.k.a Suki. I never got an answer on either, but I kept trying. In between calls I listened to Johnny Cash, to remind myself what real country music sounded like after the ungodly stuff at Tuck's. I never even made it through a single song, though, because I kept stopping the music to try another call.

The roads were clear, so I zipped south on the highway and into Columbus in good time. I got off at Hudson Avenue, well north of downtown so I never got a real good look at the skyline, and worked my way toward Indianola Avenue. Soon I was driving past tall homes built right next to each other, with light spilling between curtains in picture windows downstairs and smaller windows the higher you looked,

I found the Boone house without too much trouble. Lights were on downstairs and in an upstairs window. There was no place to park on the street, and an ancient Buick took up the driveway, so I continued down the street until I found a church with a small lot in the back. I parked there and hoofed it to the Boone residence. The chill was intense, and I was eager to find Jimmy anyway, so I trotted. That mitigated the cold somewhat, but it felt like I was breathing ice. A dog barked somewhere nearby in the darkness. He sounded big, but I couldn't tell where he was thanks to echoes off the three-story homes. I kept my eyes peeled, but the barking soon stopped and nothing came at me.

I got to the Boone home and ascended steep steps to a covered porch. It was nice to have something to block the wind. I held my hands together to form a tunnel, blew warm air through them, then rang the bell.

No answer.

I rang again. I could hear the bell inside. I could hear a TV, too.

I rang yet again. Still no answer.

Once upon a time, as a sheriff's detective, I'd have done a mental tap dance about probable cause. I'd have weighed the potential dangers of the situation against the undesired consequences of unnecessarily busting into someone's home, and I'd have tried to fudge the variables until I got a result that allowed me to justify what I wanted to do anyway. I'm not a cop anymore, though, and I had a kid to find, so I skipped the math. I just opened the screen door and reached for the knob.

The main door was not locked.

I opened it, just a tiny bit, and peeked inside. "Hello?"

The door opened onto a hallway that went straight ahead and to a kitchen, flanked by a stairway that went up and an arched opening that led to a living room. The TV sounds came from the living room, to my right. I looked in that direction and saw big red splatters against a yellow wall. Streaks reached toward the floor. It was an obscene pattern I'd seen before, and it kicked my mind into overdrive.

I rushed inside. My heart was beating out a Neil Peart drum solo, and my breathing was a bit out of control, but I rushed inside. That's what cops do, even if they are ex-cops.

I halted before a horrific scene.

A man sat on the floor, propped at an awkward angle against the wall with all the gore on it. His forehead had been shattered, and he'd been shot a couple of times in the chest. I was not looking at a suicide. And I was not, thank God, looking at a dead fifteen-year-old.

A Smith and Wesson revolver next to the dead man's hand indicated he'd attempted to defend himself.

I had not heard the shots as I approached the home, and his gun did not have a silencer, so this crime scene was at least a few minutes old, but judging by the slowly streaking blood on the wall, not too many minutes. The guy might have been killed while I was parking my truck.

I did a quick spin to explore the room. Small recliner and side table, neither overturned. Sofa by the picture window, no room behind it for anyone to hide. The wall opposite the dead man had a couple of bullet holes in it, above the TV. On the screen, fake doctors were urgently trying to save a life.

I crouched low and reached for my pistol out of instinct. It was a dumb move, because I had stopped carrying a weapon after last fall's gun incident with the high school linebacker. The choice to go without a weapon seemed rather stupid just now.

I reached for my phone, but a moving shadow in the adjacent dining room grabbed my attention. The shadow quickly became a man, and he had not decided against carrying a gun.

"The fuck!" He aimed at me.

My reaction was pure reflex. "Police!"

"The fuck," he repeated, sighting along the gun barrel.

I'd love to tell you about all the cunning calculations and clear, cool thinking that went through my mind as I decided the best way to counter this undesirable situation, but I'd be lying. Survival meant fight or flight, and I can't outrun bullets. Nor was I close enough to reach him. And I sure as hell did not have time to think. I launched myself toward the dead man's gun, and hoped he hadn't emptied the chamber.

Thunder exploded, and lightning seared my back.

I grabbed the Smith and Wesson.

More thunder. More yelling. "The fuck! The fuck!"

I rolled away from the dead guy and aimed at the shadow. I added my own thunderclaps to the deadly crescendo.

I'm not sure how many shots he got off. I'm not sure how many shots I got off, either. I only know that I kept pulling the trigger until I got clicks instead of bullets, and when it was over, he was dead and I wasn't. The carpet around me was torn up by bullets, and my back hurt like hell.

I didn't spare my attacker any more time than it took to confirm that he was dead. He was a big guy, wearing jeans and a black coat, and I'd hit him in the throat and head. I'd tried to aim for the torso, of course, but I wasn't going to argue with the results. There was no need to check for a pulse.

I worried that I'd find more death in this house, and that among the dead would be a young chess wizard named Jimmy and his friend Suki.

CHAPTER EIGHTEEN

I REACHED FOR my phone, and it wasn't there. I scanned the floor and found it. When I reached down to pick it up, blood dripped from my shoulder and smeared the screen.

I tore off my jacket and touched my left shoulder. It felt like I'd been grazed. It stung, and my fingers told me it was a long gash, but I'd probably live. That's what I told myself, anyway. Grazed. It's not like I had time to look for a mirror to check. And what am I? A doctor?

No, I'm a PI. Looking for a missing kid.

I wiped the phone on my jeans, which only made more of a mess, then tried to call 911 while running into the dining room. My phone battery picked that moment to die. All those calls from the highway had drained it.

I went back to the living room and looked at the dead man against the wall, the one I'd seen upon entering. A cell phone peeked from the pocket of his gray flannel shirt. I snatched at it, but only the top half of the phone emerged. It had been shot to pieces.

The other man, the one I'd killed, had no phone on him that I could immediately see. So, I could not call the cops. The guns just now had been insanely loud, though, and I was certain neighbors had to have heard. They'd have dialed 911 by now. Hell, they probably had called police after the previous shooting.

I was aware that this was a crime scene, of course, and that I should not be fouling up the evidence, but I had no idea what the hell had happened here, or whether there were any more gunmen in the house. I grabbed the dead man's Ruger. Job one was stay alive and find Jimmy and Suki. I could argue with lawyers about evidence tampering later.

A quick check of the gun, however, told me it was empty. I tossed it next to the corpse and passed beyond him and into the kitchen.

No one was there.

"Jimmy! Suki!"

I went through the kitchen and into the front hall, and thus full circle back to the front door. I climbed the stairs as fast as I could. The effort made me a little dizzy.

"Jimmy! Suki!"

The second floor was three bedrooms and a bathroom. They contained all the usual bedroom and bathroom things, but no scared kids and no surprise gunmen. Another set of stairs led upward.

It was an attic bedroom, and definitely belonged to a teen. Clothes everywhere. Books everywhere. Posters on the wall portraying comic book characters and movie figures, mostly looking vaguely Japanese and sporting huge eyes. No Jimmy, though. No Suki, either.

But there was a chessboard on the floor, with a game in progress.

I yelled their names again, hoping they would emerge from under the bed, or from a closet. "Jimmy! Suki! It's safe. I'm a detective. You can come out."

No such luck, of course.

Had they been here when the shooting started? That was a scary thought. Then I had a scarier one. Had one of the kids done some shooting, too?

What the hell had I stumbled into here?

I looked around for clues, and mostly saw teenage mess. None of it was riddled with bullets or soaked with blood. I heard a siren in the distance, and figured it was on the way here.

I kept scanning the room, wondering what the hell to do next. Then I saw it.

A Reds cap. On the floor, next to the bed.

Jimmy never went anywhere without his Reds cap.

I snatched it up and looked under the brim. There were big blue initials from a felt marker: JZ.

Jimmy Zachman had been here. But where was he now?

CHAPTER NINETEEN

THE FRONT WINDOW was small, but it offered a good view of the street. I saw no cops, and no more people with guns, but sirens wailed and I saw flashing lights in the distance.

No one was peering out from any windows across the street. I assumed the neighbors had all hunkered down when the shooting started. They'd likely start looking, maybe even step out of their homes, once the police had the scene under control.

I was breathing like a catcher who'd run out a triple, and my head was spinning. Eventually, though, I realized the chill at the nape of my neck was not fear, but cool air. It was cold in here.

I looked all the way to the far end of the room. The rear window was open.

A stack of paperbacks on the floor nearly tripped me up, but I made it to the window as quickly as I could. One of those hook-and-chain fire escape ladders clung to the sill.

"Good thinking, kids." I popped Jimmy's cap on my head, clambered out, and descended to the small backyard. By the time I hit the ground, I missed my jacket, because it was damned cold. I generally ignore chilly weather, but this time it seeped into my lungs and stung my back.

I remembered I'd been shot. I reached a hand behind me and it came back wet. My jeans seemed to be sticking to the back of my right leg, too. My teeth were chattering like one of those damned novelty toys.

My drained phone provided no flashlight, but a security light from a neighboring home allowed me to see a little. A fence surrounded the yard and garage. The garage was open, and there was a small Toyota in it. Nothing else. I peeked into the car, but there were no kids inside.

There was literally no place to hide. No safe place, as Jimmy's father had said.

I decided two teens fleeing bullets would get as far away as they could, as fast as they could. The choices were to go left to the driveway, where the old Buick still sat, and run down to Indianola, or go over the fence into a neighbor's yard.

The sirens grew louder.

The gunshots had been toward the front of the house, so I doubted the kids had gone that way. I decided to go for the fence. But should I go north, south, or east?

The ground beneath the ladder was a bit soft from a snow that was mostly melted away. I searched for tennis shoe marks and found a smeary track and a deep dent in the ground. No sneaker tread marks in the dent. Maybe one of the two had slipped, and gotten a muddy knee.

There were some partial tracks, though. It looked as though they'd gone east, straight through the backyard.

It was unclear how much of a head start the kids had on me. The man I'd shot probably was the one who'd gunned down the other guy, but that was just a guess. One of the two dead men, probably, was Suki's father. The other could have been a member of the household who'd grabbed his own gun after somebody else, the proverbial person or persons unknown, had started the shooting. He could even have been a neighbor who just wanted to come rushing in to see if his next-door guy was OK. Hell, almost everyone has a gun these days. I had no idea who was who. But under any scenario, it seemed unlikely the initial shots had been fired very long ago, or else cops probably would have arrived by now.

The cops, judging by the sirens, were close now, but they weren't here yet.

There was a good chance the kids had not gotten far. Maybe they were hiding in an adjacent yard or had been pulled indoors to safety by a brave neighbor.

I ran at the fence and jumped. It was less than six feet high, not as tall as me, and it should have been a simple maneuver to plant my hands on the top and vault over. I run laps on uneven ground around my pond to build up coordination and endurance so I can do things like that. It always made sense to me, as a cop, to stay in shape. But my right hand slipped on the wood and my left never even touched the fence, while my feet just dragged on the ground. I slammed into the wood, bounced back hard, and landed on my back.

My bleeding back.

Everything swirled around me, and none of it seemed to even be going in the same direction. The house was upside down, the security light was spinning and pulsating, and my head seemed to be moving independently from the rest of my body as I struggled to get up.

Oh, yeah, I remembered. I'd been shot in the shoulder—and my pants were sticking to my leg—even though I'd not been shot in the leg. Scared as I'd been, I was pretty sure I had not shit my pants. That shoulder must have been bleeding way more than I'd thought.

CHAPTER TWENTY

Linda was still catching her breath, and her eyes were closed, but she could sense that Sam was watching her intently. Sam was still breathing hard, too, and Linda could feel the exhalations against her cheek.

Rolling a little closer, she opened her eyes and planted a small kiss on Sam's nose. "That was spectacular, I must say." She whispered it, even though the two of them were alone at the farmhouse. It just seemed like a moment for whispering.

"Yes," Sam answered, before kissing her on the lips. "Spectacular is the word I was thinking."

"I'm an English teacher, you know," Linda said. "Words, and all that. Trust me, spectacular is the proper word."

She rolled away from Sam and sat up, reaching for the wine bottle, not bothering to turn on the little bedside lamp. She looked back over her shoulder. "More?"

"No," Sam said, shaking his head. "But you go right ahead."

Linda poured, then upturned her glass and drained it. She placed the empty vessel back on the nightstand and turned back to Sam. "Where were we?"

"We, my dear, were basking in the afterglow of some rather enthusiastic lovemaking, I'd say."

"Indeed."

"But . . ."

Linda leaned over and kissed Sam. "But what?"

"Well, you were totally with me a few minutes ago, absolutely no doubts about that, but now, well, I think your mind is somewhere else."

"Why do you say that?"

Sam smiled. "You sipped your beer at the bar—lovely place, by the way, fun crowd, thanks for introducing me—but you sipped slowly at the bar, but now just drained that glass like it was the last Merlot on Earth."

Linda shrugged. "I got thirsty."

"Yeah," Sam said, "and your voice is a little higher than it has been all evening. Like, a whole octave."

"So?"

"Like you are nervous."

Linda stretched out beside Sam. "Well, I am. Aren't you? I mean, when you're with someone new, it's all a big mystery, right? Expectations and all that?"

Sam scrunched up his forehead and smacked his lips in thought before continuing. "You actually didn't seem the least bit nervous, at all, going into the whole thing. No, girl. You were one hundred percent committed."

Linda blinked her eyes. "Well, yes."

Sam stroked Linda's shoulder. "I get it now, I think."

"Get what?"

"What's going on. You kind of tensed up at the phrase 'one hundred percent committed,' you know."

"I did?"

Sam nodded. "Yeah. It seemed reflexive."

Silence filled the room. It seemed like ten minutes, but probably was only a couple, before Linda spoke. "Look, things are a little complicated."

"Things are always complicated, I get it," Sam said. "You told me you and Ed were not going anywhere."

"Yes. Yes, I did. And it's true."

Sam ran a finger through Linda's hair. "But you'd like it to go somewhere, wouldn't you?"

Linda just sighed.

Sam repeated himself. "Wouldn't you?"

"I guess so," Linda whispered. "But it's not going to."

"Well, my dear English teacher slash art teacher assistant with the long legs and stunning red hair and all the . . . um, enthusiasm for love on display here tonight, I just have to ask. What the hell is his problem?"

"He's nervous," Linda said, still whispering. "He's been through some bad stuff, saw a lot of things as a cop he can't unsee, stuff he'd prefer not to think about, you know?"

"OK."

"And I just want to make things better, try to understand."

More silence, until Sam finally asked. "And?"

"And I think I tend to remind him of shit more often than I help him forget it. I try not to, but I think that's what's going on."

Sam kissed her forehead.

Linda continued. "But I'm getting better at it. Fewer questions about the past and the future, more in-the-moment stuff, just being together, all that."

"Has he noticed?"

Linda sighed. "I'm not sure. I think he's just, you know, thinking change is bad. Don't rock the boat."

Sam inhaled sharply. "Is that what you are doing with me?"

"Huh?"

"You know, with me. Are you just rocking the boat?"

Linda rose on one arm and looked Sam right in the eyes. "No." Then she kissed Sam intensely, the way they'd kissed earlier when they both had realized that things had gone too far to stop this night. When their lips finally parted, Linda whispered: "I very much wanted this to happen." She kissed Sam again.

"It's complicated," Sam whispered.

"It always is," Linda replied.

They kissed again, more gently this time but just as intensely.

CHAPTER TWENTY-ONE

TUCK FINISHED HIS deep-fried mushrooms, the only fried thing he consumed. He took another sip of his 120 Minute IPA from Dogfish Head Craft Brewery. He had two more bottles of the seasonal wonder hidden away, and he was determined to savor them. He would pour just this one tonight; the others would be saved for future quiet moments.

The 90 Minute IPA he'd poured for Ed was great, in Tuck's opinion, a stellar brew and a standout among the bedazzling number of India pale ales out there, but the 120 Minute IPA? That deserved a poem.

He laughed. "Hello, beautiful brew. I work hard and I deserve a little relaxation. Thank you for joining the party." He gazed around at the piles of books in his tiny apartment above the bar and grill he owned. Talking to himself was not an unusual occurrence, of course, and he'd once told Ed that when he talked to himself, he was talking to the universe as well, and what the hell? Maybe the universe needed to hear whatever it was he had to say. Maybe it would answer him. Anyway, talking to himself beat the hell out of talking to most people.

Tuck picked up his phone, put on his headphones, and turned on some music. "La Villa Strangiato," a little instrumental virtuosity from Rush to erase the memory of bad country music all day. Playing that hillbilly stuff was good for business, but not good for Tuck's soul. Sometimes, he berated himself for stooping so low just to make some money. Anyway, when he was alone, it was going to be rock and it was going to be loud. He used headphones, though, because he wasn't an asshole. There was another apartment at the back of the building, and the nice lady who lived there with her grandson did not need to hear Tuck's rock.

He'd been playing a lot of Rush lately, since Neil Peart had recently died. He particularly enjoyed this piece, with the slow build and Peart's devastatingly clean work on the high-hat cymbals. It was beautiful stuff.

Tuck drank to the drummer's memory, then opened up Twitter.

Tuck realized he ought to be reading one of his many books instead of monkeying around on Twitter, but he was not in the mood for Dostoevsky at the moment and so he dove into social media instead. He followed a lot of journalists on Twitter, and found it to be a pretty good way of keeping up with things. Twitter was fine for that, he mused. It's only when you try to talk to other people that Twitter becomes a problem. Then, it's proof of the devil.

"A lot of problems just go away if you avoid most people," he'd often said.

He scrolled past a few hot takes about Ohio State's loss to Clemson. "It was a catch and a fumble," he muttered bitterly. He and Ed had already decided to keep that shit in the past, and bury it, but Twitter wasn't letting it go. Tuck did not need to read any more about it.

Then he saw a couple of *Columbus Dispatch* reporters tweeting about a shooting not far from the campus.

Shootings got to Tuck, in a big way, and the nation's tolerance for shootings as long as people could hang on to their precious gun rights bothered him, too. Tuck was a gun owner himself—he kept a shotgun behind the bar, because bars often attract trouble—but he couldn't quite understand the American love affair with guns. To him, a gun was a tool, and you should always use the right tool for the right job. If you needed something that spat out hundreds of rounds in seconds, maybe deer hunting wasn't your sport.

Anyway, Tuck always read stories about shootings.

This one troubled him more than usual, though. Cops were pulling body bags from a house on Indianola Avenue.

Ed had gone to look for a missing kid, at a home on Indianola Avenue in Columbus.

Nah, Tuck told himself, sipping again at his beer. *Ed was involved in a shooting last fall. The Jeff Cotton thing. Ain't no way the universe sends another gun thing his way this soon, right? Karma ain't that kind of bitch.*

He kept reading. Reporters mentioned multiple body bags—the exact count was unknown—and cops who said nothing beyond "no comment."

Tuck shook his head and removed the headphones. "I can clear this up in a second," he said, fully aware he was talking to himself again but not really caring one damned bit. He tapped his phone a few times, to turn off the music, then to call Ed.

He got no answer.

"That ain't conclusive," Tuck told himself. "The man's busy."

He kept scrolling, but he was no longer reading. He kept remembering conversations with Ed about police work, and how a cop always had to be ready for anything. "You think you are going to tell some guy to make his dog stop barking, and you find a damned meth lab or some asshole throwing his wife around in the kitchen," Ed had said once. "Or you think everything is fine and then the nice granny who'd called you to report a missing cat pulls a switchblade because her son died in police custody years ago. You never really know what's up. And don't forget, even a granny with a knife can get in a lucky stab. One lucky stab can kill you."

Tuck tried calling Ed again. Still no answer.

Reporters on Twitter still were trying to sort things out. One of them had talked to a witness, a neighbor who had said there were kids in the house.

Ed had gone to look for a kid.

Tuck counted to thirty—after initially deciding to count to sixty—and dialed again.

He got no answer.

"Fuck," he said. "Jesus."

He called Linda. He didn't expect an answer, as she and her date had looked very preoccupied with one another while leaving the bar. But he had to try, anyway.

"Hey," Linda said, quietly. "What's up?"

Tuck panicked just a little, not sure what to say or how to say it. "Hey. Listen, have you seen the news tonight?"

"No," Linda said. "I have company. Only answered the phone because I'm in the kitchen looking for more wine."

"Oh." Tuck caught his breath. "Listen, there is a shooting down in Columbus, on Indianola Avenue."

"Oh, God."

"And Ed was going to Indianola to look for that kid, and, well, Indianola is a long, long road, but . . . Ed is not answering his phone."

"Oh. God."

"His phone might just be on a charger; it might be that he's busy looking for the kid and not noticing my calls. But . . ."

"Ed wouldn't ignore his phone, Tuck, not when he's looking for a missing kid. He'll have talked to people, given them his number, and all that. He'd be primed for any call from his client, or the cops. No way did he just put his phone aside."

"Look, don't jump to conclusions. I'm probably worried over nothing."

"No," she said, "you are trying to convince yourself your gut isn't telling you what it is telling you."

Tuck sighed. "I didn't want to scare you, just . . ."

"We need to go to Columbus. Now. I'm calling Shelly, Ed's cop friend. Maybe she can find out if Ed is involved. You come and get me. I am too drunk to drive."

"Right," Tuck said. "You got it. On my way."

He grabbed a coat and dashed out—the unfinished beer forgotten.

CHAPTER TWENTY-TWO

Answer it, Poco, goddamn it. Answer the phone.

Zip's fingers tapped nervously on the steering wheel. He didn't like this. He didn't like anything about this.

Finally, Poco picked up. He got straight to business, as was his way. "Well?"

"Goddamn it, Poco, cops everywhere, ambulance, body bag, it's a fucking mess, and—"

Poco coughed. "Calm down, Zip. Was Adam there? Did you see him?"

"Only if he was in the fucking body bag." He regretted it the moment he said it, of course. Adam was Poco's brother. Poco was worried sick. Zip raced on, hoping his boss might not notice the insensitivity. "His car is here, but . . . they took someone in an ambulance, and brought a body out of the house, and . . ."

The conversation paused for a moment, and Zip could envision Poco's steely eyes, creased forehead, and sneering face. Zip hated it when Poco was unhappy, because Poco then made everyone else unhappy.

Finally, Zip's boss broke the silence. "Are you still watching?"

"Fuck no, man! Did you hear me say cops are everywhere? I'm not kidding, man. It's a fucking FOP convention. I drove past."

"I need you to hang around. Adam might be hiding nearby."

"I haven't seen him."

Poco continued. "Or he might be in the hospital. He's my brother, and I need to know what happened to him. You understand me?"

"Yeah, man, I get it. Sorry. I'm just, well, there are a lot of cops here."

"I know, but this is important. So you are going to calm the fuck down and keep watch, do you understand?"

"Yeah. I get it. I'm turning around." Zip pulled into a side street, checked the mirrors, and backed out to head in the other direction.

Meanwhile, Poco continued talking in quiet, menacing tones that implied that he was talking to an idiot. Zip hated that. Zip had heard that tone a lot. "There's a crowd watching, right?"

"Yeah."

"People on porches, on the sidewalk, checking it out? Everyone loves a good crime scene, right?"

"Yeah. I guess they do."

"So, you're curious. You are going to blend in."

"Blend in? I got a goddamned four-inch scar on my face, and you want me to blend in?"

"Yes," Poco said. "Nobody gives a fuck about your ugly face, they're all concentrating on the shootings, right? You can even talk to people, and they'll barely look at you and keep watching the house. What's going on, you say. I don't know, they say, some people got shot. Probably drugs. It's always drugs. This neighborhood is going to hell. Maybe they say someone ran off. Maybe that's Adam. Or if Adam got shot, then maybe that's the guy who shot Adam. Or maybe that's the guy who has our money. Right? But, I'll be honest, I don't even care about the money anymore, you know? I care about Adam. I need to know he is OK."

"Yeah, Poco, sure. I'm sorry this is going on. Really."

"I want to know what's going on. You ask people, get a description of anybody who was around, find out what is going on. Hell, pretend you are a cop, or a reporter. But find out some answers."

"Yeah. I'm almost there. Oh, holy fuck . . ."

"What?"

"They're dragging out another body bag."

"Be calm."

"I got you, Poco, I got you. Yeah. OK. I know what to do. It's just . . ."

"Just what?"

"What if it is Adam in one of those body bags?"

Poco inhaled so sharply that Zip could hear it. When he spoke, his voice quivered without losing any of its menace.

"Then we'll fill another body bag."

CHAPTER TWENTY-THREE

Mostly, I heard beeps. Occasionally, a rush of air, or a whisper. But mostly, beeps.

I heard a droning voice, too, on a speaker somewhere in the distance, beyond the eyelids I didn't have the energy to open.

Then I heard a sweeter voice. A familiar one.

Linda.

"I think he's awake."

"I'll get the nurse." That was Tuck. I heard his footsteps and a door opening.

I decided to open my eyes. It wasn't quite like lifting deadweights, but it was close.

Linda was smiling at me. "You are going to be fine," she said, and she sounded like she meant it.

"Hospital?"

She nodded. "Yes, Ed, you are in the hospital. You got shot in the shoulder. Looks like the bullet went down your back. They say you lost quite a bit of blood." Linda gulped, but she kept smiling and her eyes were steady. "The paramedics did a good job. So did the doctors here. You are going to be just fine."

Tuck came into view on the other side of the bed. "Nurse is fetching the doctor. All that semi-Buddhist shit I said before? Fuck that, Ed. Start carrying a gun again."

"Found a gun," I said, although it sounded like it came from somewhere else. "Still got shot."

"There's a mean-looking cop wants to talk to you," Tuck said.

"Me first." The voice was feminine and soft. "How are you feeling, Mr. Runyon? I'm Dr. Medley."

Linda backed away and the doctor came into view. Long hair, brown turning gray, and pale blue eyes. Raised eyebrows, a gentle smile, and a nodding head combined to say all was well. "A bullet dug a shallow furrow across your shoulder and part of the way down your back. You were very lucky, because it didn't shatter bone or hit anything major, but I'd stay away from gunplay in the future."

"Noted."

"You lost a good deal of blood." She pointed to a tube going into my right arm. "This is replacing fluids and giving you some pain reliever. Police said it looked like you moved around a lot after you got shot? Maybe the activity widened the gash a bit, got the blood pumping harder. Anyway, police officers found you before things got too bad, but it was close to becoming really bad."

"Thank Jesus," Linda said quietly.

I decided to try more talking. "Shot a guy. Rolled around. Ran up a couple flights of stairs. Climbed down a ladder. Tried to jump a fence. Didn't work."

"Tough guy, huh? Your friends say you are an ex-cop, looking for a missing kid, self-defense, etcetera. Well, I'll let the police worry about all that." As the doctor talked, she looked at all the beeping things and took my pulse with her fingers. "My job is to get you better. We closed up the gash on your back. You have stitches and glue. We replaced the lost blood. You are at University Hospitals, by the way, just in case you don't know."

"Thanks." I was trying to sound tough, but my mind was racing. The bullet furrow across my back could just as easily have been a deep hole in my head, or a tunnel through a lung. I'd thought about such possibilities before, of course. Every cop does. And I'd lived through a few close calls, including one just a few months ago. But this was the closest call ever, and I kept seeing that man's gun in my mind.

It was huge. A cannon.

And it was loud. So fucking loud.

I had to wonder about the lasting impact of this, because I could tell my knees were jelly and I wasn't even standing up. Would there be a next time? If so, would reflexes take over again? Or would I freeze like a deer in headlights? What was the point of all the training and pond laps if a small piece of metal could drill all the way through you?

Should I give up this PI business and learn to sell real estate? It's a lovely cottage, Mr. and Mrs. Brown, just the cute thing a couple of empty-nesters like you need. Look at those countertops. Plenty of garden space.

Fuck that, I decided. The future wasn't happening right now, was it? No. But there was a problem here in the present that needed my attention, so I needed to stop musing about what had almost happened, or what might happen down the road, and concentrate on what I needed to do. I'd promised the Zachmans I'd find their boy. So that was Mission One. A career change and home tours would have to wait.

I'm not sure how long my mind had been wandering down dark country roads before I realized the doctor was still talking.

"We want you to stay a couple more days, at least, so we can make sure all is well, but honestly, looking at all this, you may be eligible for release sooner. You look like you work out and take care of yourself."

Was she flirting with me? Or was that just wishful thinking? I shot a glance at Linda. Linda clearly thought Dr. Medley was flirting with me, but she didn't say anything.

I decided to focus on that mention of early release. "Can I go now? I have some important stuff to do."

"Now?" She shook her head. "No need to flee. The food here is not *that* bad."

"Look, I need to—"

She put on a stern expression. It was obvious that she'd practiced it, because being stern did not come naturally to her, but it's a skill doctors need. "Not just yet, I'm afraid. I put in pretty good stitches, thank you very much, and I don't want you tearing them apart. Give yourself time to heal."

"How long have I been here?"

"You came in last night. It's Sunday morning, so you haven't been here long enough. Do you feel up to talking to Detective Gutierrez? He's been eager to hear what happened. I can hold him off, though, if you want to rest, which would be my recommendation. But I understand there are missing kids involved in this, so . . ."

"Yes, I can talk to him." I had questions for the detective, too.

"I'll send him in," she said. "This is your beeper." She held up the box with the red button, then placed it near my right hand. "You hit this if you feel pain, have questions, need to use the restroom or anything else. You probably are not hungry, but thirsty?"

"Eggs. I want eggs. And lots of water, too. I am very thirsty."

Dr. Medley smiled. It was a good smile, much better than her stern face. "I'll see what we can rustle up for you."

She walked out, and Linda filled her spot. "I have a water bottle right here," she said. "And a straw. I knew you'd be needing it. I was hoping private detectives didn't get shot at, Ed."

"Me, too." Still trying to sound tough. I wasn't sure I could fool Linda, though. I heard ice rattle around as she held the bottle where I could get at it. It took an effort to use the straw, but the cold water was one of the better things I'd ever tasted.

Tuck leaned over me on the other side of the bed. "So what the fuck happened, man?"

"I walked into something no one should walk into, and I still haven't found Jimmy." No safe place out there for a kid, Jimmy's dad had said. So far, dad seemed to be on the money.

I saw Tuck look up and back away. Another man filled the vacancy and showed me a badge. "Mr. Runyon, I'm Detective Nick Gutierrez. This is my partner, Detective Jenny Kind."

He pointed a thumb over his shoulder, where a mousy woman in a blazer and dress slacks was tapping on a smartphone. Detective Gutierrez seemed almost twice her size, bigger than me, certainly, but that might have been an illusion based on whatever drugs they were feeding me and on the fact that he was looming over me. Anyway, he seemed like a fucking giant. A bearded, brown-eyed giant. "Your friends here told me a little bit, but you know cops. I want to hear it in your words. But first . . ."

The detective looked at my friends. "Hello, again. I need you two to go get coffee or something, please."

Linda and Tuck gave me worried glances, and Linda placed the water bottle near my hand. Then they hurried out.

Once they were gone, it seemed I became the center of this detective's universe. He stared at me as if I were about to reveal the nature of God.

"Why were you there, Mr. Runyon? At the house on Indianola."

I inhaled deeply. "I'm a private detective, looking for a boy named Jimmy Zachman, who went missing from Ambletown. Have you found him?"

I did not add the words "dead or alive," but I was thinking them.

Gutierrez looked skeptical. "Two dead men. Two guns. Your fingerprints all over the guns. Your blood all over the house. What the hell happened?"

"I told you. I'm looking for Jimmy. His parents hired me. Have you found him?"

"No," Gutierrez said. "No Jimmy, nor did we find the boy that was living there, Tommy Boone."

"Tommy prefers Suki, I hear. Suki is Jimmy's friend."

"I heard that, too." He sighed and nodded. "We're looking for the kids. We'll find them. Don't worry about that. For now I want to—"

"It's my job to worry about that," I said.

I think I annoyed him, which was fine, because he was annoying me. He was a cop, with a million things on his plate, but I had one soul focus—finding Jimmy Zachman. I was beginning to feel really good about my decision to leave law enforcement.

The detective rubbed his chin. "It's my job to worry about that, too, but right here and now it is my job to ask you questions to find out why the fuck we found two dead people in a house on Indianola, and why one of them was filled with lead from a gun with your fingerprints all over it, and your prints were on the other gun, too, which was used to kill the other guy, and why there are two missing kids, and why you were found bleeding all over the backyard. Detective Kind and I have a whole big police department out looking for those kids, so you just worry about telling me why you all had a little shoot-up."

"I told you why I went there. Don't know why the shooting started. Guy drew on me, I was unarmed, I grabbed a gun no one was using at the moment, and bang bang. Self-defense."

"Self-defense."

"Yeah."

Gutierrez turned to look at Detective Kind. "Self-defense, he says."

"I told you he'd say that," she replied. Her poker face was absolutely masterful.

I was growing impatient. "Have you found the kids?"

Gutierrez sighed. "We're checking all the places Suki hangs out, calling Suki's friends and all that. So don't you worry about that. We'll find them. Right now, I need you to focus on my questions. Understood?"

I'd left a perfectly good job behind me just so I could focus on finding kids instead of answering all the questions cops had to worry about. But I decided not to bore Detective Gutierrez with those details. He'd probably read all about my shootout with Jeff Cotton and my inglorious departure from NYPD and all that other stuff, anyway. He'd had plenty of time to read up on me while doctors were refilling me with blood.

"Yeah, OK," I muttered. "I understand. I've given similar speeches."

"You were a sheriff's detective."

"Yes."

He nodded. "And now you are a PI?"

"Yes."

"Did you know your license is still pending?"

"I've paid up, filed everything."

He grinned. "Yeah, but wheels grind slowly."

"Everything is in order, and I did not want to tell the Zachmans I couldn't go look for their kid because the state of Ohio is slow at paperwork."

"Maybe it's you who's slow at paperwork."

I inhaled deeply. "Either way, paperwork is a really boring concern right now, don't you think?"

The detective stared at me for a while. "PIs give me headaches."

"Maybe I'll end up in an abandoned silo someday, eaten by feral cats."

He shook his head and tried not to laugh, but failed. "That guy, Parker. I knew him. God, I hated him. Total imbecile. He caused his own misery. I don't say he deserved going out like that, nobody does, with the cats and all, but, well, anyway, I don't wish that on anyone and I don't hate other PIs. They just give me headaches. Are you going to give me headaches, Mr. Runyon?"

"Most likely, yes."

He laughed again. "How do you know Charlie Boone?"

"I didn't. I went there looking for Jimmy Zachman. I had no idea who else might be there."

"Tell me about Jimmy Zachman," the detective said, while his partner made notes in her phone. I told him most of it, but left out the part about the blackmail. The cops would be calling Jimmy's parents soon, most likely, and I didn't need a detective to blurt out Jimmy's secrets.

"OK," the detective said. "Why did you shoot Charlie—"

"Charlie Boone was shot before I showed up, assuming he was the one sitting against the wall and wearing a flannel shirt. I shot the other guy. But whoever I shot, well, it was because he was trying to shoot me."

Gutierrez glanced at Detective Kind. So did I. Her face was inscrutable.

"Boone was the guy in the flannel shirt. And how do you know the other guy?"

"We introduced ourselves to one another at a gunfight."

He sighed. "No attitude, Runyon. I don't need you—"

"I told you I'd give you headaches. And I didn't go there looking for trouble, just looking for a kid. And now I'm stuck in here, and he's out there, and . . ."

My mind went to dark places. I envisioned the portraits of Jimmy on the wall at the Zachman home. They had skull faces.

"We'll find those kids, Runyon. Trust me on that. What made you think Jimmy Zachman was there?"

I had my doubts about the cops finding the kids, but I was glad he had talked just then. I blinked away the dark visions and explained the chess app clues.

"And what did you find when you got to the house?"

"Like I said. A man shot dead inside, gun by his hand, but not suicide because multiple gunshots to chest and face. Another guy shows up, presumably the one who shot the first guy, but I don't really know, and he decides he wants to shoot me." I took a sip of water. Talking made my throat hurt. Raising the water to my face and leaning a bit to sip hurt my shoulder. My head fell back to the pillow, and that hurt, too, but I continued talking. "I identified myself as an officer, just out of habit, I guess, because I'm not a cop anymore, but anyway he didn't seem impressed so I made a lucky grab for the first guy's gun and shot until I ran out of bullets."

"And got shot in the process."

"Yep."

"Did you see anyone else?"

"No."

"Did you recognize the vehicle in the driveway?"

"No."

"How many shots did you fire?"

"I don't know. I kept shooting until I was empty, I know that."

"What then?"

I told him the rest of it, the journey up to the attic bedroom, Jimmy's ball cap, everything up to my ill-fated attempt to vault over the fence. I didn't remember anything after that.

He tossed in some more questions, about where I parked my vehicle and how I approached the house, and he repeated a couple of inquiries to see if my answers stayed consistent. They did.

He paused for a while. "I got shot once," he said. He touched his left thigh. "Six years ago. Still hurts when it's cold outside."

"Glad you are OK," I told him.

"Likewise to you, Mr. Runyon. Ed. Listen . . ."

Detective Gutierrez began pacing. "I talked with Detective Shelly Beckworth. She's coming to see you, she says, soon as she can. I'm supposed to tell you that. She likes you. Anyway, Shelly's a damned good cop. She tells me you are a bit of a hothead, but otherwise you are a good cop, too. I am inclined to believe your version of events, especially since your prints weren't the only ones on those guns."

"Thanks."

He turned and fixed me with one of those intimidating cop stares. "But I am a skeptic, Ed, and so I require evidence to back up my inclinations before I accept them as facts. We have evidence, including your phone. You can bet we're going to dig deep into that. And if we find anything in there that tells me you are lying or withholding information, or are in any way involved with this drug business . . ."

"What drug business?"

He stared at me. I stared back. That went on for a couple of centuries.

Gutierrez grinned and turned to his partner. "Jenny, what do you think?"

She shrugged. "That seemed to me like a genuine reaction from a guy who has no idea what the fuck is really going on."

Gutierrez nodded. "Me, too. OK, Ed. I tried to sneak that in there, about the drug stuff. Wanted to see if you got flustered or your nostrils flared or anything like that. My gut tells me you are legit, and more importantly, Jenny's gut tells her you are legit. She's a better judge of that sort of thing. Went to college and all that shit."

"And they taught her to go with her gut?"

He shook his head and laughed. "No. They banged on about evidence and signs that someone is lying and statistics and all that shit, right, Jenny?"

"I use all that, too," she said. "Anyway, I don't think this guy has a clue what's really going on." She grinned at me.

"Education is good," I answered. "And I don't have a clue what's really going on. What drug business?" This did not sound like anything good.

Gutierrez inhaled deeply. "So. The guy you shot. His name is Adam Sawyer, and he's got a long record of misdemeanor assaults along with a habit of being associated in one way or another with people we bust. We bust a drug house, and he's got a tangential connection to someone there. We search a perp's known associates and find Sawyer on the list. We know he's dirty, was dirty, before you killed him, anyway. But we never had anything that could stick."

"Sounds like a not nice guy."

"And if he was there, waving a gun around, well, then, you did not just walk into a break-in or a domestic squabble."

Shit.

"We think Boone was a minor player," Gutierrez said. "He'd take heroin down south, usually, Chillicothe, Waverly, down there, probably at the behest of Sawyer or others like Sawyer, and he'd bring money and grass back. That's all shit we learned from some undercover stuff, by the way, so don't go talking about it or anything."

"I won't."

"So, what we think, anyway, is something like this. Maybe Charlie ripped off his bosses. Kept some money, kept some grass, kept some drugs, something. Maybe Sawyer showed up to correct that situation. Find whatever it was, put Charlie down, you know."

"Human Resources work can get rough in the drug business."

He nodded. "Yeah. And I think you walked in and got yourself smack dab in the middle of it."

"Jesus Christ." My head was swimming. If all this was true, Jimmy Zachman had run from one bad situation and right into the middle of one that was way, way worse. "And you've searched the property top to bottom, right? No kids? Any sign of where they went?"

"We searched, Ed, I promise you. We're still searching. No sign of anyone else getting hurt. We found the escape ladder, same as you, and we're thinking the kids just ran. They just got the fuck outta there."

"I hope."

"We're talking to neighbors, seeing if they saw the kids run off. We're checking security camera footage from neighbors, the ones who have cameras, anyway. We're talking to Suki's known friends. Got some info off the kid's iPad. We'll find them."

"I know you'll do everything you can." I probably sounded skeptical. I'd done everything I could back when I was a cop, and kids had died.

Gutierrez asked me a few more details, the usual cop routine where he repeated questions from earlier to see if I gave the same answers or struggled to recollect what I had said.

"Alright, then," he said. "You rest, get better. I'm putting my card here." He reached into his wallet and placed a card on the tray attached to the bed. "If you remember anything else that might help me, you call. Anytime, day or night."

"Will do."

"There is a number on the card you can call about your personal items, too. You can collect your phone and stuff, eventually, but it's all evidence, of course, and we'll need to hang on to it until the prosecutor figures we don't need it anymore. Those wheels turn slow. I guess you know all that, though, huh?"

"Understood. Thanks." Who knew how long my stuff would be held? If there were other parties involved, my things might stay in the state's custody until those people were arrested, tried, and convicted. And until any appeals got resolved. And, of course, the state might find reason to charge me with something, too.

It would be a pain in the ass for me, and it felt weird being on this side of the equation after years of explaining to other people why we needed to keep their stuff. The cops would want to examine the blood on my clothes to see if it all came from me, or if I'd wrestled with someone else. They'd want to match the fabric in my clothes with any bits or threads found elsewhere in the home. They'd want to check my phone to see where I'd been and who I'd talked to in the hours leading up to the events on Indianola Avenue. They'd want to see if the evidence comported with the account I'd given them, and yes, sir, we know it is inconvenient to be without your phone but this is a homicide investigation and that is some very important stuff, you know.

I'd get my stuff back when I got it back. In the meantime, I'd just have to cope.

Detectives Gutierrez and Kind left. A nurse entered with a weary smile and a tray. The tray contained something that may once have been eggs, scrambled on a plate between two slices of almost-toasted bread, and a Styrofoam cup full of cold water. She put my meal down and used the lever to raise my bed to prop me up. We made small talk until she left, then I ate enthusiastically.

Linda and Tuck came back in. Linda felt my forehead. "No fever," she said.

"Did I have a fever?"

"Hell, I don't know," she said, waving her hands. "I gotta do something, right?"

I grabbed her hand. "Thanks."

That drew a tear. "We brought you some clothes. Yours are all bloody and evidence and all that, they said. I got your spare shoes, too."

"Thanks."

"Your phone is evidence, too."

"Yeah. I was at a shooting scene where two people died. I'll get my phone back, someday. It's OK. Stop worrying."

"I brought your Buckeyes fleece. It's not warm enough for this weather, but it was all I could find in a hurry."

"Thanks, mom."

She grinned through tears. "Sorry. Just, you got shot, Ed."

"Yeah. I remember. I was there."

Tuck was trying to maintain his normal zen thing, but he wasn't doing so well. "So, look, you come work for me, right? I can't pay a lot, but hell, you can drink beer and eat my food and shit. I could use a good bouncer, and I've seen you fight, right? You just come work for me, stomp on trouble before it escalates to fucking bullets flying all over the place, and, you know, life goes on. No more walking into gun battles."

I grinned. Then I laughed.

"What is so funny?" That was Linda.

I laughed again. It hurt, but I didn't mention that to them. "Oh, I am so gonna piss you two off..."

They looked at me like I was from Mars.

"What do you mean?" Tuck said it, and Linda' expression echoed it.

"I'm blaming the pain drugs, so I might not be making great decisions, but I just thought of something that Gutierrez does not know."

"So call him," Linda said, picking up his card.

"I'll call him, sure," I said, sitting up. I could feel the trace of the bullet along my back. I tried not to groan. "But he's tracking drug runners and killers and who knows when he or anyone else on his busy police department will get around to checking on Jimmy. So I'm gonna check on Jimmy."

Linda snarled and scrunched up her face. "Jimmy is a probable witness in a couple of homicides, so don't give me that bullshit. They will definitely look for him, and the other kid, too. You are just trying to justify whatever the hell it is you are about to do."

"I think I can find Jimmy in a half hour," I said.

Linda wasn't buying it. "I know you had a couple of missing kid cases go bad, Ed, but that does not mean the cops are just going to ignore whatever it is you have to point out. You don't have to go play Lone Ranger."

"Batman," I said. "And I know. The cops will do what they can. But I can check this out fast and maybe leave the real cops more time to find all the drug people. And the nice doc said I could probably leave early because I'm tough."

Linda scowled. "Drug people? What? And she did not mean you could leave this early, damn it."

"Drug people. I can't say more. Look, if I'm right, I'm going to drive a short distance, find Jimmy and Suki, and then call everyone to tell them all is well. Then I will come right back here and let them patch up anything that needs patching or pump more drugs into me or whatever. OK?"

"We'll go with you," Tuck said.

I shook my head. I could feel the muscles in my shoulder protest, but I did not mention that to Tuck and Linda. "No, I'll do it."

Linda folded her arms. "Why can't we go with you?"

The answer to that was that I might be wrong, and some son of a bitch might have followed the kids or tracked them down for some goddamned reason, thinking they had taken whatever it was that got Charlie Boone killed. If I accidentally stumbled into another gun battle, I did not want Linda or Tuck under fire, too.

"Three adults and two kids in Tuck's tiny car, or yours? Never going to work. You guys can give me a ride to my truck. I left it at a church."

CHAPTER TWENTY-FOUR

"I FOUND SOMETHING, Poco."

"Yeah? What did you find? Did you find the son of a bitch who killed Adam?"

"No."

"Then I do not give a fuck what you found."

Zip should have anticipated that reaction. Poco had no patience. He inhaled sharply and soldiered on. "I think I found his truck, Poco. News says he's a detective named Ed Runyon, from Mifflin County, wherever the fuck that is. Reporters say that's unconfirmed, but they always hedge, right? Anyway, he shot up a kid last year, some football stud. I found a truck here, close to the Boone house. Mifflin County plates. Gotta be this Runyon guy's truck, I'm thinking."

Poco inhaled sharply. "Yeah, you may be right, might be his truck. But the news says Runyon is in the hospital, Zip. Go there and kill him."

Zip sighed. "Look. I know this is rough, man. Adam is your brother, you love him, I get it."

"He practically raised me, man."

"I know, man. I know. But a hospital? That's a lot of cameras and witnesses, Poco. Security cameras, you know? Probably cops parked outside Runyon's door. Go there and kill him? That's insane. But I got this, man. I have his truck, right? Gotta be his truck. You remember how we got Charlie? I'm gonna do the same thing."

Zip grinned, because he could imagine Poco's eyes lighting up with realization.

"That's smart, Zip. You got one with you?"

"Hell, yeah. Got one in the glove box."

"That's good. That's damned good. Do that, Zip. Sure. You are right. Hospital's a bad play. Sorry, man. It's . . . my brother is dead, you know? I can't think, man."

Zip moved the phone away from his face and sighed with relief. Then he returned the phone to his face and spoke again. "I get it, man. I cannot imagine how you feel."

Poco gulped. "It hurts, man. It really hurts. So here is what you do. Follow this guy, kill this guy, I'll make it worth your while. You know that, right?"

"I know that, Poco. I got this, man. This Runyon bastard? He's as good as dead."

CHAPTER TWENTY-FIVE

THERE HAD BEEN a bit of arguing, during which the doctor had insisted I should stay and continue running up hospital bills that I could only hope my newly purchased private insurance would cover. I had nodded ascent and pretended to give in, and it may even have been an Oscar-worthy performance, but as soon as the doctor was gone, I pulled the IV tube from my arm and bandaged myself from supplies in the drawer next to my bed. I worked quickly, and I got a little dizzy, but it certainly didn't kill me or anything, and I wasn't leaking blood all over the floor.

By the time Linda and Tuck had returned from restroom trips, I was dressed in the clothing they'd brought me. Linda had even brought my old sneakers, the grass-stained ones I wear to do yard work. She lives on a farm. There's a lot of yard work.

"All clear," I'd told them. "I promised the doc I'd be right back at the first sign of trouble, but there won't be any trouble. This will be quick, I promise you. I'm gonna go find that kid." I had rushed out after that, because I was fairly certain something beeped on a nurse's station somewhere when a patient removed his own IV tube.

Now we were driving across Columbus.

"I still think this is the dumbest goddamned thing you've ever done, Ed," Linda said. "Except for maybe driving drunk from New

York to Ohio and chasing that kid with a big gun into the fucking woods last year and . . . and . . ." Her language gets more colorful when she's mad.

She was in the front seat of Tuck's Honda. I reached from my seat in the rear and brushed red hair away from her eyes. "Yeah, I'm a dumbass."

"Ed, goddamnit. I need a cigarette. I don't believe you, either. That doctor did not say you could go. You made that up. I know it. You don't even have a coat. Just that fleece."

"The fleece will be fine," I answered. Tuck had no extra coat to lend me, and I was a lot bigger than him, anyway. Linda had argued in favor of a quick stop at a mall somewhere to buy me a coat, but I'd balked at that because I was in a hurry.

"Sorry." She fumbled through her little denim purse. "I don't think I have any cigarettes, damn it. We left town so fast." She'd given up smoking three times since I'd met her. The relapses were pretty much caused by stress related to knowing me. And yes, I do feel guilty about that.

"Maybe Sam will be less stressful," I said out loud, before realizing I probably shouldn't have.

Linda glared at me, and Tuck rushed in to change the subject and save my ass. That's what wingmen are for, right?

"You should have stayed in the hospital, Ed."

I sort of wished he'd changed the topic to literature or *Star Trek*, but what the hell.

"It's going to be fine," I said. "Really. I feel OK."

Linda shot a glance at Tuck. "Did you notice he did not deny making up that part about the doctor saying this was OK?"

Tuck nodded. "I did notice that. Yes."

I sighed. "You are the worst wingman in the history of wingmen, Tuck."

"I might have the hardest job in the history of wingmen," he answered.

We all remained silent the rest of the way, although I was fairly certain we had not yet exhausted the topic of my bad decision-making.

Tuck pulled into the parking lot at the church where I'd left my truck before walking down the street to get shot. It was still there. Cops hadn't impounded it or anything. Maybe that was because they really did believe my account. Maybe that was because a couple of drug dealers getting shot up wasn't their highest priority. Maybe someone had just not gotten around to the paperwork yet. Anyway, my truck was where I'd left it. I glanced at the cross atop the church and nodded in thanks.

Tuck, who apparently had decided he still could sink to further depths as a wingman, expanded on his previous comment. "You really are a stubborn ass."

"I know, but I have work to do. Lend me your phone?"

He handed it to me. "Same passcode."

I nodded. The passcode was 2112, the name of his favorite Rush album, plus his initials. Quite the rock hound, my buddy Tuck. Fortunately, our friendship did not hinge on common musical tastes. Give me Waylon and Willie over the Canadian power trio any day.

"Thanks, Tuck. Can I borrow a few bucks, too?"

Linda fished around in her purse and gave me two twenties and her truck key. Tuck gave me his credit card.

"You two are the best. I really mean it."

"You don't deserve us," Linda muttered. "Please be careful."

"I will."

I got out and headed toward my venerable old Ford F-150.

"Be careful," Linda said again. "Don't pull those stitches out."

"I'll be careful," I said, and I think I managed not to sound annoyed. I was not worried. The cops were tracking down all of Suki's friends, but they likely weren't as far along as I was in factoring Jimmy into their equations. Jimmy's aunt lived in Columbus, not too far from here, and there was at least a chance the kids had bolted in her direction. It was worth checking out, and the police probably did not know about Jimmy's aunt yet. It would be good for Whiskey River Investigations if I found the kids before the cops did.

It would be good for my soul, too.

I started to call Detective Gutierrez, but hesitated. I could be at Jimmy's aunt's house in less than half an hour. I could probably get to the house as quickly as any Columbus cop, and there was no goddamned way I would be diverted to handle some robbery in progress, active shooter, or any other call that would make a civil servant jump into action. I had one mission: find Jimmy Zachman. So that's what I was going to do.

Singularity of purpose made decisions easy, I decided. I'd drive to the aunt's house, and with any luck I'd find Jimmy and Suki there, probably eating chocolate chip cookies dunked in milk or whatever else aunts gave visiting nephews and their friends. I'd call Gutierrez with the results of my quest. Ed Runyon, knight errant, triumphant. No need to call the detective now. It was better to wait and give him solid results.

I'm fairly certain that I'd have felt entirely differently if I still were a detective with the Mifflin County Sheriff's Office and a PI involved in one of my cases lied his way out of a hospital so he or she could check out a potential lead that had not been mentioned to me at all, but screw it. I decided to live in the now.

Tuck waited until I'd reached my truck before he pulled away. Sunday morning services apparently had ended, and people were exiting the church. I got more than a few stares of the "who are you" variety. Nobody came forward to tell me about Jesus, though, or ask me if I'd been saved. I considered that a good thing, because proselytizing is kind of rude. I waved and smiled at a couple of the people who stared at me.

I slid behind the wheel and hoisted the phone Tuck had lent me. I did not have my notes, because those were on the phone that Columbus PD had taken into evidence after I'd unwisely inserted myself between a drug mule and his unhappy employer. I had a cloud account, though, so boom, hello notes. I dialed Becky Zachman's number.

No answer.

I fired up the truck and moved to pull out of the lot. There was just one way out, and several vehicles ahead of me, so this process took a while. I found myself staring at the cross atop the church.

I decided to try my hand at prayer again. *Dear God, let Jimmy and Suki be safe. Let me find them healthy and unharmed. Let me reunite Jimmy with his worried parents. And let me find a place for Suki, too.*

Those prayerful thoughts reminded me of Jimmy's parents. *Shit, I probably should call them,* I realized. They may have heard the news about the shootings, they may be in a panic. Columbus police may have called them already, but who knows how that went. I needed to call them. I was taking their money, after all.

A car horn honked, and I came out of my reverie. I was holding up traffic out of the church lot. I offered to let a surly-looking fellow in an ancient white Chevy van with a dented fender cut in line in front of me, but he shook his head no. I pressed forward, other church people followed me out and soon everyone was headed to their destinations. Probably Bob Evans or IHOP for the church crowd. Becky Zachman's house for me.

Once I'd navigated my way out of the lot, I called Tammy Zachman, Jimmy's mom. It went straight to voicemail, so I left a message.

"Mrs. Zachman, this is Ed Runyon. I am calling from a different phone because mine is unavailable. I am tracking down a couple of leads. I'll call you again with an update as soon as I can."

I tried calling Bob, and got voicemail again. I left a similar message, and figured maybe they were on the phone with one another. Or, possibly, they both were talking to cops who wanted to know why their son was at a house where drug traffickers had a deadly disagreement. I hoped I'd be able to give the Zachmans some good news soon.

I tried to put myself in the Zachmans' position, and found I couldn't. Not being a parent, I could not imagine the pain and angst they were going through. I have no close family alive. Linda and Tuck are pretty much my family. I knew I'd be going through hell if one of them were missing, possibly in danger, but I imagined the genetic bonds between parents and child were infinitely stronger, and the worry infinitely greater. I could not truly feel what they were going through, but I could feel my resolve to help them growing, blood loss and doctor's orders be damned.

I concentrated on traffic. With any luck, I'd have the best possible news for the Zachmans within the next thirty minutes.

CHAPTER TWENTY-SIX

LINDA WAS RIGHT. The fleece wasn't heavy enough.

I jogged toward Becky Zachman's front door, hoping to generate some warmth, but I felt the jolt of every step in my back and eventually gave up the jogging. Walking would suffice. I was glad Linda was not here to see me reduce speed and wince in pain.

Becky Zachman's door was like all the other front doors in a row of identical apartments not too far from The Ohio State University. I rang the bell.

No answer. I rang again, and listened. The bell was working. So was a TV, or maybe a stereo. As I waited, it became clear I was listening to music, on good speakers. Jazz.

The last time I'd listened to recorded sounds while standing outside a door, I ended up with someone ventilating my back with a gun. I tensed up.

I stood away from the door and to the side, just in case a bunch of bullets came ripping through it. It seemed unlikely, but I thought erring on the side of caution was a good plan going forward. Always expect a hail of bullets. That's my philosophy. I'm Ed Runyon. Thanks for coming to my TED Talk.

Nobody came to the door, so I tried calling Becky Zachman's number again. I heard it ring within.

She answered almost immediately. "Hello?"

"Becky Zachman? Hello. It's Ed Runyon, the detective you talked to. I'm on your front porch. Has Jimmy come here?"

The door opened suddenly. "No. He's not here. Come in." She dashed back inside, and I followed.

Becky Zachman was slender, mid-forties, and wearing a huge, furry bathrobe. Her hair was a wet mess, and I could smell pot from somewhere within the bowels of the apartment. The furnishings were mostly spartan, but there were plenty of books arranged neatly on shelves. A genuine vinyl record spun beneath a needle arm.

"Sorry I did not answer right away," she said. "I was busy trying to force myself to relax. I'm just very worried about Jimmy. I'm a jumble of jitters."

"Understandable." I decided right then and there that Jimmy had not come here seeking shelter. "I tried to call ahead, but I did not get an answer. I'm sorry if I came at a bad time," I said.

"It's not a bad time. I probably was completely submerged in the tub. Trying to relax, as I said."

She went to the stereo and stopped the music. She kept talking while she lifted the record from the turntable and slipped it into its sleeve. Miles Davis, *Bitches Brew*. Not country music or bluegrass, but I'd liked what I heard. She looked over her shoulder while she tucked the album back on top of a shelf full of Thelonius Monk and Charlie Parker. "So, you haven't found him yet, I can see. Do you have any clues?"

"I came close to finding him, but . . ."

She sat on a divan, and pointed toward a recliner. "Sit."

I did. "Do you want to change?" The robe was not very secure.

"No," she said, tucking the bathrobe around her. She looked at me like a president's press secretary, waiting for a reporter to stop jabbering and ask an actual question. She had a question for me, though. "So what have you found?"

I wasn't sure how much to tell her, but she paid attention to me without blinking, and I kind of got the idea she could handle things, despite her being a little bit on edge. So, I told her all of it.

She stared wide-eyed through the entire story, gasping and shaking her head. Once I finished, she took a deep breath and spoke. "Oh my God. And you are sure Jimmy was there?"

"Does his Reds cap have his initials under the brim?"

"Yes."

She gulped. I'd seen her brother do the same gulp. Mira Sorvino Syndrome aside, it looked better on her.

I tried to set aside any thoughts about how she looked and whether the robe might slip open again. "I found the cap, so I am certain Jimmy was there," I said. "But apparently, he and his friend got away, using a fire escape ladder. I was hoping they'd run here, that maybe Jimmy would seek his favorite aunt."

"They didn't. I wish they had. Oh God, I wish they would." Shaking a bit, she opened a compartment in the arm of the divan and pulled out a custom-made cigarette and a lighter. "Would you like to . . ."

"No," I said.

She lit up. Definitely pot. I supposed it paired well with Miles Davis, but I didn't really know.

I leaned forward. "Have you heard from Bob?"

She shook her head.

"He apparently failed to mention he'd left work early the day Jimmy disappeared."

I'd said that precisely so I could gauge her reaction. She gave me a blank stare. "So?"

"So, it just seems weird when people don't tell detectives everything. Especially when their kid is missing."

She grinned, but sadly. "So, you're the suspicious type? And here I am with a joint. Are you going to turn me in?"

"Of course not. But I am wondering if you have any inkling what Jimmy's dad might have been up to that he didn't want cops or his wife to know about."

She tensed and closed her eyes. I could tell she was battling with something, so I waited.

Finally, she looked up at me. "Bob and I were close once, but . . . we don't really talk now. It's . . . complicated. When we did talk, and by *talk*, I mean online, because he seldom calls me and I seldom call him, it just . . . didn't go well."

I nodded, as though I understood, though I wasn't sure I did.

She closed her eyes, and her jaw tightened. I suddenly felt like I was intruding on a private moment. I'd felt that way before, as a cop. In that job, you see people at stressful times, and ask questions that can open old wounds. Thinking about the lost relationship with her brother clearly was causing Becky Zachman some pain.

She opened her eyes and looked at me. "I'm sorry," she said.

"Nothing to apologize for," I replied. "It's tough times, right? Politics and all that, we're all at one another's throats, and little things become big things. I've seen it a lot. Maybe things will get better."

I'd heard similar things when I was still a cop. Families ripped asunder by the great goddamned divide of modern politics. Everybody focused on the concerns of their culture wars tribe, and forgetting the things they had in common. It was one of the reasons I liked living in my tiny trailer in the woods, with hawks and deer for neighbors. I tried to sound like I believed that last part I'd told her, about things getting better, but I wasn't sure I did. I'd heard a whole lot more stories about families splitting these past few years than I'd heard about happy reconciliations. The data did not support the idea that we'd get past that shit, so I preferred to live in the woods and limit human contact as much as possible.

She continued. "Everything, and I mean everything, comes back to religion with Bob. Politics, science, Disney movies, I mean everything. We try to communicate, and it turns into an argument, whether it's football or cooking or gender rights or . . ."

She wiped away a tear. "Anyway, we don't communicate much. When he asked me about Jimmy, that was the first time we'd communicated at all in, probably, three months."

"I see," I said.

She looked up at me. "I am not sure you do. Surely you don't think there is a connection between whatever Bob's doing and Jimmy and all this drug stuff, right?" Her eyebrows arched, the way Spock's do when McCoy says something illogical. "Try to focus on the big picture, Detective. I mean, come on. I don't talk to Bob, and he doesn't ever, ever hear anything I say, but he's a good person. Really. He is not possibly involved in anything sordid, or illegal. No way."

I nodded. I think every person I've ever arrested has at least one family member who earnestly avows their innocence. Even after years in prison. Even after a signed confession. Hell, I'd once arrested a guy whose fingerprints were on the knife we found in the victim's neck. He confessed. In court. Four times. His mom still swore there was no way he'd done it.

My own initial impression of Bob made me doubt he had done anything wrong, but a cop's gut can be mistaken, too. It's always best to look for evidence.

And the evidence was that Bob had not mentioned leaving work that day. And that did not look good.

I shrugged. "I know what you mean, I really do. And you probably are right. But you'd be astounded to find out how big the big picture really is and how sometimes things that don't seem connected really are. Sometimes, they're not. But sometimes . . ." I shrugged again. "Anyway, Bob is hiding something, and it may be connected to Jimmy's disappearance."

"I don't see how."

"Neither do I, at this point. But as an outside observer, let me lay this out. Bob Zachman is keeping secrets, and his kid ran away. Bob worked at a bank. Has he been doing something illegal? Jimmy Zachman ran away to the house of a guy who apparently pissed off nasty drug people with guns. Is whatever Bob is hiding connected to whatever sent a killer to the Boone house? Or is it all a coincidence? I don't know. Maybe it's all connected, maybe not. Probably not. But we have two kids, from two households, and those kids are connected. Maybe other stuff is connected, too."

She shook her head. "I'll never believe Bob is involved in anything shady, let alone criminal. That's just not Bob. Trust me."

I was surprised to find that I did trust her. She seemed to exude honesty, and nothing in my cop radar indicated she was lying.

"I suspect you're correct," I said. "Bob's probably not a drug lord or anything. But I have to prepare for the worst and hope for the best, you know. I need to dig in and unearth all the wormy secrets. If I don't end up needing to tell anyone else about those worms, I'll keep my mouth shut. But if I need to squeeze the worms to find out where Jimmy is, by God, I am going to squeeze some fucking worms."

I must have gotten a tad intense, because her joint flared very brightly but didn't seem to be calming her nerves. "I see. That makes a sort of gruesome sense, I guess."

"So what is Bob hiding?"

"I can't see him doing anything with drug people. Really."

"An affair?"

She shook her head. "I don't see it. I mean, I know sometimes these guys who are very preachy are shitty people when it comes to marriage, and I know some of the ones who are anti-gay and all that—I read his blog, even if we don't talk—I know they turn out to be really, really gay. You know, flaming, but in secret. It's a thing, I guess. But that is just not Bob."

"OK." I made a mental note. She'd brought up the possibility Bob was gay, unprompted by me.

"And he loves Tammy. He really, truly does. I know that. He'd never cheat on her. Never."

"Does he gamble?"

"He buys a lottery ticket every Christmas, then writes a long apology on his blog for dipping a toe into the evil world of gambling."

"Hmmm. Well, he's hiding something. If you think of anything, please let me know. And if you hear from Jimmy . . ."

"Of course."

"I appreciate your help," I told her.

"I appreciate your . . . oh, shit, I didn't even ask. You got shot. Are you OK? Should you be doing this? I mean, the cops can do this, right?"

"I should be doing this, absolutely. I'll be fine. Take care."

She gave me an appraising look, then nodded. "Then go find those kids."

She watched me as I returned to my truck. I tried to walk like the cold wasn't seeping through my inadequate fleece and down into my bones through the gash in my back. I know the doctors closed it up, but it still felt wide open.

Oh, well. I had a kid to find.

As I climbed into the truck, I noticed a white Chevy van parked down the street, behind me. It looked familiar. I couldn't see anyone inside it, but it had a dented fender and I was pretty certain it was the same van I'd seen when I left the church lot.

Was Detective Gutierrez having me followed?

I thought about it for a moment, and decided if I were still a cop and I were investigating a crime scene where people got shot to death and a couple of kids had vanished, I'd have me followed, too. It just made sense. And that explained why the police had not impounded my car. They wanted to see what I was going to do next.

I thought about waving at anyone who might be in the van, but decided against it. They were just doing their job.

I didn't need to make things easy for the tail, though. I casually turned down a side street before the van had even pulled out behind me, then hit the gas once I was out of sight. I made a couple more turns with no regard at all for where I might be going. Just random moves.

A few minutes later, assured that I could now move freely about without any civil servants on my trail, I called Bob Zachman again.

CHAPTER TWENTY-SEVEN

"Hey, Poco."

"Yeah, Zip."

"It's working, man."

"Yeah?"

"Oh, yeah. Like a charm. Better than you would think. It's pretty sweet."

"Good. You are following Runyon?"

"Yeah, I am. Hey, Poco?"

"Yeah?"

"Sorry about Adam."

"You said that before."

"Yeah, but . . . you know."

"Yeah. Just keep at it, stay focused. Follow Runyon. It's working good?"

"Oh yeah. Real good. Ain't no fucking way he gets away from me."

CHAPTER TWENTY-EIGHT

Bob Zachman answered on the first ring, but he sounded suspicious. "Hello?"

"Mr. Zachman, Ed Runyon."

"Oh, God, have you found Jimmy?"

"No, not yet, but I am in Columbus and I am working on it."

"The cops called us, from Columbus. We hear Jimmy was at a drug house?" He sounded as though he'd heard aliens had planted probes in his neighbor's cat.

"Yes," I said. "But I have no reason to think he went there because of drugs."

Bob replied in a torrent. "The cops sure think he went there because of drugs! They seem to think he's the one shooting everyone! I don't understand any of this! Jimmy is not on drugs, he is not associated with drug lords, he's never fired a gun, he's no . . ."

"Bob," I said.

". . . drug runner or gangbanger or whatever it is the cops think . . ."

"Bob," I said, a little sharper.

". . . he is, I can tell you that. I know my son."

No, you don't, I thought, but didn't say it. Instead, I said: "Bob, let me get a word in, please."

"I'm sorry," he said. "I'm just beside myself."

"I know," I said. "No need to apologize. Jimmy has a young friend, who lives at that house, and he went there to see his friend. I don't think Jimmy went there for drugs, or took any drugs, or anything like that."

"He has a friend at a drug house? And people got shot?"

"Yes, sir. But not Jimmy. He got away, along with his friend, it looks like. And I have no reason to think Jimmy's friend is into drugs, either." I had no particular reason to think Jimmy's friend wasn't into drugs, but this did not seem to be the time to say that.

"You got shot." I could visualize Bob spitting. He was still worked up.

"I got grazed. I'm OK, and I am still poking around for Jimmy. I have some avenues to explore."

I really had only one avenue, the chess app. My plan was to explore that next.

I could hear a sigh. "Thank you. Please, just find him. Look, I am sorry if I sounded off when I answered. Strange number, and I thought it was maybe a ransom demand or a hospital or . . ."

"I understand. I am using a borrowed phone. Mine's in evidence. Mr. Zachman, I need to ask you a question."

"Of course."

"Where did you go the afternoon Jimmy disappeared? You left work for a while."

Silence.

"It was a private matter." He whispered that. Tammy must have been nearby.

I adopted my no-nonsense tone, developed after years of working as a cop. "Look, I'm not your judge or anything like that, but I am the guy who got shot looking for your son and if you are up to anything, and I mean anything, that might be relevant to his disappearance then you ought to just level with me."

"How do you know it is relevant?"

I would have face-palmed, but I had one hand on the wheel and the other holding Tuck's phone to my head. "I don't know that it is. But your kid ran off for a reason, and maybe that reason is whatever it is you don't want to tell me. And his motives for leaving might damned well tell me what his next move will be, so, I'm sorry to be kind of rough here, but . . . what are you hiding?"

"Hold on."

I listened as Bob shouted, "Honey, I'm going to spread more salt on the walk." I could not hear her answer, if there was one.

I waited and heard a door close, followed by some heavy breathing. "It's cold out here," Bob said.

"No doubt. So what is going on?"

I was prepared for him to confess to an affair, or that he watched porn, or that he was gay, or that he watched gay porn while having an affair. I was not prepared for what he said.

"I was having coffee with an atheist."

The way he said it, he made it sound way worse than starring in a gay porn movie his wife didn't know about.

I sighed. "Coffee? With an atheist? I'm afraid I'm not following you."

"Look, Mr. Runyon, Tammy will bust my chops good if she knows I'm doing this."

"Is she afraid you will get some atheist on you? I don't understand."

"No, no, no. Look. I write a blog, I try to share the Word, and . . . and . . . well, I get into discussions. Sometimes really intense discussions. A lot of the time, it's doctrinal stuff, salvation by works or by faith, the nature of the Trinity, things like that. But sometimes, it's defending the very core of my faith, you know, and some atheist is trying to rattle my belief."

I started to answer with a heartfelt, "Jesus Christ, you are kidding me," but I caught myself in time. "And these discussions bother your wife?"

"She says they make me tense. She's always on me to stop. Wants me to stop blogging, too. But it's important, you know? A Christian needs to be able to defend the faith. Spread the Word."

"Yeah, I see that, but . . ."

"And sometimes I like to divert things from online, you know, where misunderstanding is so easy."

And where your wife might see it, I thought.

He continued. "You can make a difference if you can look in someone's eyes. I firmly believe that. So I invite the guy for a coffee, and we get together and discuss whatever issue it is that is making him deprive himself of a relationship with Jesus."

"I have to ask, why do that during office hours?"

He sighed. "Well, I go home for lunch every day, unless I meet Tammy somewhere, so that's out, and if I do it after work she'll ask where I've been and I don't want to lie to her, so that's out, too. I've been at the bank a long time, I do good work and things get done, so I just tell people I have a meeting somewhere, or maybe I'm not feeling well, and I just go. They trust me."

"Well, OK, then. I assume your atheist friend can confirm all this."

"He can, yes, and he'll do so, if you ask. He's a good person, just misguided. His name is Andrew, Andrew Jenkins. I can text you his number."

"Thanks. Please do. The police are going to ask you about this, too, by the way." I was kind of surprised they hadn't already, since Spears knew of the discrepancy. But the Jimmy Zachman disappearance was just one of God knows how many cases Ambletown PD had on its plate, so maybe that question was still on the detective's to-do list. Spears didn't think Bob had anything to do with his son's disappearance, anyway, so maybe it was low priority.

This case was my only priority, though, and I mentally congratulated myself for leaving the sheriff's office and striking out on my own.

Even though the police weren't beating down his door, my question got Bob's attention. "Oh. Really? The police?"

"You might want to be proactive, Mr. Zachman, and call them. That way they won't come knocking to ask you about it in front of your wife. Ask for Detective Dillon Spears."

"I guess I just don't see it as anything—"

"Sir, your boy disappeared and you've been withholding information about your own movements on the same day. You told cops you were at work. When people don't tell cops where they really were or what they were really doing, it makes cops very grumpy and very suspicious and that makes them come around to ask a lot of questions. Cops hate unanswered questions. Sometimes they drag you to the station to ask those questions. And sometimes they will make you sit and squirm for a while, hours maybe, until they are satisfied you are finally giving them the whole story."

"I see," he said.

"It would be tough to explain to your wife why the cops are so interested."

"I understand. It feels a bit uncomfortable, to be honest, being grilled like this, but I guess you have a difficult job and I can understand why things are this way. Tammy doesn't need to know about this, right?"

I could imagine his pacing and worried wide eyes, and I tried not to laugh.

"No, sir. She won't hear it from me, or from the cops if they don't grill you in front of her. Unless it somehow ends up being relevant to Jimmy's disappearance, this can all remain between you and me and your atheist friend. And I don't think Jimmy left home because you were trying to teach somebody about Jesus."

"It was Anselm's Ontological Argument."

"Anselm? I thought you said his name was Andrew?"

He actually laughed. "No. Andrew is the atheist friend. Anselm is an early Christian thinker who sought to prove God exists through an argument. God is the being who is greater than any other being we can possibly conceive. A being who exists in reality is greater than a being who exists only in our minds—"

I stopped him, because I remembered reading that on Bob's blog. It didn't sound any more convincing over the phone, but he clearly was smitten. "OK, look, Mr. Zachman, I am going to go find your son."

"Thank you. And you won't tell Tammy . . ."

"About your coffee klatches? No. None of my business."

"Thank you. She'd kill me. I told her I'd stop doing that."

"Yeah, that's between you and her and Jesus. I'm going to stay out of it."

"Thank you. Goodbye."

I drove on and wondered how anyone could take the time on the phone to define somebody's ontological argument for God to a private investigator who was looking for his missing son whose last known location was a house where two people got shot dead, but I gave up on trying to understand religion a long time ago. I just talk to God sometimes and hope he, or she, is listening, and I figure if God wants me to know something, well, God can find a way to tell me.

Life seems simpler that way.

CHAPTER TWENTY-NINE

I PULLED OVER in a small neighborhood park and dug out my charger cord. I plugged in Tuck's phone and downloaded the chess app.

After a few moments of logging in and poking around, I found a very pleasant surprise.

"Hallelujah! Well, hello, Suki!"

Wunderkind had accepted my challenge, and was waiting for me to make the first move as White.

I advanced my king pawn two squares, then hit the chat icon. It turned out that initiating the chat required more thought than choosing my opening move in the game.

How should I do this? If Suki had been Jimmy's chosen port in a storm, then Suki likely knew about Jimmy's situation with the extortionist, or at least some of it. Jimmy was ducking new conversations online, and had instantly rejected my chess challenge. Suki had accepted my request, but if my first message seemed in any way suspicious, the kids were likely to think I was the asshole trying to track Jimmy down and threaten him some more. The bastard had already tried to get to Jimmy through Ross Mason, at the chess club. Maybe he'd reached out to others, too. Maybe Jimmy and Suki had caught wind of that, so maybe they were primed to be suspicious.

My elation at Wunderkind's decision to play against me evaporated. I could not afford to blow this, and without knowing what kind of trouble Jimmy and Suki were in, I had no patience to wait. So I just stared at the damned phone screen and tried to decide what to type.

In chess, it's called paralysis by analysis. Unable to choose between a wide variety of options, you freeze. That was me, frozen.

I inhaled deeply. If Suki was playing chess, Suki probably was somewhere safe. Presumably, Jimmy was with him.

They probably were OK. Kids who are dodging bullets don't take time to play online chess.

I told myself to relax. Just think about what to say, and say it.

Suki's queen bishop pawn leapt to C5. The game was on, and I was about to get my ass kicked. Tuck says I just fart around with chess instead of really studying it. I say games are supposed to be fun, and shouldn't require a doctoral degree. Anyway, it didn't matter. I just needed to talk to the kid.

My chat icon turned green, and a red dot appeared next to it. I had a message.

I read it. "Thanks for the challenge!"

My heart started pounding. I know it's a dumb move to read too much into a chat message, but it was difficult for me to believe that a starving kid trying to stay warm between a couple of alley trash bins while hiding from drug dealers with guns would take time to accept a chess challenge and say a polite hello.

I typed: "Hi. How are you?" I felt like a damned middle-schooler. Then I moved another pawn.

Suki replied. "Been better tbh."

Well, I don't doubt that, I thought, exhaling a gush of air.

Suki moved a knight. The kid certainly wasn't spending a lot of time analyzing my moves.

I decided to play it cool, rather than rush the conversation. "Sorry to hear," I typed. Then I moved a bishop out into the field of battle.

"Thnx. Gotta go, ttyl."

Shit!

I stared at the phone screen, willing Suki to come back and make a move. That didn't happen.

I pounded the steering wheel, and my wounded shoulder immediately pointed out that was stupid. I winced, reached behind me under the fleece, and my fingers came back without blood on them.

I asked the phone to find a burger place with a drive-thru window, aimed the truck that way, and then called Linda.

She answered quickly. "Are you OK?"

"Yeah, no new wounds or anything. I feel—"

"Did you find the kids?"

"No."

"Shit, Ed."

"Yeah, I know." I told her about the aborted chess game.

"Well," she said, voice full of hope, "you have a line of communication and that is great!"

"Yes, it is. Just frustrating. I need to find these kids, hon."

She was silent for a moment, and then I realized I'd called her "hon." I probably wasn't supposed to do that anymore. Linda was dating someone else.

She decided not to bring all that up. "I know it is frustrating, but think about it, Ed. The kid is playing chess online. So presumably somewhere safe, presumably not mourning his friend or anything like that, right? They probably ran to one of Suki's friend's houses or something."

"That's my best guess, yes."

"And the kid isn't going to make a couple of moves and then just stop playing the game, right?"

"Considering how fucked up my position is right now, no, Suki will come back and continue beating the living shit out of me. I estimate I have maybe three or four moves left before the kid embarrasses me to the point of me becoming a recluse, probably living in a forest shack somewhere."

"You mean like you do now?"

She had a point. "Touché."

She laughed a little. "If he beats you, just ask for a rematch and keep talking if you have to."

"Yep. Oh, and guess what? Jimmy's dad has a deep dark secret."

"Oh my God, is he boffing the church secretary?"

"*Boffing?*"

"I'm trying to clean up my language."

"Why?"

She laughed. "Fuck if I know. Is he fucking the church secretary?"

"No. He's trying to bring atheists to Jesus over coffee, and he promised his wife he'd stop doing that because she says it makes him surly."

"Holy shit."

"Yep, secret coffee meetings and deep discussions of epistemology and all that."

"I'll be damned," she said. "Are you sure you want to drag Jimmy back to that house? I mean, if he's gay? I read some of his dad's blog. Holy shit, he is not very down with the whole LGBTQ thing. Calls them 'Alphabet People' and all that. That's really fucked up, Ed. Pisses me off."

"I thought you were cleaning up your language. And maybe you should go back to reading about the weird virus that's coming."

"Stop it, Ed. That virus is going to suck bad, if this blogger knows anything. I might just stop reading blogs and anti-social media altogether. People like Bob, so against other people's rights just because of their sexuality, that just make me so mad. And dad's attitude probably is why Jimmy ran off in the first place."

"Well, not necessarily. There are other issues, too." I thought about the blackmail threat. "But it might be a contributing factor. Bob's Jesus ain't your Jesus, Linda, and I don't much like all that shit he says, either. I doubt I'll be having beers with Bob Zachman anytime. But he loves his kid and just wants him back safe and sound. Maybe love will prevail and dad and mom will be all accepting and everything, you know? Traumatic experiences bring people together and all that."

"I sure hope so, I really do. I'll pray for that."

"Good. Listen, I'm staying in Columbus."

"Of course. You going back to the hospital?" She made it sound more like a command than a question.

"No, not unless cops drag me there. There's probably an APB out on me."

"Ed, don't be a mule."

"I gotta find these kids, Linda. You know that."

She sighed. "Yeah, I guess I do. If you are going to be a mule, be a careful mule."

"I will. Tell Tuck I'm sorry, but I am going to need his phone for a while longer."

"I'll tell him, but I am sure he will just say keep the phone and do what you gotta do. You know how Tuck is."

"Yeah. Just apologize for me, OK?"

"I will."

"And, um, thanks for coming to my rescue."

"What else would I do?"

"I'm almost to the magic box where I can order a burger. I'll let you know what I find when I find it."

"You be careful. Praying for you, too."

"Thanks."

I turned a corner and pulled into the Wendy's drive-thru lane. My peripheral vision caught a glimpse of a white Chevy van. It had been behind me, but now it continued northward down the road. I wasn't certain it was the same one I'd seen earlier when I'd left the church, but it was conceivable. Apparently, Detective Gutierrez's tail had picked me up again, but the guy didn't want a hamburger. He probably wanted to see what I was up to. One other possibility: he was tailing me and waiting for backup to take me into custody. My flight from the hospital probably did not look good in the eyes of one Detective Gutierrez. Cops hate that sort of thing.

Once the van was out of sight, I pulled away from the drive-thru lane and exited the lot without getting a burger. I headed south. I could find another burger anywhere, but chances to teach a cop that I'm not that easy to tail? Those don't come along every day.

CHAPTER THIRTY

"WELL?"

"I had him, Poco, but he's slippery."

"Go get him again."

"I will. He won't disappear, you know?"

"See that he doesn't. I am getting impatient, Zip."

"I know, man."

"He killed Adam."

"I know, Poco, I know. But it's been nothing but witnesses all day, you know? Broad daylight, all that?"

"Stay on him. You will get your chance."

"Oh, yeah. I'll do it, man. You'll see."

"Good. I want it to hurt. I want it to hurt bad, Zip."

"It will, Poco. It will. I promise you, man. He will suffer."

"Adam used to take me to ballgames," Poco said. "Back when we had time for ballgames."

"I know," Zip said. "I know, man. You guys were tight."

"Brothers," Poco said.

"I know, man. I know. I'll make this Runyon guy pay."

Poco sniffed. "Thank you. Kill him, man. Just kill him."

"I will."

CHAPTER THIRTY-ONE

I'D WATCHED THE phone screen while eating my Quarter Pounder, but so far there had been no moves from Suki, aka Wunderkind. I was sitting in a mall parking lot, eating bad food and watching the phone and keeping an eye out for a cop in a white van. I was growing surlier by the minute, and thinking about driving up to visit the sheriff's deputy who'd smacked Tuck around. Donnor Brogan could still use a bit of thrashing, and I could use someone to thrash.

An honest-to-goodness straight up fight might do me good, I thought. I could burn off some of this pent-up energy. I spent a few enjoyable moments imagining myself tossing him, huffing and puffing and bruised all over, into the back of his shiny hillbilly wet dream of a truck.

I didn't have time for that, of course, and I'd promised Tuck I'd stay out of it. Sometimes Tuck really annoys me.

Suki's bishop jumped across the board, attacking my knight. I left the doomed piece where it was and hit the chat icon, then typed as quickly as I could.

"U OK?" I do not ordinarily approve of such text message spelling, but I wanted to get my message out before Suki could go away.

"Yes. Why?"

I sighed. "You disappeared fast last time."

"Had to do some stuff. It's cool."

"Glad to hear. Can I tell you something?" I took a deep breath. If this question set alarms ringing, Suki might shut down the conversation.

"What?"

I tried to look three or four moves ahead in this conversation, the way I knew Suki was looking several moves ahead on the chessboard.

I typed: "I need you to trust me. I'm a private detective. My name is Ed Runyon. Jimmy's dad hired me. I need to know Jimmy is OK. I know he ran off with you. I just want to know Jimmy and you are both safe."

I held my breath, read it twice, wondered if this was the right move or not, then hit *send*.

As soon as I did that, I started typing again. "Call Jimmy's dad or mom, they will confirm they hired me. Please. Everyone is worried sick."

I watched for an answer. None came.

Fuck.

I stared at the goddamned chessboard, and looked for a way to save my knight. I had to prolong the game, if I could, and keep the line of communication open.

I moved a pawn to support my knight, then went back to the chat.

"Think about it, please. I only want to help. Call me."

I entered Tuck's phone number. I entered the URL for my company website, too.

Then I waited.

Then I waited some more and then I texted my gorgeous cop friend.

CHAPTER THIRTY-TWO

THIRTY MINUTES LATER, I was on the other side of town and knocking on Detective Shelly Beckworth's apartment door.

"Come on in," she yelled. "And then explain to me why the hell you are not in the hospital. You got out of there before I could even come and see you."

I entered, as bidden, and found Shelly pouring beer at a counter that separated the small living room from the small kitchen. "I have a missing kid to find."

She gave me a skeptical glance. "Are you sure you are up to this?"

I nodded. "I'm OK, really."

"I'm not convinced, but I am not carrying you back to the doctor." She placed a mug on the counter. "I am not your momma. Great Lakes, the IPA. Commodore Perry, your favorite, right? I went to the corner and nabbed some. You need a heavier coat, tough guy. It's cold out there."

"Mine's in evidence, along with my phone."

"Ah. That's why you texted from Tuck's."

"Yep. Where is your girlfriend?" I tossed my fleece on a sofa, then started tapping at Tuck's phone. I'd given Suki my website information. Maybe the kids would reach out to me that way. I changed the website to foreword notices and calls to Tuck's number as Shelly and I talked.

"Lana? She should be home soon, so if you stick around you can meet her." She smiled. "But take your threesome dreams and toss them right in that trash bin over there. It ain't happening."

"I was not thinking that."

"It crossed your mind," she said, grinning.

She was looking pretty good, so yeah, it had crossed my mind. "Apparently, it crossed yours, too," I answered.

"Only because I know how your Neanderthal brain works."

"Did Neanderthals do orgies?"

"I think the evidence is lacking on that, Ed."

"Enough of that, then. So let me update you on this case I'm working on."

"Yeah, sounds scary." She poured some mixed nuts into a bowl.

I laid it all out for her. "I don't know if Suki is going to keep talking with me or not. I don't even really know if Jimmy is with Suki, that's just an assumption. There is evidence, though. I found Jimmy's ball cap in Suki's room."

"Yes, so your assumption is a good one. No reason they would separate after running away from the house. But it's weird. When you asked if Wunderkind was OK, the answer seemed pretty chill, you know? I mean, the kid's dad just got shot dead, Suki and his extortion victim buddy, Jimmy, escaped in the night from a house riddled with bullets, they're hiding out, and Suki says everything is cool?"

I nodded. "I thought that was bizarre, too, but, well, you can't really tell from a chat message. He could have typed it with shaking hands and tears in his eyes for all I know. Their hands, their eyes, I mean. Suki's preferred pronouns."

Shelly finished sipping her beer. "It's all kind of scary, Ed."

"Yes, it is, and the sooner I find the kids and wrap this up, the better. Any advice?"

"Let me swirl it around in my head for a while."

I popped some nuts into my mouth and took a swig of IPA. Then the front door opened and a blonde supermodel walked through, wrapped in a bulky coat and carting a couple of plastic bags. "Oh, hello, Ed! I am Lana, and I have really been dying to meet you!"

She carefully put her purse on the floor and the packages in the closet, then took off the big coat to reveal a sweater that was just as efficient at hiding the curves I'd seen on that previous FaceTime call but did not obscure her rear end. I tried not to ogle, but I stink at that.

Then Lana trundled across the room and wrapped me up in a big hug. "Did Shelly let you look at her monster book?"

"Not yet."

Lana went to kiss Shelly, and I resumed failing at not ogling. When they separated, Shelly and Lana exchanged a glance that seemed fraught with meaning. "I have to go take care of something upstairs," Shelly said. "Sorry, Ed, it will take a little while. But you and Lana can get to know one another."

"Sure," I said. "No problem." My hackles were up, though. Lana and Shelly seemed to be sharing a secret, and Shelly scurried away with a bit of a guilty look.

Lana and I made small talk while Shelly ascended the stairs. Once we heard a door close above, Lana poured herself some wine and looked at me with raised eyebrows. "So, don't be mad, but Shelly told me a little bit about this case you are working on, and that's why I ended my shopping early and rushed home as soon as I heard you were coming."

"I trust Shelly."

Lana smiled. "Good! So, this boy you are looking for, he got lured into an extortion trap?"

I nodded. "Yeah, some kind of mutual masturbation video chat, I guess, and now the guy on the other side of the conversation is threatening to share a supposed video if Jimmy doesn't pay up."

Lana actually growled. "And the kid is fifteen?"

"Yeah."

"Man, I hate that. I have no sympathy if some adult gets caught in a deal like that, especially a married adult. You know? He ought to know better, and ought to keep it in his pants. But a kid . . ."

"I know. It's pretty brutal."

"Yeah. Just completely predatory."

She paused, and I started wondering why Shelly had to be absent for this conversation. "What's going on, Lana?"

"Did Shell ever tell you how we met?"

"No."

"Well, there's a guy, used to work in the police forensics lab. He had a major crush on Shelly for a while, but before that, he had a major crush on me. Shell and I met through him, and we bonded over his pursuit of our charms." Her eyes twinkled as she said that.

"Did the poor fool survive being shot down?"

Lana blushed. "Shell shot him down. She's not into guys. I'm more flexible, and me and Mike did hook up for a while. None of those sexy details are really relevant, though." She grinned. "Maybe some other day. What is relevant now is this. Mike is a certified ethical hacker, and a software developer, a very good one, and he's no longer working for the cops."

"Ethical hacker?" I went to the fridge for another beer.

"Yeah, one of those people who check company IT for problems. Like, he hacks a company's computers and then tells them how he did it, so they can fix things and keep someone else from hacking them the same way."

"Interesting."

"Yeah, and he's really good at it and charges them a boatload of money for it. I mean, he's really ninja good. One other thing, he really hates people who victimize kids. Especially ones who blackmail kids."

"Does he, now?" She had my interest. "Do you think he'd help out Jimmy?"

"I'm sure he would. He used to set up stings for the cops, to catch creeps who met fifteen-year-old girls online and lured them to hotels. Mike is a pretty gentle person, you know? Nice guy." Her eyes gazed at the ceiling for a moment, and she seemed to shiver for just a second, but she was smiling. "Wonderful guy, really. But when he was busting creeps like that, or anyone who preyed on kids, he totally changed. He got all intense. Scary, almost. Takes it very seriously, like it's his mission in life."

"Is that why you and he are not an item anymore? Because he's scary?"

She shook her head. "No. It's because Shelly is Shelly." She glanced up the staircase.

I nodded. "Fair point. So, how could this hacker guy help Jimmy?"

She laughed. "I don't know the details. I'm not a tech-head, and stuff like that bores me. I prefer art museums. But . . . I talked to Mike about Jimmy already, after Shelly told me about it. I hope you don't mind. I did not use any names—well, I gave him your name. He says he probably can help—maybe, but—"

"But what?"

"Well, the means may not be exactly certifiably ethical, if you know what I mean."

"So, he might do something illegal."

"Yeah."

I nodded. *So that's why Shelly had to leave the room. Plausible deniability. She didn't want to be associated with what might be an illegal approach. Shelly was doing a bit of a tap dance.*

I took a swig of beer. "I am not certifiably ethical, either. I am no longer a cop, and I fucking hate people who pick on kids, too, so if Mike can do something to get this son of a bitch off Jimmy's back, I'm all for it, legality be damned. If I can afford it. You said he makes a lot of money." It occurred to me this might be expensive. The Zachmans might not be able to pay for it, and I sure as hell couldn't. I also had to wonder whether it was a good idea to involve my clients at all in some sort of illegal hacking activity. As appealing as this sounded, it might not be the solution, after all, and I couldn't afford a lawyer to help me navigate all this.

Lana smiled and shook her head. "I don't think Mike will charge you a lot, if anything. He makes good pay, and he does not go after these assholes for money. He says messing with child molesters and pervert predators is the best hobby in the world. I'm going to give you his number. You call him, and he'll tell you what he can do and what he can't. He did tell me there were no guarantees."

"No guarantees. Got it. But it sounds like a fighting chance."

"There is a certain amount of luck involved, he says. But if anyone in the world can help Jimmy, it's Mike. You didn't sleep with him, though." She winked. "So you will have to address him as Miguel."

She got up, went to a sticky pad by the fridge, and jotted down a phone number. She tore off a sheet and gave that to me. "Keep that in your wallet or whatever. Might be best if you don't add him as a contact in your phone or anything." She winked. "He likes to keep a low profile." Then she ran to her purse, took out a phone, and started tapping. I assumed that was the all-clear message to Shelly. A second later, the door upstairs opened and Shelly descended.

"Did you two have a nice talk?"

"Yes, we did," Lana said, winking at me. The winking wasn't as cute as she thought it was. I mean, it didn't spoil the overall stunning look, but she'd be better off if she stopped doing it, in my humble opinion. Shelly's viewpoint on that was the only one that really mattered, I guess, so I kept my thoughts to myself.

Lana spoke. "He's a good guy, Shell, and not bad looking. Are you sure you don't want to have a little . . ."?

Shelly kissed Lana to shut her up. "Don't even joke about that shit," Shelly said, laughing. "If anything like that happens, it'll have to happen in Ed's head."

Lana laughed. "I was kidding, of course."

"Of course," I said, without a hint of sarcasm, because I always take it well when gorgeous women laugh about not having sex with me. I started to proffer another comedic rejoinder, maybe even change my mind about mentioning the annoying wink, but decided against it when the phone buzzed.

It was a notification about an inquiry on my detective agency website. The message said only "I need help." But it included a phone number, and I clicked on it.

I got an answer on the first ring. "Hello?"

It sounded like a young woman, not a runaway boy. I sighed. "Ed Runyon. I'm a private investigator. You left a message on my website."

The caller hesitated. "I'm looking for a private detective?"

"I'm a detective. What do you need?" I rolled my eyes.

"I think my husband is cheating."

"Cheating husband. Look, I'm kind of booked up for now." I was not going to get sidetracked by an infidelity case. "Where are you?"

"Um, Columbus."

"I can give you a couple of names, good detectives. Guy named Andy Hayes, a woman named Roxane Weary. Both have been at this longer than me, and I've talked to people who say they get the job done. Maybe one of them can help you, but I don't have time now." I had no idea whether either of those pros had any interest in a routine infidelity case, but I sure as hell didn't.

The woman on the other end of the call didn't want a referral. "I want you," she said. "I was hoping to meet up with you and talk."

I sighed. "Look, if you feel the need to call a private eye to tail your husband, the relationship is probably over anyway and you should just get up and leave him. This is my professional advice. Just get up and go."

Shelly scolded me.

The woman on the line paused. "But I—"

"Sorry." I hung up.

Shelly grimaced. "Can you afford to chase off customers?"

"Yeah." I held up Tuck's phone. "Don't suppose you could get my own phone out of—"

"No way, cowboy. You know how slow the wheels of justice grind."

"Had to try. I'm in a mood. And I may still be under the effects of pain medicine from the hospital."

"I do not doubt that. You are moving well, but, anyway. How is the shoulder?"

"It'll heal. How is your leg?" The last time Shelly and I had worked together, she had taken a bullet from Jeff Cotton's rifle.

"I have a scar, otherwise all is well."

"I'll kiss the scar later and make it all better," Lana said, before kissing Shelly and heading up the stairs. "Nice meeting you, Ed."

"Nice meeting you, too." I watched her all the way up the stairs. When I turned back to look at Shelly, she was shaking her head.

"You can at least try not to use X-ray vision on her clothes, Ed."

"Yeah, I'll work on that."

My phone buzzed again. Another website notification, again a vague message with a number. I called.

"Hello?" It was a decidedly male voice this time.

"Ed Runyon, private detective. You just reached out to my website."

"Hello, yeah. Do you do missing person investigations?"

"Yes, I do," I answered. "But I am currently engaged. What's going on? Maybe I can refer you to someone."

"How much do you charge?"

I told him my rates. "Please give me an idea what's going on, and I'll refer you to someone. I don't have time for your case now, but I know a couple of good PIs."

He hung up.

I looked at Shelly. "Well, at least I was nicer to that one."

"Yeah," she said, skeptically.

"It was a missing person case."

"Could even have been a missing kid case. Your specialty. Did you think of that?"

I had to admit I hadn't. "I can't find them all at the same time. The Zachmans hired me first."

"Fair enough," Shelly said.

I started pacing. "Where were all these inquiries when I didn't have a priority case?"

"How often do you get calls like that, Ed? I was under the impression things were slow, but you've had two inquiries in the span of a couple of minutes."

I stopped and blinked at her. "Holy shit. You are right. I haven't often had two calls in a day, let alone . . ." I went to the counter and raised my beer. "I think I have it, by Jove." I took a swig.

"Well, Mr. Holmes?"

"The chess masters are analyzing the position," I said. "They're calling to see if I'm legit."

"Son of a bitch. Smart kids."

"One caller was female, and the other sounded older, though. Maybe it's not them."

"But maybe they have friends?"

"Maybe. I mean, that makes sense. If Suki has time to play chess with me and chat, they've got to be holed up safe somewhere, right? That could imply friends."

I looked at the numbers that had called. Two different numbers. I called the second number, the one for the missing person case. No answer.

I called the other number. No answer on that one, either.

"They probably used a virtual number app," Shelly said. "That's what I'd do if I wanted to stay anonymous. They've probably abandoned those numbers already and gotten on with their lives. I fucking hate virtual number apps."

I knew what she meant. A simple app could give you a fake phone number from any area code you wanted. Criminals love that shit. "Yeah," I said. "So, maybe it's not Jimmy and Suki checking me out. Maybe it's someone else."

"Like who?"

I paced, and thought. "I did recently walk in on a homicide scene involving druggies, and I shot a guy dead."

"Maybe a little paranoid, but maybe legit. Sounds like something in a crime novel, though."

I raised my eyebrow. "I do read a lot of those, and it pays to be paranoid when everyone is out to get you. So, if the kids are checking me out, I hope I sounded like a legitimate private investigator who gets fed up with bullshit calls when he is working on something important. If it's bad guys, I hope I sounded mean and scary like someone they should not fuck with. By the way, when I get messages from people who think the CIA is hacking their phones? I don't call them back."

Shelly smiled. "I do not blame you a bit. Do you get a lot of those?"

"Jesus, yes," I answered. "You know what, though? If the kids are checking me out, that means they haven't written me off."

She smiled. "That's right, cowboy."

"So maybe I am on the scent." I drained my beer. "I sure hope it was them."

CHAPTER THIRTY-THREE

"HELLO?"

"Hey, Poco. I got him again. This thing works like a fucking dream, man."

"Good. Fucking kill him."

"It's a neighborhood. He went inside someone's place."

"You got a silencer, don't you?"

"Yeah. But not with me."

Zip heard Poco slamming things around and cursing, probably through gritted teeth. Then the boss resumed talking. "Why don't you have your silencer?"

"Because before you called me and said go check what's going on at Indianola, I was out having a drink with a guy. I went straight from the bar to go see what was up with Adam, like you asked. The situation seemed urgent. I did not go home to get my silencer."

"I don't believe this," Poco muttered. "OK. I get it. Yeah. Sure. You don't go around with a silencer all the time."

Zip hated it when Poco was like this. The boss could be very unreasonable when emotions set in. Zip tried talking quietly, and calmly. "There's probably other people there, too."

"I don't fucking care, Zip. He killed Adam."

"I know, but . . ."

"But what?"

"I liked Adam, man, but not enough to take a lethal injection, you know what I'm saying?"

"Yeah . . . but . . ."

Zip inhaled deeply. "I'll get him. He can't get away from me. I'll get him."

"You promise?" Poco sounded like he was crying.

"Yeah. Wait. He's coming out."

"Kill him now!"

"Hang on."

"Kill him now, I said."

"Hang on. It's going to be kind of a long shot, man. I don't know if this will work. And I'll have to be moving, need to make a quick getaway. I don't like this."

"Get out of the fucking van, walk up to him, put the gun right to his fucking head, and pull the goddamned trigger. How hard can it fucking be?"

"It can be real fucking hard if you don't want to go to prison on a death sentence," Zip said. "Just wait!"

"Don't fuck this up, Zip."

"I won't. He's across the street. Once he passes, I'll get him from behind, and . . . fuck."

"What?"

"Police, man."

"What?"

"Fucking police! Coming down the street!"

"Are they coming for you?"

"Don't know, don't know, don't know . . . Jesus. Hang on."

"Goddamn it, Zip. What the hell is going on?"

"They passed. Just a patrol, I think."

"So go kill the son of a bitch."

"He's back in his truck, pulling out."

"God damn it!"

"He did not see me. I'll follow. Don't worry, Poco. I'm going to kill this asshole. His luck can't last forever. He's as good as dead."

"Make sure of it, Zip. Make sure of it."

CHAPTER THIRTY-FOUR

BACK IN THE truck, I put in a Waylon Jennings disc and tried not to think about Lana and Shelly and how happy they seemed together and how Linda seemed ready to move on. Waylon was singing about getting back to the basics of love in Lukenbach, Texas. I skipped ahead to "This Is Getting Funny (But There Ain't Nobody Laughing)." It suited my mood.

I checked the chess app. There were no new moves or messages from Wunderkind, aka Suki. I checked my website. There were no messages from Jimmy or Suki, or from anyone wanting me to follow an adulterer or rescue a cat from a tree.

Since it looked as though I was not going to find Jimmy right now, and no one at Shelly's apartment had invited me to sleep over, I decided to look for a hotel. I needed a bathroom, and a shower, and to be honest, a chance to stretch out on a bed and rest my back. I found a Marriott nearby, picked up a six-pack of Commodore Perry IPA at a gas station, then went to the hotel and checked in. I remembered telling the Zachmans I would pick the cheapest hotels, but I was too tired to look for something less expensive. I decided not to bill them for this.

Once I was in my hotel room that looked like every other hotel room I'd ever seen, I checked my phone again. Still no good news. I hit the shower.

I stripped while the water got hot, and used the mirror to check out my shoulder because it hurt like a son of a bitch and felt rather stiff. I had not realized how long the scar was. It looked like a red river running from the top of my shoulder and down to the middle of my back. The stitches were ugly. But the gash wasn't torn open or seeping or bleeding, so I counted that as a good thing.

After the shower I dressed again, then ordered a pizza with lots of mushrooms from Tommy's. I was piling on expenses here—hotel, food, a mysterious hacker named Mike, I mean Miguel. I decided I was going to need some way to track that kind of stuff, then decided I was in no mood to figure that out now. It could wait until after I found Jimmy.

Waiting for my pizza, I mostly paced and ran the case through my head while checking the phone over and over. Ravenous as I was, I would have gladly traded the upcoming pizza for a message from Jimmy that said "come get me." At least I could be certain that I would not be assigned some sort of theft case or get called out for SWAT duty or be lectured about how far behind I was on my paperwork. Those were all things I did not miss about working for the sheriff's department. There was a downside, though, because all I could really do at the moment was obsess about finding Jimmy. And that was driving me batshit.

The pizza guy called. I met him in the lobby and took my pizza back to Room 402. I ate too much, decided not to drink another beer, and then made sure the phone volume was all the way up. I swapped out Tuck's Metallica wallpaper for an image of Johnny Cash. Tuck was going to hate it.

I set an alarm, then sprawled across the bed and took a nap. My dreams alternated between supermodel smiles and frantic phone calls from a kid who was being chased by zombies. My dreams included a lot of phone scrolling and digital chess moves, too, so I am not sure how much time elapsed between the ding that signaled an incoming text message and me realizing that it was a real ding, not a dream ding.

I grabbed the phone. It was a message left at the Whiskey River website.

I did not recognize the number.

The message said this: "If you want to find Jimmy, be on the Oval, High Street end, where all the sidewalks come together. 9 p.m. Come alone. No weapons. No cops. I'll find you."

I jumped out of bed and checked the time. I had a couple of hours, but it was already dark. Night comes too early in winter.

I called the number. No answer.

I checked Google Maps. The Oval was a large grassy area on The Ohio State University campus, and yes, I always capitalize the "T" in "The" when referring to the college, and I don't care if you think that makes me snooty. The student union was tucked between the Oval and High Street. A lot of sidewalks came together at one point not far from that. It was out in the great wide open, surrounded by buildings, and thus a damned fine place to put someone if you wanted to leave him entirely exposed to a sniper shot or some damned thing.

The fleece I had couldn't really keep out the cold. It sure as hell wasn't going to slow down bullets.

It sounded like some sort of trap.

But I now had a clue that might lead me to Jimmy, so . . . well. I was on my way to the Oval.

CHAPTER THIRTY-FIVE

A REFLECTION AND a shadow proved to be the difference between life and death.

I saw the shadow and the reflection in my truck window, as I was preparing to get in my truck to leave the Marriott parking lot. I stepped to my left, and the knife that would have been planted low in my back ruined the paint on my truck door instead.

I threw an elbow and smashed the bastard's nose. He stumbled backward, and I whirled to face him.

He leaned against a Toyota, which had kept him from falling. He still held the knife in his right hand, while his left covered his bleeding nose.

I do not waste time in a fight. That gives the other guy a chance to figure out how to kill me. I'd rather keep him worried about me killing him.

I moved toward my assailant and used my right hand to grab the wrist of his knife hand, then jerked him forward as hard as I could as I turned. The knife slid harmlessly past my ribs, and I rammed my left fist above his elbow while providing a counter-pull with my right hand. I did not succeed in snapping his arm, but I heard the knife fall.

My attacker screamed. "Fuck!" I found that wondrously satisfying as I grabbed his coat collar. Spinning, I drove his head into my truck window. The bright parking lot light revealed spider-web cracks. I hoped there were similar cracks in this fucker's skull.

I pulled him backward and slammed him against the Toyota. The car was white, so the blood splatters showed up prominently. This guy could not possibly have much fight left in him.

Somewhere in the back of my mind, I realized I was taking out my frustrations on this guy who probably just wanted my cash, and intellectually I realized that the proper thing to do was to finish subduing this clown and call the cops. With luck, this guy's progress through the criminal justice system might eventually lead him to some program that mitigated the societal forces that had led him to ambush a stranger in a parking lot.

Or not.

By the time those thoughts had processed in my gray cells, though, I'd already thrown the son of a bitch to the ground and kicked him in the ribs. My attacker kicked at me, and I slipped on ice as I backed up to avoid the blow. I went down hard and banged my left elbow in the process. That was going to leave a big purple bruise. All this action was tugging at the stitches in my back, too. I felt blood streaming down my back. I wasn't sure if that was reality or just my imagination. It hurt, either way.

Knife boy was up and running by the time I got back to my feet and clutched at my back. He did not slip on any icy patches. I started to chase him, but he was fast and had a good head start.

And besides, I had a more important errand.

I checked my hand—no blood, thank God. I picked up the knife, using just two fingers to grasp the blade near the point. No need to cover up any pretty fingerprints on the hilt. I clambered into my truck, put the knife in the glove box, and tried to remember the last time a guy had gotten away from me. I was feeling sore and slow, and a touch at my elbow told me I had a nice fresh scrape. I could still use the arm, though.

I probably should have listened to Dr. Medley and stayed in the damned hospital, but I had no time for regrets.

I looked about, but saw no sign of my assailant. I started the truck and rolled out of the lot.

I pondered for a moment, wondering if this ambush had anything to do with the text messages I'd received. I decided it probably didn't. Cities are full of people who need money for drugs or some other damned reason and are willing to kill for it. That's why I live in the country.

But I knew I could be wrong. It was possible that the last text message had been designed purposefully, to get me to leave the hotel and allow some fucker to ambush me. It did not sound like the kind of thing Jimmy might do, but it sounded like the kind of thing the drug people who'd killed Suki's dad might do. I had no idea how those drug pushers could have found me at the hotel, but weird shit happens. I couldn't discount that possibility.

That possibility was not going to deter me, however. No, no, no.

I considered calling Detective Gutierrez, but decided against that. He would simply ask me a lot of questions and insist I stay at the hotel until cops arrived. He'd have thrown up a bunch of roadblocks that would have delayed my rendezvous on the Oval. Hell, he might even be mad enough to drag me off to jail or back to the hospital. He had a job to do.

I'd left my job at the Mifflin County Sheriff's Office to avoid red tape and people telling me what to do.

So instead of calling Gutierrez, I called 911. "Hi. I just saw a fight in the Marriott parking lot over on Olentangy River Road. I think a guy was mugged or something." I described the guy with the knife to the best of my ability, which wasn't much because I'd seen little. I suddenly had empathy for all the people who'd given me really vague descriptions when I was a cop.

I knew the cops would record the phone call and eventually trace it to Tuck's phone and then to me. I also knew that would take a while. In the meantime, they'd maybe collect the bastard I'd fought in the parking lot, and I would go to the Oval. The police could tell me who the fucker was later, if they decided to do so.

And, in the meantime, there was a chance that by the time the cops tracked me down, Jimmy and Suki would be safe.

I had work to do.

CHAPTER THIRTY-SIX

"DID YOU GET him?"

"Fuck no, Poco. I'm sorry, man."

"Jesus. What happened?"

"I almost had him. I swear."

"You sound drunk. What happened, Zip?"

"I am not. I am not drunk. I got punched in the face, and slammed against a truck. My fucking head hurts like a motherfucker. He roughed me up, Poco. He just . . . he's big, Poco. And fast. He . . ."

"Calm down. Talk to me. How did you get punched in the face? Shit, Zip! Did you use the knife?"

Zip waited silently while Poco muttered curses on the other side of the call. After a few seconds, Poco spoke again. "Why didn't you go get your silencer and shoot him?"

Zip sighed. "I wanted to do this fast, man. I thought going across town to get the silencer, well, that would take time, you know? I know . . . I know this is rough on you." *And besides, the silencer fucks up my aim,* Zip thought, but did not say aloud.

Poco sighed. "Alright, yeah, I get that, I guess. I just want this guy dead, man. He killed my brother."

"He's very fast," Zip said. "Strong, too. But I will get him. I will. Adam was my friend."

"OK. Thank you."

"I tried to do it quiet, with the knife instead of the gun. It seemed the right call. That was a mistake, I guess. Anyway, I had to get close, and he's fast, Poco. He was too fast for me."

"Let me do the thinking. That's what I do. That is why I run things and why you go out and get your hands dirty, see? So, you're tracking him. You have time. Go get the silencer. Use the gun next time. Where are you now?"

"In the van. I can trail him. He won't escape me again."

"See that he doesn't."

"He won't. And I will use a gun next time."

"Good."

"He hit me really hard, Poco. All I could see was flashing lights in my head, you know? I think he broke my nose, and maybe my forehead. I'm a mess, man. All bloody and shit. Hurts like fuck. Still some flashing, now and then. Christ. Hurts like a motherfucker."

"Be strong, man. Do this for Adam."

"I will. I promise. I will shoot him as many times as it takes."

"I want him dead."

"I know."

"He killed Adam."

"I know."

"Kill him, Zip."

"I will kill him."

"If you can't see to aim because you got flashing lights in your brain, you stick the gun in his fucking mouth and you pull the trigger, you got me? Be strong."

"Yes, I got you."

"Goodbye."

"Goodbye."

CHAPTER THIRTY-SEVEN

I DIDN'T WANT to be seen driving up in my truck, so I'd paid a guy to let me park at a frat house, then hoofed it the rest of the way to the Oval. I thought a stealthy approach best.

I was at the rendezvous spot ten minutes early.

My shirt was sticking to my back, so I was pretty sure I'd torn something loose back there while fending off my attacker, after all. It hurt like the devil, too. But I'd have to cope with that later. I didn't have time for distractions.

Ohio had decided to be cold, and I wished I had more than the fleece Linda had brought me. My breath made little clouds that drifted on the breeze. Flurries danced in the air, too, slicing through my breath fog. Nearby lampposts pushed away the darkness, but one of them blinked on and off. It made little zapping noises, like those lights that kill mosquitoes.

I stood there in the cold for probably five minutes. No one shot me.

The Oval was not a busy place at the moment, but there were students about, walking from study sessions or bars or hookups or whatever. A tall skinny fellow approached from one of the many sidewalks that converged here. I glanced at him, but he ignored me and passed on by.

A few seconds later, a black girl walking rapidly and carrying what looked like a Mace canister in her right hand approached from another direction. I strolled away in another direction, because I did not want to look as though I was waiting for her to pass closely by. Women have to worry about such things, which is why they carry Mace and learn to use keys protruding between their fingers as improvised weapons. I didn't want to scare her, and I didn't want to get Mace in my face. I went through that in training a couple of times. It sucks.

She ignored me, too, and kept walking without a backward glance.

I went back to my waiting spot. I spun, slowly, looking for places where a sniper might hide. I was a sniper myself, when I worked with the Mifflin County Sheriff's Office SWAT team, so I knew where to look. The buildings were distant, and the darkness was a factor. So were the flurries. I decided a long-range shot would be a low-percentage move unless the shooter had good training and infrared goggles and something that could spit out a lot of ammunition in a hurry. Such things are pretty damned easy to buy in these United States of America, so I kept moving, changing direction a lot and telling myself I'd have to be ready to run if bullets started flying. Like I could outrun bullets. Still, there was no need to make it easy if some idiot decided to gun me down from a rooftop, and even if he didn't have adequate training and great equipment, a lucky shot can make you just as dead as an expert shot.

I knew I was being somewhat irrational, probably worrying about nothing, but my parking lot assailant had left me skittish. And, of course, I'd been shot recently, so there was that. I had a right to be nervous.

I had a right to be thankful, too; despite my close call at the Indianola house, I was here, taking a risk but doing what I needed to do and joking with myself about making any sniper waste a lot of ammunition in trying to kill little old me. I wasn't sitting in my truck, trying to calm my quaking knees and imagining myself trying to sell a fixer-upper to some cute young couple.

It was one little victory, and I was going to take it.

I noticed someone approaching from the south. I turned to face them, then heard rapid footsteps from the north. I spun to see the skinny fellow from a few moments ago walking toward me at a brisk pace.

Footsteps behind me got my attention, and I spun again. It was a tall bald fellow, with a backpack on his shoulder and an earring flashing in the lamplight. He had earbuds in; I could just make out the cords dangling from his ears.

A voice behind me got my attention. "Hey."

I turned, expecting to see the tall skinny fellow, but it was a different guy, taller than me and wider in the shoulders. I had no idea where he had come from. I hoped he wasn't a Buckeye linebacker, because no way do I want to get hit by one of those.

He was holding a pistol, aimed at my face.

I got very, very still. The gunman was about eight feet away from me. Close enough to make me consider a dangerous move, but far enough to make the odds of success nil. And I was surrounded. So anyway, I didn't try any heroics.

Another voice broke the darkness. "Hello."

I hadn't been shot yet, so I very slowly turned my head to see who had spoken. It was the girl from a few minutes before, the one with the Mace canister. She was aiming it at me, but too far away for a spray to be effective in the swirling flurries. Her voice sounded eerily familiar.

"Hi." That was the bald guy, with the earbuds. He was pulling those free from his ears. "Are you Runyon?"

I spun to face the tall skinny guy.

I was surrounded. One of them had a gun, one of them had a Mace can. I had no gun, no Mace, no knife, and no chance.

"Yeah," I said. "I'm Ed Runyon. Who the fuck are you?"

The guy with the gun smiled. "We're the Bad Bishops." His accent was foreign, but I could not place it.

"Who?"

He shrugged. "We're a chess club."

CHAPTER THIRTY-EIGHT

I LAUGHED AND felt it in my wounded back, so I stopped. I don't know that laughing is the appropriate response when one is surrounded by a college chess club with weapons, but . . . well, this was my first time. "You're a what?"

"We're a chess club," said the girl with the Mace. "And we want to see some fucking ID right now."

"OK," I said. "I think I know where this is going. I do not actually have my ID, honest, because it is in police custody." I wondered if that sounded as fishy to them as it did to me. "Did I talk to you on the phone, miss?"

"My husband's cheating," she said.

I knew it. She'd called Whiskey River Investigations, checking me out.

"Toss the ID to me," the skinny guy said. "Not to the girl with the Mace or the guy with the gun."

"I really wish I could comply, but I do not have an ID on me, I swear." I had to chuckle a bit, because I'd only heard that a million times as a cop. "The cops have my stuff because I was involved in a, um, altercation, and so my phone and wallet are in evidence. I have a borrowed phone and some other things tucked into my pockets, but no ID to show you. My picture is on my website, though." I'd been reluctant to put my photo on the website, actually, but Linda had insisted. She said I had an honest face, and it would be good for business. "You guys are already familiar with my website, right? I mean, you've been checking me out."

The skinny guy started looking at his phone. The light from the screen illuminated his face, and a dangling earring glittered. He glanced up at me. "Why are you looking for Suki?"

I smiled and nodded. I was apparently on the right track. If I could keep these young Kasparovs from killing me, I might actually succeed. "I'm hired to look for a boy named Jimmy, and I think he's with Suki so I'm looking for both of them. Is Jimmy with Suki?"

That got no answer, so I spoke again. "They are both running scared, and I just want to help them."

He stared at me like I was roadkill. "And why should we trust you?"

"Fuck if I know," I said. "I've been told I have an honest face, and I showed up here without a weapon and without cops like you wanted. But if you are in contact with Jimmy, or Suki, well, they can call Jimmy's dad and mom to confirm my story."

He shook his head. "Jimmy ain't calling his dad."

I inhaled sharply. "Look, I get it. Jimmy is worried about how his dad is going to react to some shit. I understand. Maybe you know about that, maybe you don't, I don't know, but I understand Jimmy's reluctance. I do. But his dad loves him, and his mom loves him, and they just want assurances he is safe. They need to know he is alive."

"What about Suki?"

I sighed. "Yeah. I don't know much about Suki's situation. I know Jimmy and Suki are friends, and it looks like Jimmy called Suki for help. And I know Suki's dad was into some drug shit, and someone got pissed and killed him. And I know I walked into the middle of that situation and got shot, and I killed a guy before he could kill me, and the kids climbed down a fucking ladder and ran off and, apparently, found themselves a superhero chess club for defense." I felt like I was rambling a little, but it seemed justified under the circumstances. "You guys are doing great, by the way. Nice little chess trap here, dangling your queen so I'd take the bait and then putting all your pieces in position. You win. If I'm a bad guy looking for Jimmy and Suki, you got me. But I'm not, and if you call Jimmy's dad, he'll confirm."

"I got this, Joey," the girl said.

"Yeah, Madison?"

"Yeah." She had put away the Mace, probably in a coat pocket since she wasn't carrying a purse. Now she was wielding a phone. "I'm looking at this Runyon guy's photo online."

"I'm looking at his website," Joey answered.

"Which could be fake," she said, sighing. "Anyway, he's been in the news, so that's where I am looking. Shot a kid in the fall. So, news photos along with his website photo gives us more data, which is always good, right?"

Joey let out a huff of foggy breath. "Don't lecture me, Maddy."

Madison smiled prettily. "Can't help myself. Anyway, this guy here really is him. Ed Runyon. He's a PI from Ambletown. I didn't know they needed private investigators in Ambletown."

"We don't get a lot of chess club ambushes there," I said, "but the Scrabble gangs are getting way out of control."

"No shit," Joey said.

"No shit," I answered.

"Well, then. Excuse me a moment." He turned away, walked a few paces, and started talking on his phone.

Madison grinned. "Kind of walked right into it, didn't you?"

"Yes," I said. "You set your trap very nicely. What the fuck is a Bad Bishop?"

"A bishop on the wrong-colored square, unable to attack any of the opponent's pieces because it is blocked by its own pawns," she said. "Kinda like you right now. Useless."

"Useless," I said. "A guy with a knife over at the Marriott didn't do as well as you guys. He might be in the hospital by now."

"You can share a room with him if you are lying to us," said the big guy with a gun. I still could not pin down the accent.

"I'm not," I said.

"He's not," Madison added. "He really is who he says he is."

Joey, the skinny guy, pulled his phone away from his head and spun around. "Jimmy says we're cool. He'll meet with you."

"Well, I'm honored."

"Doesn't mean he's going anywhere with you," Joey said. "He's got his reasons. Follow me. It's not far."

The guy with the gun put it away and smiled. "I wouldn't have shot you, you know. The threat is stronger than the execution."

"Huh?"

"Nimzowitsch."

"Who?"

"Chess grandmaster. He said a threat is stronger than its execution, meaning the threat, on a chessboard, mind you, is usually more bothersome to your opponent than actually carrying it out. Anyway, I wasn't going to really shoot you."

"That makes me feel better." Honestly, it did. Every vibe I got from these chess nuts said they were protecting the kids. I didn't know why, exactly, but I figured I'd learn that soon enough.

"Lead the way," I said.

CHAPTER THIRTY-NINE

THANK GOD MOST of the Bad Bishops had dropped off by the time we got to Joey's apartment on Lane Avenue, because the apartment made my tiny trailer in the woods look like the kind of dream cottage I might be showing empty-nesters someday if I decided getting shot at was too much of an occupational hazard.

Small couch. Small desk with a rolling chair. Standard-issue corner lamp with three bulbs and no shades. Naked light shining on naked women smiling from centerfold posters on the walls. A couple of naked guy centerfolds, too, which, honestly, I did not need to see. Stacks of books, mostly about psychology. A speaker on the desk that started playing something vaguely resembling music as soon as Joey tapped a bit on his phone screen. And a chessboard on the desk. A nice one, built of wood with drawers to hold the pieces when not in use. There was apparently a game in progress. Two kings, two pawns each. A race against time to see who could first reach the finish line and crown a pawn as a new queen.

I was about to cross a finish line, too.

"Suki? Jimmy? Come on out."

At Joey's call, a door in the rear corner opened. A kid with blue hair peeked out. That had to be Suki.

"Tell Jimmy it's OK," I said. "Really. I'm Ed Runyon. I am just here to help him."

Suki didn't say a word. They vanished, and the door closed.

"Suki and I play a lot of chess," Joey said. "Mostly online, but we've met up to play in parks or at the union. Good kid, very smart. Damned shame what they were living with—the dad, I mean. Anyway, they called me when the shooting started—well, after they got away, I mean—and I told them to meet me. They've been hiding here ever since."

"Yeah," I said. "Good of you to give the kids a shelter. I wish I'd known more about that situation, with Suki's dad, but I was looking for the other kid and knew nothing about Suki, really, other than that they played a lot of chess with Jimmy."

"They're both pretty good players." He pointed at the board. "Jimmy's going to win that pawn race. I probably should resign the game, but I'm stubborn. And I might, just might, be able to stalemate."

The kids had not emerged yet.

I counted to ten.

I never got to ten, so I don't know whether or not I would have lost my patience entirely and shoved Joey aside and kicked open the door to drag Jimmy out of there. The door opened without the help of my foot, and there he was.

Jimmy Zachman. A tired, scared version of the boy I'd seen in the pictures in his home. Taller than I'd expected, because in my mind I'd kept envisioning a helpless child. Jimmy in reality looked more mature than the Jimmy I'd been seeking. Still, his Reds T-shirt was streaked with black, and there were fresh rips in the knees of his jeans. He'd obviously been through a lot.

"I would give him fresh clothes, but I got nothing to fit," Joey said. "My roommate went home this weekend and has a younger brother, so he's bringing some stuff for both of them."

"Hi, Jimmy. I'm Ed. Your parents hired me to find you and bring you home."

"I don't want to go home," Jimmy said, although his eyes told a very different story. He was shaking.

"I think you do want to go home. And I think you should. I know some of what's going on, and I think I can help. And I have an idea why you don't want to talk to your dad."

I'm not sure I'd ever seen eyes widen so far so fast.

"Joey, can you turn that shit off?" I pointed at the speaker.

"Sorry. Habit." He tapped his phone and the wailing from the speaker stopped.

"I'm not going to judge you, Jimmy," I added quickly. "I know there is some stuff going on that your mom and dad might not understand at first, and I know it is going to be a very uncomfortable conversation when you get home. Such things are part of growing up. We can talk about that some. But here's the thing, Jimmy. I looked both of your parents in the eyes. I heard the love in their voices. I think it's going to be OK. Really."

No answer from Jimmy.

I sighed. "You got into a conversation online, right?"

He ignored that.

"With a guy," I said.

He ignored that, too.

I still wasn't sure who knew what or how much of Jimmy's secret I should spill, but Joey spoke up. "We've talked about it," he said. "Everyone here knows what is going on."

I sighed. "So, I think this is all going to work out, Jimmy. I really do."

Jimmy looked doubtful. Then he took a deep breath and looked me right in the eye.

"Yeah," he said. "I messed up. I messed up big-time. I trusted a guy, I showed him some . . . things I should not have showed him.

Now he's saying he'll show everyone else. My dad, my mom . . ." He swallowed. "I'm just trying to deal with all that."

"And I want to help you deal with it," I said. "You are not the first teenage boy who messed up, I guarantee you," I said. "I'll help Suki, too. I can't imagine what they're going through, the shooting and everything."

"I didn't know that would happen!" That was Suki, still behind the door, but obviously eavesdropping. I'd have listened in if my frightened friend who was being blackmailed was talking to a PI, too.

"Come on out, Suki," I said. "Is there anyone, an aunt, uncle, cousin, friend? Anyone who can take you in, give you a safe place to stay?"

Suki popped out to stand by Jimmy. They were a head shorter than Jimmy, and plump. Their clothing was in disarray, too, and it looked as though they'd been wearing the same outfit for maybe a week. Their T-shirt featured some sort of demonic cat, cartoonish and frightening at the same time. The cat's tongue was dangling to his knees, and the weird creature was surrounded by lettering I assumed to be Japanese. "My cousin Matt, in California. I can go to stay with Matt, if I can afford to get there. He'll let me stay with him. He's awesome."

"Good," I said, much relieved.

Jimmy took a deep breath and looked at me. I would describe his expression as determined. "I am not going with you," he said.

I shook my head. "Don't be that way, Jimmy. Your parents are worried sick."

"Not as worried as they'll be if they find out what I did." He stared at the floor. "What I am."

I stepped toward him, slowly, and put a hand on his shoulder. "I think maybe you are underestimating them," I said. "I know your dad has some particular views, but I don't think he's going to disown you or ground you for life or beat you with a belt or anything."

The boy looked up at me with wet eyes. "I am not worried about any of that."

"What are you worried about?"

He tried to speak, then swallowed his words. This happened three times before he finally got something out more coherent than sobs. "They'll believe I'm going to hell," he said quietly.

I did not know how to answer that.

"They're worried now, I know," Jimmy said. "But anything that happens to me on Earth won't be as bad as going to hell. That's eternal. That's what my dad believes."

I did not know how to answer that, either. Suddenly, all of Bob's theology stuff seemed way more relevant than his secret coffee klatches with atheists. This was a real-world impact, a genuine consequence in a young man's life, and Bob probably was oblivious to it.

Jimmy lifted his chin and put on a brave face. "I'd rather they think I vanished or got shot than have them find out I'm gay. I can't let that happen. I won't let that happen."

I paced. "Look, I don't think hell works that way."

"Neither do I," the boy said. "But Dad believes it. Maybe not Mom. But Dad does. That's the part that matters. It will break Dad's heart if he finds out I'm gay, whether he is right about hell or not; and if Dad's heart breaks, so does Mom's, whatever she believes."

I shook my head. "Jimmy, they are in hell right now, not knowing what happened to you."

"I'll let them know I'm OK, once I come up with a plan," he said. "I need a plausible story, that's all. I don't know yet. I'm still figuring all of this out. My brain is pretty much frozen by all this. I just need to figure things out."

I was not figuring anything out and was more than a little confused. "So, wait. If you don't want me to take you home, then . . . why did you have your chess team superheroes check me out and lead me to you? I don't get it."

"Well, you are a private detective, right? So, we're hoping you can track down the blackmailer and do something about him."

I am fairly certain my jaw dropped. "Like what?" Memories of Bible Bill and his gay hooker Salvador came flooding back.

Jimmy stammered. "I . . . I don't know. Isn't there something you can do? Track the guy down, make him leave me alone, I don't know. I've never been involved in anything like this before!"

"Tracking down blackmailers is not exactly my specialty, either," I said. "And this guy is almost certainly using fake names and phone numbers. He could be anywhere in the world, Jimmy. But don't lose hope. There may be a way out of all that."

The boy's eyes went even wider than before. "Like what?"

"Well," I said. "Maybe. Just maybe. I can contact a guy, a very good hacker, who might be able to help us."

His eyes lit up. "Great!"

"But," I said, "I'm not going to do that until you are safe and on your way home."

"But if the hacker can stop him, then I can go home and Mom and Dad will never have to know. All I need to do is come up with an explanation for why I ran off."

"And why you stole from your mom," Suki added.

"Yeah," Jimmy said, sighing.

I jumped in. "You did that to pay the blackmailer, right?"

"Yeah," Jimmy said, with another sigh.

I sighed, too. "Jimmy, I guess I don't really care what you tell your parents, although in my experience a painful truth now is better than a much more painful truth later once you get caught in the lies.

You tell them what you will, but I advise coming clean. Whatever you decide, though, I'm not leaving you here and letting your parents worry and letting you get out of my sight again. I'll contact the hacker. His name's Miguel. He hates blackmailers and it sounds like he'll be happy to stomp on this guy. But I'm not calling him unless you go home."

I wondered if this was going to be a stalemate. We stared at one another for a very long time.

I crouched a bit so our eyes would be at a level. "How are you going to eat? You can't camp here with Joey forever."

"I am going to graduate, probably," Joey said. "I'll move then."

Jimmy looked at Joey. "Do you want me to go?"

Joey shook his head. "Look, you and Suki can stay with me as long as you like. Really. I don't want you running around loose and getting into trouble. But mostly I eat cheap spaghetti and canned soup and once in a while I can scrounge up just enough money betting on chess to buy White Castles. I can't afford to feed you, and I'm not ready to be a parent." He said it gently.

I looked up at Joey. "I'm guessing you'd like to bring a girl here now and then, too?"

"Girl. Guy. I'm flexible." He grinned. "But, yeah, that's not gonna happen with kids in tow."

Jimmy was shaking his head, and his lips were pressed tight together. "No," he said, through clenched teeth. "I'm not going home yet. There has got to be another way. There has got to be."

I stood up, suddenly wishing I could just recite Jimmy's Miranda rights, clap some cuffs on him, and drag him to my truck. "Jimmy, here's how it is. You ran away from home and went to a house where people got shot dead. I don't think this is a situation where I can call your parents and say hey, Jimmy's fine but he's kind of worried about some things and so I'm not going to tell you where he is or what he's doing. That's not happening. They are worried sick. They need to see you alive and breathing and standing right in front of them so they can grab you and hold you tight and probably never, ever let go of you again, but that is your problem. My problem is I have a job to do so I need to wrap this up. You can come with me voluntarily, or I can carry you, but you're going home."

He looked at me the way he probably assesses a chessboard, analyzing things to calculate whether I could make good on my threats. I focused on not wincing from the pain in my back.

This went on for way too long before Jimmy finally spoke up. "Maybe I'm out of options."

I nodded. "Maybe home is your best option."

He thought for a while. "Are you going to tell Mom and Dad about the blackmail?"

"Not if I don't have to. As far as I'm concerned, that's your call."

That seemed to settle it, for the moment. "Can Suki come with me, for now? I don't want to leave them alone."

"Yeah," I said softly, though my head was spinning. "That's as good a plan as any, I guess. The cops are going to want to talk to both of you, though, right away. You'll need to tell them what you know about what happened. You are witnesses, you know."

"Yeah," Suki said. "Witnesses."

"We'll talk to the police, and then I'll drive you both to Ambletown. We'll call your mom and dad, Jimmy, and if they object to Suki staying with you, which I don't think they will, but if they do, then I'll find someplace nearby for Suki, someplace nice, and we'll contact this Matt in California and figure out what to do next. The important thing now is to get you both to a safe place and let everyone know you are OK. A lot of people are worried."

Jimmy nodded. Suki nodded. They looked at one another and hugged.

I looked at Joey, who shrugged. "You seem trustworthy enough," Joey said. He looked at Suki. "You trust this dude, Suki?"

"Yeah, I do, if Jimmy does."

Jimmy nodded again.

I felt like a million bucks. My first missing kid case since setting up shop as a PI, and I'd found the boy alive and well, and another kid as well. Two-for-one day. I felt so good I almost considered not charging the Zachmans, but then I remembered I had bills to pay, including some coming from the hospital. So, maybe I'd just give them a tiny discount.

"Let's go," I said. "We've got a way to walk to my truck. You two can tell me all about what you've been through. You two are either very lucky, very clever, or both."

"Both," Suki said.

"Yeah," Jimmy replied. "D&D was good prep."

The kids high-fived.

Suki went to Joey and gave him a high five, as well. "Thanks for helping me out, man."

Joey nodded. "My pleasure. Stay away from drug dealers and gunfights. And don't forget you still owe me a game. Jimmy, nice to meet you, man. I hope it all goes OK with your parents."

Jimmy looked doubtful. "I gotta work on that. Not sure it's going to work out."

"I think it will," I said. "Love conquers all, right? You know, I firmly believe that a person's theological views can adapt once they see cold, hard facts."

Joey laughed out loud. "You're not on Twitter, are you?"

"I just think Bob has probably never talked to a gay person—or even met one. Well, knowingly met one. Statistically, he met a bunch, but he may not know that. But his own son? I think that is going to make Bob think hard about some things."

I wished I felt as confident as I had tried to sound. I'd read enough of Bob Zachman's blog to know he was not real keen on the idea of homosexuality and transgender identity. I had no idea where Jimmy was on that whole spectrum, to be honest, but I was guessing it wasn't where his dad would have preferred. I was banking on Bob being so relieved to have his son home that he'd allow for some heartfelt, open discussion, but maybe bringing blue-haired Suki along would just throw gas on the fire. Bob might react badly.

I was a little pissed that such thoughts even had to be considered, but this is the world we live in these days. No safe place is guaranteed, not even for what should be a happy reunion between parents and their runaway son. Linda wasn't here to do the praying, and Tuck wasn't on hand to offer some Buddhistic perspective to ease my doubts, so I just closed my eyes for a moment and did my own praying, internally. I don't know if there really is anyone out there listening, but there might be, and I know it made me feel better to do it. What the hell. Couldn't hurt.

Someone took my hand, and I opened my eyes. "I'll pray with you," Jimmy said.

I gulped. "Thanks. Just finished. Let's go."

CHAPTER FORTY

THE SLEET FELT like it was cutting deeper furrows in my cheeks than the one a bullet had left in my back. My young companions did not seem to mind it, though.

"I paid a frat house around the corner to let me park my truck there," I said. "Not too much farther."

We were on High Street, along with dozens of students looking for hot coffee, gooey donuts, quick hookups, beer, pot, you name it. Traffic was probably lighter than usual because it was Sunday night and, this being January, classes might not even be in session. But High Street still was a fairly busy place and noisy enough that I'd decided to wait until we reached the truck to make my first call, to Jimmy's parents. Besides, my hands were cold and jammed into my fleece pockets.

I had a long list of calls to make. Detective Gutierrez would want to talk to the kids about the shootings on Indianola, of course. Detective Spears in Ambletown would appreciate knowing he could take cops off the Jimmy hunt and let them handle other police business. Jimmy's aunt deserved a call, as did Matt in California, who I hoped was not another drug dealer, and you can bet I was going to check that out before Suki went anywhere.

I wanted to call Linda, too. She'd be worried about me, and I wanted to let her know I'd succeeded. I was looking forward to hearing her say, "I knew you would." Because I knew she would.

I smelled marijuana as a couple of girls passed us going the opposite way. One of them grinned at Jimmy.

"She thought you were cute," Suki said, after the girls had passed.

"I am cute," Jimmy said. "But I am not her type."

They both laughed, and I even joined in. Some resilience in these kids, considering what they'd been through. Maybe the universe wasn't such a bad place, after all. We should all maybe listen to the kids.

Of course, one of them had stripped for a blackmailer, so . . . maybe not.

"Turn here," I said, and we headed up Fifteenth Avenue.

One frat house looks pretty much like any other to me, but I managed to remember the one where I'd left my truck. A grill was going on the porch, and I could smell bratwurst and beer. Students gathered around the heat, and on the lawn, and in the driveway. They were drinking, smoking, eating, and making out.

I saw the guy who'd taken my money earlier, when I had paid way too much to park a truck for a couple of hours, and approached him. "Thanks," I said, digging out my cash and handing him a fiver. "Had a good day, so here's a tip."

"Aw, thanks, dude, totally not necessary at all." It took him about four times longer than necessary to get all that out through the beer haze. "Wanna brew? Four coolers on the porch."

"Maybe some other time. I have to drive." I did kind of want a brew, and I felt like I'd earned it, but here I was, trying to set an example for a couple of kids.

"OK, man," the frat rat said. "Safe travels and all that good stuff." He wandered over toward a brunette, who was wandering toward a much taller fellow holding a bottle of gin and a hot dog.

I opened the truck door, then grabbed my bowling ball case and put it behind the seat. "Slide in."

Jimmy jumped in first and slid all the way over by the passenger door. "You bowl? I like to bowl."

"I like to bowl, but my friend says I suck at it." Tuck says I throw the ball down the lane way too hard to have any real control. My therapist once told me taking out my frustrations on a few bowling pins was better than breaking people's noses. I decided long ago to listen to the therapist, since I was paying her. Anyway, I throw the ball hard.

"I want to go to college," Suki said as he clambered in next.

"For the girls?" I was watching a brunette who was wearing way too little to fend off the cold.

"And the boys," Suki said. They winked at me. "But mostly because I want to learn stuff."

"That is, of course, what they want you to say." I felt pretty juvenile at that moment, and took it out on the thin coat of ice on my windshield. Once I'd scraped the glass clean, I navigated the truck past all the horny drunks and all the girls who were too young for me anyway and took up my borrowed phone to call Jimmy's parents. My phone buzzed before I could do that, though.

"Ed Runyon," I said.

"Runyon, goddamn you, Detective Nick Gutierrez. Where are you?"

"Finding Jimmy Zachman," I said. "And I did. He is safe and in my truck right now. How did you get this number?"

"I'm not stupid," he said. "Once I found out you'd skipped out of the hospital, I figured you'd borrow a phone from one of the two people in the world who liked you enough to show up there when you got shot. Jimmy's OK? Suki, too?"

"Yeah, safe and sound." I decided I liked Gutierrez. Another cop might have focused on me not being in the hospital where he'd left me, but this one seemed genuinely concerned about the kids.

"Glad to hear that. Where did you find them, and how?"

"Chess," I said. "The Royal Game. The gymnasium of the mind." I was feeling a little sassy.

"I was hoping for a more coherent answer," Gutierrez said. I explained, briefly, how I'd tracked Jimmy down and survived an ambush by the Bad Bishops.

"Jesus Christ," he said. "Well, the kids are OK. You phoned in something about a fight at a hotel. And why aren't you in the hospital?"

"Which question do you want me to answer first?"

"Fuck you. I know why you left the hospital. You had work to do, and you are exactly who Shelly Beckworth said you are. So, tell me about the hotel fight. Patrol found a little blood on a vehicle, but they did not find anyone where you said they should look. Are you fucking with us?"

"No, there was a fight. Someone jumped me, I roughed him up. I did not want to stick around, though, because I was on my way to get Jimmy and Suki."

"You said the kids are OK. Are you OK? Injured from the fight?"

"I'll be fine."

"Where are you? I want to talk to those kids. Bring them in."

"It's Sunday night, and with all due respect, I care more about the Zachmans than I do about your paperwork. I want to get Jimmy home. I was about to call the Zachmans when you called me, in fact. They don't even know their son is safe yet."

"You can call them, but we're investigating some shooting deaths, remember? I need to talk to those kids, and I need to do it now."

"You can send someone to Ambletown in the morning," I said. "That's where they will be."

"Now listen, Ed, you need to—"

I clicked off. I was starting to think I could get used to being my own boss.

"That was the cops?" Suki asked.

"Yeah," I said.

"I'll talk to them," Suki said. "I know what Dad was doing." He glanced at his phone. "Shit. Battery's dead."

"Mine, too," Jimmy said.

I sighed. "I have to ask, Suki. You knew your dad was running drugs, but you brought your friend into that situation?"

"I didn't know anyone was gonna get shot," the kid said. "Honest. Jimmy was in trouble and I just wanted to keep him safe, you know? So I went and got him. I didn't ever think anyone would come shoot up the place and kill my dad. My dad did that shit for years and didn't get shot, you know?"

"You do not sound overly broken up about your father's death," I pointed out.

"Yeah, well, we don't all get great dads." He crossed his arms across his chest.

I let the silence fill the space, figuring Suki would elaborate. The youngster did, eventually.

"He used to hit me. And left me at home by myself, sometimes for days. It just, it wasn't really ever . . . we weren't close."

"OK," I said. As a cop, I'd run into a few shitty dads. "You guys got away, though. When the shooting started."

"Yeah, we had the fire ladder and just got out of there as fast as we could. I knew Joey and the Bad Bishops would help us."

"Why didn't you call your aunt, Jimmy?"

"She would tell my parents what's going on," he said, quietly. "I don't want them to know."

Suki touched Jimmy's shoulder, and changed the subject. "I know some of the people my dad did it for, the drug runs, I mean," Suki said. "He talked to them on the phone sometimes. A guy named Zip was one. Poco, I think. Maybe Pogo, or Pongo. I'll try to remember more."

"Good," I said. "That will help the police, I'm sure."

"I won't mind putting some of those drug fuckers in jail."

"You want to talk to this cop?" My phone was buzzing. Gutierrez again.

"Yeah," Suki said.

"OK." I answered. "Stay by your phone, Detective. Suki's going to call you."

"Listen, Runyon, you tell him—"

"Suki goes by *them*, not *him*," I said. I ended the call, then gave Suki the cop's number. "You talk to the cop, but keep it down. I'm calling Jimmy's parents."

"OK." Suki plugged the charger cord into their phone.

Jimmy pleaded. "Do we have to call them now?"

"Yes," I said. "They need to know you are safe. They are terrified, and I don't blame them."

"OK." He did not sound like it was OK.

I did not want to lecture the kid, but I felt the need. "You could have saved them a lot of worry, you know. Just a call to say you were OK."

"I didn't want to talk to them," he said. "I don't want to explain."

I decided to cut Jimmy some slack and called his mom instead of his dad. I managed to get the number out of my notes before I had to merge onto I-71 North.

Jimmy glanced at me. "Can that hacker really fix this?"

"I don't know, Jimmy, but maybe. Keep in mind I'm a dumbass who gave up a steady government job just so I could start my own business without really knowing how. I definitely do not have all the answers."

"A leap into the unknown," Jimmy said, "is sometimes the only way forward."

Jimmy sounded like Tuck all of a sudden. "Um, sure," I said while listening for his mom to answer my call.

She didn't even say hello. "Have you found him? Is he OK?"

"Yes, and yes. We are in Columbus, and headed north now. I'll have him to you in about an hour."

"Oh, thank God! Thank God! Thank God! Just . . . thank God!"

"Jimmy's sitting next to me, along with a friend. I'm going to hand Jimmy my phone."

"Yes! Oh, thank God! Bob! Bob! Come here!"

Reaching across Suki, who sat next to me talking to the detective, I handed my phone to Jimmy.

"Mom?"

"Oh, thank God! Thank God! Thank God!" She was animated, loud and sobbing. I could hear her, even though I had not activated the speakerphone option. "Jimmy, my boo, are you OK?"

"Yes, Mom. I am OK. Don't call me your boo."

"Oh, thank God."

"Mom, I need to tell you—"

"Wait," she said sharply. "You can tell me all of it when you are in my arms again. OK, my boo? You don't have to explain anything now. Not anything. Your dad is coming."

That sounded like a warning, and then it hit me.

The sharp look she'd given her husband at the mention of homosexuals. Her comments about Jesus and forgiveness. Her urging Bob to stop blogging and arguing on social media.

Mom knew. Mom knew her son was gay.

Tammy Zachman might not know about the masturbation video, or the extortion threats, but she knew her son was gay, and she suspected that was why he'd run away, and she was worried about how Bob might react when he found out.

I grinned. *Moms, man.*

Bob might well shit his pants and start preaching at Jimmy, but I had a feeling Tammy was going to get between father and son and lay down some law. And I suspected that just might work. Bob was already half scared of her anyway.

My thoughts had distracted me from the phone calls, and with both kids talking in whispers beside me, I could no longer catch much anyway. So, I just drove.

Suki's call to Gutierrez ended first.

"Everything OK?"

He nodded. "Yeah. I'm not supposed to go off to California until I've given a full statement."

"We'll figure that out," I said. "It won't take you long to give your statement. I'm sorry you went through all this."

"Dad was a loser."

I decided not to pursue that line of conversation any further. "I'm sorry about what happened. And I'm damned glad you and Jimmy got out of there."

"Me, too."

We covered a mile or so in silence before I took another stab at conversation. "You have a job or anything, Suki? Or school tomorrow? Anyone we need to call?"

"I'm homeschooled." They laughed. "Sort of. I do it all on my own, really. I do all the studying—and not just the unbelievably dumb shit the school gives me, but actual real history and real science—and Dad just signed some shit now and then. Or I signed it, faking his signature."

"Wait, you are a Christian homeschooler?"

"Kind of. Mom signed me up for that, before she . . . well, a long time ago. I decided I liked being home more than going to school, so once she passed away, I just faked some signatures and pretended Dad was signing everything."

"You are kidding me, right?"

"Nah, I'm serious. I could handle the course of study, if you want to call it that, in my sleep, in way less time than they expected it to get done, anyway. Dad didn't care, and no one from the school ever checked up on me, really, as long as I got the checks sent on time. I don't think those schools are well regulated, you know?"

I shook my head. "And you don't have a job?"

"No job, but I want one."

"Maybe your cousin can hook you up in California."

"Yeah. He works at a winery. He might be able to get me a job there. That would be cool."

We got quiet, while Jimmy whispered into Tuck's phone. He was crying. I felt like an eavesdropper, and tried not to listen too much. The interstate was in pretty good shape despite the sleet, but orange and green flashing lights way ahead told me the trucks were out spreading salt and brine. The sky was starless, and I figured the weather was going to get shittier before it got better. But the truck handles such things well, so I was not too concerned.

"Bye, Mom. I love you, too."

Jimmy reached across Suki and handed me the phone. I gave it a glance. "Juice is almost gone. Suki, I need the power cord. Can you plug this in for me?"

"On it."

"Mom and Dad happy, Jimmy?"

"Yeah," he said. "Yeah."

"Good. Do me a favor, now, and call your Aunt Becky. She's worried, too."

I handed the phone back and Jimmy started tapping at the screen. Apparently, he knew the number by heart. I heard her answer. "Did you find him?"

"It's me, Jimmy."

"Oh, thank God! Are you OK?"

"Yes."

"Yes?"

"Yes. Not hurt. I'm with Suki, my friend, and we're with the detective."

I started a quiet conversation with Suki to prevent myself from further eavesdropping, and after a couple of minutes, Jimmy reached the phone to me. "She wants to talk to you."

I took it. "Hi, Becky."

"I am so thankful you found him," she said. She was crying. "Just, thank you so much."

"I'm glad it turned out fine," I said.

"Yeah. Good news is something we can all use, right?"

"Right." I had a feeling she was working up to something. I was correct.

"Listen," she said. "Um, do you think we could get together and talk some more, sometime? I mean, after Jimmy's home safe and you've had a doctor look at that ripped-up back again and all that. We could, I don't know . . ."

An image of Linda and Sam flashed in my mind. "Yeah," I said. "I'd like that."

"Yeah?"

"Yeah." I gave her my real number. "It's going to be a while before I get that phone back, though, probably, so I'll call you, soon."

"That'll be nice," she said, before ending the call.

OK, so I got shot and attacked in a parking lot and ambushed by a vicious mob of college chess players, but on the plus side, I had found the kid and I was going to get a paycheck and, apparently, at least, one date. Things were looking up. Maybe I didn't need to schedule myself for a seminar on how to sell real estate just yet.

"The fuck is this?" Suki was holding up one of my Doc Watson CDs.

"Old people music," I said. "Now shut up."

CHAPTER FORTY-ONE

"YOU BETTER BE calling me to say you killed him."

"Not yet, Poco. There are always witnesses."

"There are always excuses!"

Zip sighed. Poco was impatient and he understood why. "Poco, listen, man. I got him. I found his truck. I waited. He came back with kids, man."

"I don't give a fuck about kids, Zip." Poco was losing it.

"I know, I know. But the truck, it was parked at a party. Some kind of college frat thing. Witnesses fucking everywhere, man."

"You disappoint me. I thought I could count on you."

"You can, Poco. You know you can. Didn't I take care of that bastard Jimenez? Remember him, huh? Where is he now, Poco, huh?"

"That was then. This is now."

"OK, OK. Look. He is not going to escape. Runyon is not going to escape. We are going north, out in the middle of fucking nowhere. Just a few cars. Sooner or later . . ."

"Sooner, Zip."

"Jesus, look man, there is a truck—you know, the salt truck with the bright lights. They have the radios, man. If I just drive up by this guy and shoot him, the salt truck guy will call the patrol and then, boom, I am surrounded and on the run. This shit requires patience, Poco."

"I am out of patience."

"That's why you need me, man. I know how to do this shit. You, it has been a long time since you had to get your hands dirty, right? You sit in your home with your phone and you forget there are real problems and circumstances out here in the real world where the bullets are flying. It's been a long time for you. But I've done it before. I can do it again. I know what it's like out here. Chill."

"You chill, goddamn it. And you kill him."

"I will kill him. I can track him, OK? I will kill him. Stop worrying."

CHAPTER FORTY-TWO

We drove in silence for a few minutes. We were heading into that stretch of interstate between Columbus and Cleveland where there is very little to see even by daylight, let alone on a dark night like this. Other than the salt truck way ahead and a few sets of headlights a hundred yards or so behind me, we were alone on the northbound lanes. The southbound lanes had a bit more traffic, but not a lot.

The sleet in my headlights made it look a little like I was taking the *Millennium Falcon* into hyperspace, but so far nothing interfered with traction. No worries. This was Ohio, and I'd grown up here. I could drive in this crap.

I was in a good mood and I really wanted to play some Willie Nelson, but I did not think a couple of fifteen-year-olds would be into that and, frankly, this pair had been through enough.

In the silence and with nothing else to distract me, I thought about how quickly I'd agreed to see Becky Zachman again, and wondered why I'd done that. She was attractive, but there hadn't been any kind of spark. And, truth be told, it had been Linda's face in my mind as I'd agreed to see her. Had I agreed to make a date with Becky just to get back at Linda for going out with Sam Briggs? Was I just being petty? Was I that fucking shallow?

Did that even matter? I mean, it was just going to be coffee, right? No big deal. It didn't have to lead to anything. And if Linda was enjoying a romantic adventure, well, why couldn't I? I mean, we'd never even really agreed to be exclusive, when you got right down to it, Linda and I.

If Tuck had been with us, I'm sure he'd have offered me some sort of ethical road map. And he'd have kept expounding on it until I told him to shut the fuck up. Then we'd have talked about *Star Wars* or football. That's what friends are for.

But here I was with a couple of kids, and they had their own problems. No need to tell them mine, and Jimmy's dating scene was more messed up than mine anyway.

Oh, well. If I couldn't figure out my love life, I could at least fill my stomach.

"There are food stops off the exit up here," I said. "Are you guys hungry?"

"Hamburgers?" Suki smiled.

"Yeah, hamburgers," Jimmy chimed in. "McDonald's?"

"Wendy's?" Suki parried.

"Jesus," I muttered. "You two fight it out, otherwise we're going to whatever I see first."

Jimmy gave in, so we were bound for Wendy's. I hit the exit.

Once we had burgers and fries and Frosties, we rolled north again.

I was not eager to pursue this next line of inquiry, but I felt the situation demanded it. "So, Jimmy, I have to ask."

"Shit."

"Yeah, I know. Bum deal. You are a smart kid. How did that whole blackmail thing happen? Didn't you smell a trap?"

Jimmy looked down at his Frosty. "It started with playing chess. Just talking about stuff. This guy challenged me to a game, and I accepted. He said he was in Uruguay."

"Yeah?"

"Yeah. We played, and we talked, chatted I mean, and he seemed cool. General stuff, you know, and . . . it was someone to talk to. I don't have many people to talk to, you know. I mean, I have friends and stuff, but, no one who would understand, no one who would get how I feel. You know?"

I remained silent.

"Anyway, online chess is how I met Suki, and they are cool as fu—really cool. So, I talked to this guy. He told me about Uruguay, I told him about Ohio, we joked a lot, and we got to know each other. Or, I thought we did. We talked about all kinds of things, and . . ."

He paused.

I prompted him. "And?"

Jimmy sighed. "He hinted he had a secret. And then he said he was gay. I did not say anything at first, but . . ."

"But?"

"But we kept playing and chatting, and he said again he was gay and I said I think maybe I am, too, although I'm not sure, I guess, but I just . . ."

"It's OK," I said. "Skip ahead a bit."

Jimmy's voice was almost a whisper.

"So, he said we could talk better on Google Hangouts."

"OK."

"We started talking on Google Hangouts and then, well, he showed me a video."

"OK."

Jimmy was whispering now. I could barely hear him. "It was a . . . naked video."

"Naked?"

"Yes. He was getting out of the shower."

"OK." I was gritting my teeth at this point. I wanted to shout at Jimmy and ask him why the hell he didn't just shut down contact at this point. A chess player ought to see that trap being set up, right? But I kept my mouth shut. When I was fifteen, I did dumb things, too. I couldn't list all the ridiculously stupid places I'd taken a girl to make out when I was that age, and it was sheer dumb luck I hadn't gotten caught or gotten anyone pregnant.

So, like I said, I kept my mouth shut.

"And I trusted him, I guess, so I . . . did a video for him."

Jesus. "And then?"

"And then everything changed and he was just mean. He says I have to pay him or he was going to show that video to everyone!"

"Holy hell."

Jimmy was crying now. "He started going on and on about his sick kid and how he needed money to buy medicine and he didn't want to hurt me but he wouldn't have to hurt me if I would just help him."

"How much money did he want?"

"I sent him a hundred dollars."

"How did you do that?"

"Amazon cards. I spent a hundred bucks on Amazon cards, and scratched them off and gave him the numbers. That was his idea."

"Damn."

"Yeah. I thought he'd leave me alone after that, but he didn't."

Of course, he didn't, I thought. Why would he? It's not like he was going to become a decent human being all of a sudden.

"You sent him more?"

"Yeah." I could barely hear him.

"You got that money from your mom's purse, didn't you?"

"Yes," he said, as quietly as I'd always imagined an admission in a confessional to be, not that I knew anything about that. "I wasn't going to do that, but he just kept pressuring me."

"How?"

"Text messages, mostly."

"He had your number?"

Jimmy nodded. "I gave it to him, when I thought he was nice."

"I see."

"He messaged me over and over. I blocked the number, and he'd just get a new number and message me again. It was all the time." Jimmy was sobbing again. "All the time, and I wanted it to stop. I knew it would be bad if he sent that video to anyone, my mom and dad would see it, it would be horrible, so I took Mom's money. I'm very sorry about that."

"I know you are," I said.

"That was wrong of me."

He was shaking now.

"Well, you were scared."

"Yes," he said, gasping for breath. "Still am."

"After you took that money, what happened?"

He sucked snot up into his nose, and reached for a napkin. After wiping, he said, "I bought more gift cards for him."

"Damn. How much did you spend?"

"All of it."

"Seven hundred dollars?"

Jimmy nodded his head. "He just wanted more money and kept right on threatening me. All the time. I didn't know what to do."

"Did the clerks at the stores wonder why the fuck you were spending so much money on gift cards?"

"Yeah, actually. I just said they were prizes for a church raffle."

"Really?"

"Yeah."

I shook my head. "And then what?"

"He just wanted more money, and I realized there was no reason at all for him to stop asking me for money." Jimmy sucked up a lot of snot, then let out a deep breath. "So, I told Suki I needed help."

"You called Suki?"

"Chess chat," Jimmy said.

"Yeah, chess chat," Suki said. "Jimmy told me what was going on. I was like, what? But Jimmy is my friend. So I decided to help, you know, any way I could. I stole my dad's car and went and got him." Suki seemed proud of that.

"You stole your dad's car? Do you have a license?"

"What are you, a cop?"

"Not anymore. Do you have a license?"

"No," Suki admitted. "Learner's permit. Is that really an issue right now?"

I laughed. "I guess not. Chalk it up to cop reflexes. Carry on,"

Suki nodded. "Sometimes Dad would take me somewhere and he'd get all drunk or high and I'd have to drive us home. Fucker. Anyway, that's how I learned to drive."

Jesus, I thought. *No safe place, indeed.*

"I don't know what I am going to do," Jimmy said. "My dad will hate this."

"Your dad is a big boy, Jimmy. I think he can handle this. Is the blackmailer still bugging you?"

"Yeah. Message after message after message. New numbers all the time. I answered back this morning, just hoping I could get him to stop. I told him I was trying to borrow money from a friend to pay him more. That was Suki's idea, just to get the guy off of my back. He let up, a little bit, but he thinks he is getting five hundred bucks by Friday."

I nodded. "That sounds like maybe you've bought some time, then."

"With the blackmailer, maybe," Jimmy said. "I have no idea what to do about Dad. His own boy, bound for hell? That will kill him."

Jesus, I thought. *This poor kid. This poor family.*

I had entertained some silly notions of staying out of the family drama, but Jimmy's situation didn't just tug at my heartstrings, as they say. This kid's plight had thrown a goddamn grappling hook into a ventricle and was now pulling my heart and my whole cardiovascular system right out of me. I spent the next mile trying to decide what the hell to do.

After the devil on one shoulder and the angel on the other failed to find consensus, I decided to do what I was hired to do. I wasn't a counselor, and I wasn't a clergyman. I was a PI, and I was hired to find Jimmy Zachman and bring him home safe. So that's what I was going to do. Bob could work out his theological demons on his own.

"Jimmy. Did you tell your parents about this, all this extortion stuff, just now, on the phone?"

"No. Mom sounded like she knew something, though? Maybe? She's smarter than Dad thinks she is."

"OK." My mind was racing. "Tell Mom first. Away from Dad. Tell her. She'll protect you." I'd seen the looks she'd directed at Bob. I was convinced she already knew her son was gay. And I had little doubt that Bob would fold like an umbrella if she got in his face.

"OK."

"In the meantime, I'm going to call the hacker guy about this blackmail situation."

"OK." Jimmy sounded more enthusiastic this time.

"This is no guarantee," I said. "I don't know this guy. He was recommended by a friend of a friend. I have reason to trust them, but . . . if I talk to this guy and it sounds sketchy, well, it might not be the solution after all."

"I understand," Jimmy said, the enthusiasm waning.

I picked up the phone, still plugged in, and punched up the number Lana had given me. Mike the hacker. I was supposed to call him Miguel, because I was not his lover.

"Hello." Even in just two syllables, he sounded like he should be narrating a commercial for fine Portuguese wine.

"Is this Mike? I mean, Miguel?"

"Who is calling, please?"

"My name is Ed Runyon."

"Yes, Mr. Runyon. I have been expecting your call."

"So, you know I've got a young friend in trouble. Lana says you may be able to help. I'm wondering how."

"Yes. She explained to me the blackmail situation. I have experience with these motherfuckers," he said. "I know how to hurt them, and I love hurting them. They are excrement. They deserve no mercy, and I show them none. But there are no guarantees. Whether I can help or not depends on the details. It depends on some luck. It depends on how smart or stupid this person is. Is your friend still in contact with this motherfucking son of a bitch?" Miguel's thick accent made even the phrase "motherfucking son of a bitch" sound exotic. He continued. "I need some sort of channel of communication, some way to get at them. If they've gone ghost, then it may be that there is nothing I can do."

"They have been texting. Hang on, I'm with the kid. I'll ask if there is anything else." I asked.

"Just text messages, lately," Jimmy said. "Not Google Hangouts, not chess. Just texts. Different numbers all the time, but lots of them. Threats and demands."

I relayed that to Mike.

"How did they communicate before?"

"Uh, a chess app, and Google Hangouts."

"Is this shameless son of a whore still on Google Hangouts?"

I asked Jimmy. "He was as of yesterday," Jimmy said. "I checked and his account was still there. I did not talk to him. I do not know if he is still on the chess app. I blocked him there."

I shared all of that with Miguel.

"Excellent. Then there is a chance I can help," Miguel said. "If I can communicate with them, I can learn things about them. And if I can learn things about them, I can hack them."

"You are good at that, I hear."

"I am very good at that. Large, rich companies hire me to break into their sophisticated systems so they can learn how I got in and block all those entry ports. Your average extortionist? He does not have a sophisticated system. I will need very little intel before I can make him so unhappy he pisses his pants and cries on his mommy's breast."

Miguel sounded gleeful, like he was planning a child's birthday party and was going to surprise her with a pony. "This sounds good," I said.

"If I can hack them, I will delete whatever they have on their victims. Just poof. Spoiler alert. They always have other victims. This is what they do. They play online all day, they find potential victims, they betray their trust. These are the scum of the worst people."

"Yeah," I said. "I'm not a fan."

Miguel laughed. "But I have skills, my friend, and after I have deleted whatever they have on your young friend, I will have a little fun. Have you heard of ransomware?"

"Yeah," I said. That was a computer bug that could turn someone's data into an unreadable mess, unless they had the secret key to unlock it, and they had to pay a ransom to get that key. "I have heard of ransomware."

Miguel laughed. "If I can hack him, I can make him fall to his knees and make him wish I had simply deleted the pictures and videos he uses to extort people. I will wipe his entire system clean. And by that, I mean turn his computers and his phone into useless junk. And then I will be the cat, playing with a mouse, and he will be very,

very sorry he decided to prey on kids. It will be as though the guts of his phone melted, his computer system burnt to a crisp. I will turn every device he uses to hurt people into a goddamned fucking paperweight."

Miguel sounded like he could not wait to get started.

"What's this going to cost? That might be a problem."

"No no no," Miguel said. "You do not understand. Did Lana not tell you? Once upon a time, I knew a young man, a sweet boy, very close to me, who fell prey to those people. He put a gun to his head. Thank God someone found him before he could pull the trigger."

"Shit," I said.

Miguel inhaled sharply. "The boy is OK now, mostly. He is still coping, trying to get past what they did to him, but he is doing better. I hate these fucking people, Mr. Runyon. I could not possibly convey to you the depth of my hatred for them. I look into my young friend's eyes, and I still see what they did to him. So, I make them pay, Mr. Runyon. This is my hobby. I will do this for free. I will take down these motherfuckers, for the sheer, unmitigated joy of it."

"You've done this before?'

"I do this all the time. There are people in Ghana and in the Philippines who would curse my name and hunt me down, if they only had means to do so. But I am a ghost. I am the wind. I am the night, dark and mysterious."

"Free sounds very reasonable. Well, then," I said. "What next?"

"I will text you an email address. Have your young friend contact me. I'll gather some details. No guarantees, but if I can help your young friend, I will do so."

"Thanks." I ended the call. "Were you able to hear enough to get the gist of that, Jimmy?"

"Yes! Can he really do that?"

"I don't know, but he was highly recommended. And he sounds like a fricking cyber Batman."

Suki chuckled. "Like Aragorn! 'You have my sword!'"

I nodded. "We'll have to talk this over with your mom, Jimmy. I mean, I think she should know if you are dealing with an international hacker, I guess. Don't you?"

"Not . . . really?"

"Really."

"OK."

The salt truck was still ahead of us. I glanced at the speedometer and realized I'd slowed down a bit, something I tend to do without noticing when I talk on the phone while driving. Linda teases me about it. She drives eighty miles an hour at all times. I decided to pass the truck and pressed a little harder on the gas pedal. I wanted to get these kids to the Zachman house and then go have myself a few celebratory beers.

I checked my rearview mirror before changing lanes. There still was a pair of headlights back there, about a hundred yards off.

I did some calculating. I'd been on the phone a while, which meant I'd been driving in grandpa mode. Why hadn't that vehicle passed me? There was some sleet, sure, but the roads were not bad.

Maybe it was a grandma behind me, just driving slow. Maybe it was someone from Florida, who had no fucking idea what sleet was and just hoped to survive the journey. Maybe it was a mobile meth lab, with a careful driver who just wanted to take it easy and not blow shit up, which is a thing that can happen when you are driving a mobile meth lab on wintry roads.

Or maybe someone was following me.

Well, then. I decided there was no reason to assume good intentions from anyone until I got Jimmy home. No need to take unnecessary chances.

I drove past the salt truck, and we all blinked a bit as the bright lights illuminated the truck cab. When I glanced in my rearview mirror, the headlights were still there.

I accelerated. So did the car behind me.

None of that proved anything, of course. It was dark. There was some sleet coming down. Maybe the car behind me was just using my truck as a beacon, an easy way to tell if there was a curve ahead. I'd done that kind of thing before myself, hoping that the driver ahead of me was familiar with the local roads. But . . .

Don't ask me why this stuff suddenly popped up in my mind. Maybe I would have noticed things sooner had I not been laser-focused on finding Jimmy. Now that I'd found my quarry, some dots were starting to connect in my brain. Tuck says brains are melting pots. A lot of stuff goes in, interacts, and you never know when something might bubble to the top.

Anyway, I'd seen a white van in a couple of places earlier. At the time, I'd thought it was one of Gutierrez's cops, tailing me while they investigated the shootings at Suki's house. But a Columbus cop wouldn't have tailed me out of town like this. I was out of any Columbus cop's jurisdiction. So those headlights back there were not a Columbus cop.

Had Gutierrez asked another jurisdiction for help? Maybe, but why? I'd probably irritated him, but no way was I a prime suspect in whatever had happened at Suki's house. Gutierrez and his partner knew the players involved in that fiasco, and they knew I'd just stumbled into it.

I remembered the guy who had jumped me in the hotel parking lot. Maybe he hadn't been looking for spare change to buy some heroin. Maybe he'd been looking for revenge. I'd killed a man, after all. A dangerous man. Dangerous men have dangerous friends.

Gutierrez had spelled it out, but I hadn't really registered it at the time because I was focused on finding Jimmy. I'd killed a guy who was part of a lucrative drug operation. It had not been my intent to kill anyone involved in a lucrative drug operation, but I doubted any drug lords would really care about my intentions.

Shit. No safe place, indeed.

And here I was with two kids in my truck, on a lonely highway.

I smacked my forehead and wondered if maybe I was too goddamned stupid to be rescuing wayward kids.

"You OK?" That was Jimmy.

"Maybe. Hold on, you two." I sped up and took the next exit, then floored it. I wanted to put as much distance between me and the trailing vehicle as I could, because I was getting close to my home turf and I knew a couple of things. I knew, for instance, this two-lane road I was exiting onto bent to the left just ahead. And I knew there was a crossroad there. If I could reach that before the other vehicle caught up to me, well, good luck to some Columbus drug dealer trying to find me on Mifflin County back roads in the dark. Home-field advantage, goddamn it.

I reached the crossroad and turned hard to the right. That was the wrong way to go for anyone headed to Ambletown, but it was the right way to go if I wanted to shake a tail.

I slowed down, because the road followed a creek path and that meant it meandered quite a bit. And there was the sleet to deal with; no salt truck or plow had come down this road recently. They prioritize roads leading to hospitals and those that get a lot of traffic, not those that meander past a few farms and a couple of Amish households.

I glanced at my rearview mirrors. There were no headlights behind me.

Of course, I didn't really know that I'd been followed. It all could have just been paranoia on my part. But I preferred to think I had just exhibited some private eye genius.

"What the fuck was that about?" Suki's voice quivered. "You always drive like that?"

"I swerved to miss a rabbit," I said, aiming the truck eastward at the next crossroad. "And kids are not supposed to cuss."

CHAPTER FORTY-THREE

"DAMN, IT IS dark out here," Suki said. He sounded worried.

"Yeah, cloudy night, no buildings or city lights around, surrounded by trees, gets dark," I answered. "Nothing to worry about, though. I know this road very well."

Indeed, I did. We were heading east on Gossert Creek Road, with a tree-covered hill sloping above us on the left and a steep drop to the creek on our right. Not that I could really see either in the dark, but this was my stomping grounds and I knew they were there. All we could really see were the road, the guardrails, and the occasional yellow sign with a curvy arrow telling me to go to the right or the left. One sign told me to slow way down and then go left, then right, then left again. I complied.

I was pretty sure I'd left any follower behind, so now all I had to do was keep an eye out for deer or, perhaps, an Amish buggy. The Amish forego amenities like electricity and cars, but they don't let that stop them from going where they need to go. Sleety cold weather and darkness were not going to keep them homebound if a neighbor was in need or anything like that. This road, however, was not one of their main routes, so the odds of running up on one of the black buggies in the dark were reasonably low.

I started to relax. "There is a creek down there," I said. "Not much of one, really, but a nice place to hike. You two like hiking?"

I might as well have asked if they liked differential calculus, based on the silence.

"Oh, well."

I envisioned the Zachmans, hugging one another tight and praying in thanks, maybe rustling up Jimmy's favorite snacks. It gave me a warm feeling inside.

I decided to give Linda a call. She answered within seconds.

"Ed, are you OK?" Her voice was pitched a bit higher than usual, probably because she was trying not to sound overly concerned.

"Yes, and I found Jimmy. Found his friend Suki, too. We're headed to Jimmy's house."

"Did you say you found him? You are breaking up a little," she said.

"Found him," I said. "Safe and sound. A little tired, kind of worried, but safe and sound."

"Oh, thank God," Linda said. "That is wonderful. You are still breaking up some. Where are you?"

"We took a roundabout way. We're on Gossert Creek, headed toward Flyman, and then we'll go through Jodyville. So, crap signal. Sorry, I should have waited to call you."

"No, I'm glad you called. I was . . . curious and . . . well, a little concerned, of course."

"I'm OK, Linda. Really."

"Good. You are taking a long way around, aren't you? Are you planning to stop at Tuck's?"

"No, and it is Sunday night, so Tuck is closed. Which sucks, because I have earned a few beers."

"So why the long way?"

I sighed. I didn't want to mention I thought we'd been followed, and a quick glance at the rearview mirror convinced me I'd shaken the tail, anyway. No need to worry her, I decided. "I'm going to stop at the trailer, grab a couple of things before I take Jimmy home."

"I knew you'd find them, Ed. I knew it. Is your shoulder really OK?"

"Thanks. Yeah, no pain, for now," I told her, glad she hadn't asked what I was going to pick up at home because I had no fricking idea how to answer that plausibly. "I appreciate your support, Linda. I really do. Maybe we can get together and—"

I stopped talking because a flash of headlights showed up behind me. Whoever it was, they were coming too fast for this road, even without the darkness and the sleet.

"Hey," I said. "Phone's cutting out again. Gotta go." I ended the call and dropped the phone in Suki's lap. "Hold that for me." Then I stepped on the gas.

"Hang on, kids."

I told myself this was not anyone who'd followed us from the interstate. I was confident I'd shaken any followers. Most likely, this was just an idiot, maybe a drunk driver, going way too fast. I didn't want to be involved in whatever crash that maniac ended up in, though, so I put some distance between me and whoever was following. There were a few spots ahead where I could get out of the fool's way, if I could spot them in the dark.

The vehicle behind me sped up.

I took the next curve as fast as I thought my truck could handle, and did some mental math. The headlights behind me reappeared several seconds sooner than I thought they would. I could not make out any details of the vehicle. Just the headlights, staring at us like glowing monster eyes. They were accompanied by an engine growl, which I could now hear above my Ford's engine.

The fucker was getting closer.

I did a little more mental math, this time factoring in my run of recent luck, and decided the odds now probably favored a whitetail deer dashing into my headlight beams, or a dark Amish buggy suddenly looming in the road ahead.

"Heads down, you two."

"Are we being followed?"

"Heads down, I said!"

I heard two sharp thunder cracks, and something smacked my tailgate.

Gunshots. The fucker was shooting at us.

"Are those gunshots?"

"Yes, Suki! Stay down!"

I floored it, and the truck's rear tires slipped a bit on the wet road. In my head, I heard Tuck admonishing me. "Start carrying a gun again, Ed."

It was too late to take that sage advice. I was on a dark country road, with two kids and no weapons, being pursued by someone who did have a gun.

Not good.

But I had home-court advantage. I knew this country, and odds were, my pursuer did not. I ran that thought through my head a few times. It did not inspire as much confidence as I'd hoped.

Another crack of gunfire was followed by a thunk on the roof, just above my head. Jimmy screamed. Suki erupted in a series of heartfelt F-bombs.

"Suki, call 911. Give them my name, tell them we are on Gossert Creek Road . . ." I had to pause and slow down at the next bend, but I knew there was a straightaway after that. Rather, there was what passed for a straightaway in this part of Mifflin County. It was still not a good idea to drive it at high speed on a dark winter's night. It was better than getting shot, though. Maybe.

Suki fumbled with the phone. "What road?"

"Gossert Creek! Heading east toward Flyman. Call them!"

"Screen's locked!" He sounded panicked.

"2-1-1-2-5-8," I said.

Bless him, he got it on the first try. "OK, unlocked!"

I floored it while Suki called. My wheels spun a bit, then grabbed hold of the road. Snowflakes looked like fat fireflies in my headlights. Then we hit a pothole, and the whole truck bucked like a meteor had hit it. Loud thunks beneath the truck sounded like hammers.

"Fuck!" I got the truck under control while Suki yelled into my phone. "Gossert Creek! Help us!"

My mind raced. Mifflin County Sheriff's Office would currently have two cars on patrol. There probably should be more than that, if effective law enforcement was to be achieved, but budgets are budgets and taxpayers are taxpayers. If we were lucky, one of those two cars would be close by, and we'd see some flashing red and blue lights soon.

That would take a whole lot of luck, however, and I don't often have a lot of that.

As if the universe was trying to prove that point, something red flashed on my dashboard.

I was running out of gas.

Impossible. I'd filled the tank . . . shit. That pothole—or maybe a bullet. I was probably streaming gas all over the road behind me.

We weren't going to make it to Flyman Road.

Headlights loomed behind me.

My mind raced. I had no gas. I had no gun. I had no police lights flashing up ahead. All I had was two scared kids, a borrowed phone, and a fucking bowling ball.

An idea came to mind. A crazy, idiotic, no-chance-it-could-work idea. But it was all I had.

I spent about twelve seconds trying to talk myself out of it.

Another gunshot cracked behind us. The bullet smacked the tailgate with a loud metallic pop.

So, I was suddenly resolved to put my decidedly crazy plan into action. "Suki, you can drive, right?"

"Yeah." His voice was quivering, so that single word was about six syllables, mostly nervous laughter.

"Good. Look. There's an old rail bridge ahead. Around a curve. We'll go under it." I sped up.

"Yeah." Five syllables.

"I'm going to do a hard stop after we pass beneath it. You with me?" I was trying to sound really calm, like a zen master explaining proper meditation. I sounded more like a nervous gerbil.

The gas dial crept closer to the "empty" mark.

"No," Suki said. Three syllables.

"Yes. Listen. I'm putting as much distance between us and the crazy person as I can. I'm going to stop the truck, and jump out, and you are going to drive."

"There's a fucker with a gun chasing us."

"I'm going to stop him."

"Fuck!" That was Jimmy.

"No choice, guys. Look, you got out of a tight spot before, right?"

"Fuck!" Jimmy again.

"Fuck!" That was Suki. Probably nine syllables.

I adopted my stern cop voice. "We're doing this!"

I slowed for the sharp curve. The overpass loomed. I drove under it and applied the brakes. Thanks to the sleet, the truck went a good fifteen feet farther than I'd wanted and nudged up against the guardrail.

I reached behind me for the bowling ball case and jumped out. "Go go go! Until you run out of gas, then get into the woods! Follow the creek! Take the phone with you!"

The smell of gasoline told me I'd surmised correctly. The truck was leaking fuel.

Headlights from behind illuminated the underpass, and turned the leafless trees into looming skeletons. "Go!"

Suki slid behind the wheel and went.

I ducked behind the overpass pillar and pulled the bowling ball out of the case. I could hear the pursuer approaching. Headlight beams bounced up and down. Shadows did dervish dances all around me.

I lifted the bowling ball over my head and muttered a prayer. My feet wanted to slide around beneath me. My right heel found a large stone embedded in the ground, so I braced against that, like a pitcher using the rubber on the mound.

I laughed, nervously, a little in awe of my own audacity. The newspaper accounts of my death were going to be fucking hilarious. I hoped Farkas would spell my name right.

A bright blinding light rushed at me, like a Steven Spielberg special effect. I could only assume there was a vehicle behind it, and not some powerful alien spaceship. I sure as hell could not see past all the brightness.

I launched the ball. Sixteen pounds of what I hoped would be destructive fury. I could hear Tuck in my head, telling me I suck at bowling because I hurl the ball too damned hard.

I threw it really damned hard this time.

Blinded by the damned headlights, I could not see where the ball hit, but I'd aimed above the beams and I could hear the impact. I could not see the spider-web cracks, but I could hear them crawl across the glass.

The vehicle—a van, as I should have guessed, probably the same one that had haunted me before—veered hard to the right as I jumped in the other direction. Metal screeched, and something flew past my head and smacked a tree behind me. Headlight beams rolled drunkenly in the woods. Bits of guardrail tumbled in the light before hitting the ground, lying still like dead metal snakes.

The van rolled out of sight. I landed hard on my stomach, nearly knocking the wind out of me.

I waited, caught my breath, and wished I had my fucking phone.

Eventually, after thanking God a million times in my head and thinking I'd have to maybe concede a couple of theological points to Linda, I crept to the empty spot where the guardrail used to be. Down the slope, the van rested on its side, wheels toward me. Headlights brightened the tree trunks to the east, and taillights turned the westward trees red. Both flickered now and then. The van was mostly a box-shaped shadow between the lights.

I knew this spot pretty well. The van couldn't be more than a few inches from teetering over a sharp drop and plunging into Gossert Creek. I kind of wished it had.

Once upon a time, when I was a sheriff's detective, I might have radioed in to report this situation and then rushed forward to see if anyone in the van needed immediate medical attention. I might even have tried to brace the van with fallen timbers or stones to prevent any tumbling, so anyone inside could get out.

But I was a private eye now, and whoever was in the van had just tried to kill me and two kids, so I decided I didn't really care. Let the van tumble and take anyone inside it into the icy waters of Gossert Creek.

Being my own boss was great.

Snowflakes, big wet gobs, smacked my cheeks. I noticed the bullet furrow on my back was colder than the rest of me. I reached back there and my fingers came back wet and sticky. I'd probably ripped the damn wound open again, but then I had just rolled in snowy mud. Everything on me was wet and sticky. Maybe I was imagining things.

I spun around, hoping to see the flashing lights of a Mifflin County patrol car. I didn't.

Then, I heard a sharp gunshot.

I dove for cover and landed on my back behind an oak. The pain in my shoulder upon landing left no doubt about the status of my wound, but I was relatively certain I had not taken another bullet. I knew what that felt like now.

I risked a peek.

Someone in the van was climbing out of the driver's-door window, waving a gun. He was climbing vertically because the van was on its side, and it reminded me of a prairie dog popping out of a hole.

I began to wonder if I was getting delirious. And I couldn't even find my fucking bowling ball.

CHAPTER FORTY-FOUR

"No no no no no no no . . ."

"What's wrong?" Jimmy looked back at nothing but darkness beyond the faint red glow of the truck's taillights. "Why are we stopping?"

"Gas is gone." Indeed, the engine was sputtering in death throes.

Suki pulled to the side, and the truck started to tilt into a ditch. "Shit!" A hard counterclockwise twist of the wheel brought the slowing vehicle back onto the road, where Suki braked and put it in park.

Suki looked at Jimmy. "I don't think we got far enough."

"I don't see anything back there, Suki." Jimmy swallowed hard. "I don't really see anything anywhere."

"Well, we are shitting ducks right here."

"It's sitting ducks, not shitting," Jimmy said, laughing nervously. He wondered if Suki was just being silly to relieve tension.

"Well, I am literally shitting ducks right now!"

Suki's voice had gone up a couple of octaves and nearly choked itself off at the end. Jimmy decided that sounded like real fear. He opened the passenger door. "Ed said to get into the woods. Let's go!"

Once they both were out beneath the falling snowflakes, they realized it was too dark to discern any clear path. Suki used the phone's flashlight function. "Should we go up or down?"

"Down to the creek," Jimmy said. "Ed said follow the creek, so let's go down to it."

"OK."

The phone flashlight proved to be an uncertain guide, wavering back and forth and up and down as Suki stumbled and slid on the muddy ground and ducked beneath branches. Jimmy slid and dropped on his ass twice, once dropping six or seven feet before stopping with his feet against a maple trunk. Suki felt lucky just to have been able to hang onto the phone.

It seemed an eternity before they reached the creek bank, where they halted to catch their breath.

"I hate hiking," Suki said. "Just in case we ever see Ed and he asks again."

"Me, too. Where is the sheriff?"

"I dunno. I can try to call again." Suki had called 9-1-1 as Ed had instructed, and managed to blurt out what was going on and even remembered the name of Gossert Creek Road, but the call had dropped before the dispatcher could ask any more questions.

Suki tried again, but the phone indicated there was no signal available. "Well, this sucks." They showed the screen to Jimmy.

The friends stared at each other, the faint light from the phone screen illuminating wide eyes and heavy ghosts of fog as they struggled to catch their breath.

Suki's teeth chattered. "Do you think there are bears?"

"No," Jimmy said, uncertainly. "Maybe coyotes."

"Coyotes, like, as in plural?" Suki's teeth chattering grew louder.

"Well, they hunt in packs," Jimmy replied.

Suki spun around slowly, shining the phone lamp into the confusing array of trees, underbrush, and shadows. "Hunt? Did you say hunt?"

Jimmy's teeth started clacking, too. "My dad used to take me camping sometimes," he said. "Dad said wildlife is always more afraid of you than you are of them."

"I seriously fucking doubt that!"

"Shush!" Jimmy put his hand over Suki's mouth. They both got quiet, and Jimmy listened. He heard the creek lapping past below them, the branches scratching against one another in the wind, the chattering of Suki's teeth beneath his hand and his own heartbeat.

But there was something else.

Something moving through the dark tangle of woods.

It came from behind them, where they'd left Ed to fend for himself.

Jimmy crouched low, almost slipped in doing so, and removed his hand from Suki's face.

"What was that?" Suki whispered it, and seemed to have trouble getting the words out.

"I don't know," Jimmy answered, almost silently.

They heard it again. Sort of a crunch, followed by something that sounded like a rake shuffling dry leaves.

"Maybe it's Ed," Suki said, nodding hopefully.

Jimmy shook his head. "Ed would call our names. Don't you think?"

"Shit," Suki said. "The gun guy, then?"

Jimmy shook his head. "Don't know."

"Coyotes?"

"Don't know. Hush!"

They stared at each other, but they heard no more ominous sounds. Just water, woods, and wind.

Until they heard the engine noise.

"Fuck!" Suki said, way too loud.

"Shut up!" Jimmy looked back up toward the road. There was, indeed, a vehicle engine echoing through the woods.

And then he saw something else.

A flash of lightning—*no*, he thought. *Lightning isn't red.* And then it was blue. Next, he realized beams of alternating blue and red were filling the woods.

Jimmy exhaled sharply. "I think the deputies are here."

CHAPTER FORTY-FIVE

I TRIED TO control my breathing. I didn't want the shooter to hear me and discern where I had landed. But my every exhalation seemed to echo among the trees. Sounds seem to carry farther on cold Ohio nights.

I realized how lucky I'd been. I hadn't seen the gun before the shot came. Had the aim been true, I'd likely be dead right now.

But there was some karmic balance, too. Had I seen the gun first, before the shot, I might well have frozen. Even now, an image of the gun that had left a bleeding trail across my back on Indianola Avenue filled my mind. If I'd seen the shot coming, would I have shut down? Would I have stood there, quaking, gawking, while the shooter fired again, certain in the knowledge that there was no goddamned way I was going to get lucky enough to survive being shot at twice in one lifetime, let alone one week?

I'd never know if I'd have frozen or not, because that hadn't happened. I'd heard a shot, and reacted out of reflexes, and now I was still alive.

And slowly, the fight-or-flight-or-just-stand-there-and-die lizard brain in my head was yielding to rational thought.

Or delirious thought. Like I said before, blood loss is a bitch and I was certain I was leaking pretty good right now.

"Where you at, motherfucker? Come out so I can kill you!"

It was a male voice, slurring heavily. Perhaps he'd taken a blow to the head in the van's tumble. I doubted my bowling ball had shattered the windshield and clobbered him. I wasn't that lucky.

I did not answer, but I risked another peek. The van was on its side, undercarriage toward me, driver's side up. The guy cursing my name was not out of the van yet. He was lifting himself upward, through the door window, one hand to either side as the rest of him slithered like a snake out of its hole. He clutched the gun, a pistol of some kind, in his right hand, and that made his climb awkward. But he seemed spry enough, and clutching a gun wasn't going to slow him down much.

Me? I was sweating, despite the chill and the snow coming down. Salty fluid stung my eyes, and I could feel my blood-soaked shirt sticking to my back. The cold seemed to freeze the gash on my back, and I could actually feel the path of it. If I'd had a sheet of paper, I could have drawn it precisely without looking at it.

The crazy man yelled again. "Where are you, motherfucker?"

I decided to distract him, because that sounded like a better plan than letting him just climb out and shoot me. My fingers found a large stick, and I flung it into the darkness. It rattled and rustled through the tree limbs, and he raised the gun. He did not waste a shot, damn it, but he did sink down a bit into the van.

I cursed silently. That trick always worked in the movies, goddamn it.

The van guy started muttering. "Fuck, man. Where are you? I'll find you. Can't track you now, but I will find you. I will find you, you son of a bitch motherfucker son of a whore. I will find you."

I dismissed most of that as the rant of a madman, but I zeroed in on the words "can't track you now." If I lived long enough to see my truck again, I was going to have to search for a GPS tracker. The bastard probably had placed it on my truck while I was in the hospital. That would explain how he kept showing up. This, of course, was further evidence to bolster my conviction that modern technology was mostly designed just to annoy me.

I wished I had my phone, though. I wanted to call Jimmy and Suki, to make sure they were OK. I wanted to call Linda and Tuck, to talk to them again just in case this son of a bitch got out of the truck and shot me dead. I wanted to call in a fucking air strike.

But all I could do was lie there in the wet cold mud, staring alternatively between the man who wanted to kill me and the surrounding trees that were not, goddamnit, being illuminated by the shining beacons of a sheriff's patrol car. Goddamn those cheap ass voters, anyway. Mifflin County needed more deputies on the road, and they needed them right goddamn now.

The van's lights went out.

I counted six heartbeats in the darkness, then the lights came back.

I heard my attacker resuming his climb, so I risked another look. It was too dark to tell if he was bleeding, but he definitely was breathing heavily. And the shadowy bulk of the van definitely was rocking a bit. His every move made it teeter, just a bit. He was on the verge of sending it over the edge, on down through the trees and into the icy water below.

I saw his right knee come up. It would not be long now. He'd be out of the van, on the ground and mobile. He had a gun, and I did not. If he found me, I was dead.

So, I decided not to wait.

I got up, as quietly as I could. It was not as quiet as I would have hoped.

He roared. "Fucking dog! You killed my friend Adam, you motherfucker!"

I guessed Adam was the guy I'd shot on Indianola Avenue, because, well, I don't shoot so many people that it is hard to keep track.

He raised the gun and fired, snapping a branch somewhere behind me.

By the time he was halfway through the word "fucking," I was halfway to the van. By the time he got to "dog," I'd flown into a Captain Kirk–style flying kick, with both feet aimed at the van chassis. By the time he fired the gun again, the van was rolling, bouncing, and tumbling, headlights and taillights turning the woods into a bizarre nightmare light show.

I had fallen on my face. I looked behind me. I could see just enough to tell the gunman still was hanging partially out the window, and I'd been to enough accident scenes as a sheriff's detective to know what kind of mess that was going to make of him.

The truck tumbled. No more gunshots. No more shouting. Lots of crunching and thumping.

I sat down on the cold ground and prayed. I could hear the van tearing its way through the trees. It was even money whether it would rip through saplings and find the creek or butt up against a big oak and stop. But there was no doubt I could stop worrying about getting shot.

Whoever the son of a bitch was, he wasn't going to shoot anyone. Ever.

Eventually, I heard a splash, and all the noise stopped.

I think my heart rate had slowed to something near normal by the time the woods filled with red and blue flashing lights. I glanced uphill and saw headlights. The silhouetted remains of the twisted guardrails pointed at the sky.

I don't remember much after that.

CHAPTER FORTY-SIX

Tammy Zachman wrapped her arms around her son.

"You are safe at home, boo. Safe at home."

Bob was still in the living room, talking with the deputies who'd brought Jimmy home. The friend, Suki, was out there, too. Tammy was taking Jimmy to his room to change his muddy clothes and find something for Suki to wear, but Jimmy had teared up and turned to her. They stood together now, ice melting from the boy's clothes and dripping mud onto the carpet. Tammy didn't care about that. Her son was safe.

Jimmy started talking, in apologetic sobs. Tammy just listened, and before long she had at least a picture of what had happened. Jimmy told her all of it. She did not fully understand, of course, but she had the big picture.

"Oh, boo," she whispered.

"Don't tell Dad," Jimmy said.

"We have to tell him, but not now," she answered. She kissed his forehead. He had a scrape, apparently acquired after he and Suki had run into the dark woods once the truck's tank had emptied. She wiped it gently with a thumb. "Need a Band-Aid for that. And some Neosporin."

"Don't tell Dad," Jimmy pleaded.

"No, not now," his mom replied. "Not now. For now, let's just say you took the money to buy a gift for a girl, OK? Someone you met online."

"We're going to lie to him?"

Tammy inhaled sharply. "I don't like it, but yes. This is all . . . too much for our little family to handle in one night. So, we'll just go with a girl, say that's why you took my money—you are paying that back, by the way, and don't think you won't—and we'll let your dad cope with that. Then you and me, we'll come up with a strategy for easing him into the truth."

"It'll kill him," Jimmy said.

"No, it won't," she whispered. "He'll learn. I wouldn't have married him if I didn't believe that." Then she had a horrible thought. "Your friend, he's not spilling the beans out there, is he? He's not going to blurt out anything about you and this blackmailer and all that?"

"No," Jimmy said. "They're cool. They're not going to say anything."

"*They're*," Tammy repeated. "*They're*. Pronouns. I'm going to have to work on that. I'll probably slip up a few times, you know. Habit. But I'll try."

Jimmy smiled and hugged her. "It's OK. As long as you are trying."

CHAPTER FORTY-SEVEN

"I AM GETTING very tired of waking you up in hospitals, Ed." Linda gave me a swift kiss. It was a bit sisterly for my taste.

"Me, too. Jimmy and Suki, are they OK?"

"Yes," Linda said. "You did good. The kids are just fine. Scared shitless, but just fine. They have been here a couple of times, along with Jimmy's dad and mom. They might all be in the cafeteria, still. Bob likes the egg salad sandwiches. Tuck had to go back to the bar, but he's been here, too. I'm supposed to call him when you wake up."

"I'll let you know when I do." I closed my eyes again.

"You didn't get shot this time," Linda said. "Thank God."

"Indeed." I opened my eyes again. I was in the hospital in Ambletown. I'd seen these rooms plenty of times, usually asking questions of crime victims.

"You tore open the wound in your back," Linda said. "Lost blood again. Gonna have to take you shopping—you are ruining a lot of clothes." Her jaw quivered a bit, but she was holding up pretty well, I thought. She continued talking. "Got more tubes in your arm, more fluids. I told them to give you stronger pain medicine this time, something to keep you in your goddamned bed." She picked up the thing with the button to call a nurse. "The doctor in Columbus is mighty pissed, and I don't blame her."

"I found them, Linda."

"Yes, you did."

"That's all that matters." I left out the parts where I'd found them safe among friends and then dragged them back out into the world where a gunman was chasing me down for killing his drug-dealing friend. I thought that might make me look kind of bad.

"It's not all that matters," she said, choking a bit on the words. "But it's a lot. You did good. Still, you should have stayed in the hospital."

"Not sure I'd have found them if I had," I said.

"Maybe," she said. "Still."

"I'm going to nap," I said.

"Good," Linda said, squeezing my hand.

I didn't fall asleep, although I felt as though I would at any moment. Instead, my mind replayed a few of the scarier scenes from the last few days. Diving for a gun while someone took aim. Shooting the son of a bitch while his bullet carved a furrow in my back and the only sounds in the universe came from guns. A van roaring beneath the underpass, bearing down on me like a dragon emerging from its cave. Me, with a bowling ball instead of a magic sword. Headlights obliterating the darkness and everything else, then rolling away in a tumult of twisted metal and shattered glass.

Me, dropkicking a goddamned van.

As the slow-motion movie played in my head, I felt cold. I'd used up three lifetimes of luck in just the last few days. It didn't seem a sustainable way to make a living. Maybe I should stick to tailing cheating husbands, or go into real estate after all.

But I'd found the kid. Hell, I'd found two kids. That's worth some risk, in my book.

There was another bright spot, too. After getting shot in the back, I'd wondered how I might react if I stared into the abyss again. I'd wondered if I'd freeze up, if the reflexes would fail me, if I'd just shut down.

Well, I had stepped right up to death and thrown a bowling ball into its face. Take that, bastard.

If you are wondering how I felt about killing two people, well, I'd have preferred not to do that, but I had been a sniper for SWAT in Mifflin County, so I'd long ago come to grips with the idea that I might have to kill someone someday. And they both were trying to kill me, too, so I was not going to be drowning my sorrows over their demise.

I might soon be drowning my sorrows over the sudden realization that life could end very, very quickly, though. I was suddenly very fucking aware of that.

I was aware that Linda was still squeezing my hand, too.

A nurse entered the room and said, "How are we doing today?"

I opened my eyes. "I am very sleepy."

Linda stepped aside. "He's coherent, though. Been talking a little."

The nurse stepped up and started checking my pulse. "Not surprised you are sleepy. Any pain?"

"Just dull aches," I muttered, "I feel kind of high right now. What did you give me?"

"Pain relievers," she said. She was cute, a redhead with freckles, but she looked at me like I was some kind of dumbass and that, frankly, spoiled the attraction. "And muscle relaxants, so you don't move around and tear open your shoulder again. We patched up your shoulder and a bunch of scrapes. I don't know what you did, but I would not do it again. Your pulse is OK; other vitals look good. I'm going to go tell Dr. McLanan you are awake."

"OK."

The nurse left, and I looked at Linda. "My eyes are kind of blurry, so I couldn't tell. Is the nurse hot?"

She smiled. "Yeah, I guess so."

I think I smiled. It was difficult to tell. I couldn't feel my face.

I heard footsteps. "Mr. Runyon, I'm Dr. McLanan. I want to check some things."

He was black, and short, and scowling. That was all I could really discern. He made me count backward from ten. He made me count fingers he held up in front of my face. He glared at the monitors nearby and checked the connection between the IV bag and my arm. "I hear you have a habit of leaving hospitals against the advice of your doctors."

"One time is not a habit," I said, although it kind of sounded like "Undine is not a rabbit." Either way, he did not seem impressed.

"If you pull that shit on my watch, there will be hell to pay."

"Got nowhere I have to be now."

"You have to pee now? We'll get you some help with that."

"No, I mean, well, yeah."

He left. Linda held my hand and some burly orderly with tattoos covering both of his arms came to help me get to the bathroom. That was kind of embarrassing, so I shan't say more.

After that, I drifted in and out of sleep. I could tell Linda was holding my hand the entire time, though, so that helped. That went on until I woke up and said something that, well, I had no idea what I said, but Linda heard it and she said, "Tammy Zachman is here, Ed. Can you talk to her?"

"Sure." I tried to will myself to alertness.

Tammy Zachman rushed forward.

"Mr. Runyon, thank God for you, and may God look after you!" She loomed over me, peering into my eyes. Then she whispered. "I made Bob go get flowers so we could talk. He'll be here soon. I wanted you to know, Jimmy told me what is going on. I mean, everything that is going on. Oh my God. Teenagers. I mean, Jesus. We called that man, Miguel, the hacker. Bob does not know. Miguel thinks he can help. But everything is going to be OK, I promise you that. Jimmy won't have to worry about Bob."

"I didn't think he would," I said, "but thanks for confirming. Tell Jimmy I want a chess game when I'm out of here." That's what I tried to say, anyway. Tammy Zachman just looked confused.

"Sure."

Bob entered with flowers, and Jimmy and Suki followed. We all engaged in a lot of happy small talk that somehow ended with me drifting back into sleep.

CHAPTER FORTY-EIGHT

MIGUEL LOOKED AT the screen and smiled, then reached for his cognac. He always drank cognac when he was playing with his prey.

The hacker always listened to music, too. Tonight, it was Corelli's *Trio Sonata Op. 2 No. 11*. Arcangelo Corelli was a frequent choice for Miguel at such moments. *Such beautiful music*, he thought. *A necessary countermelody to the sordid people I must deal with while enjoying my hobby.*

Jimmy's info had been good. The fool of an extortionist was, indeed, still using the same Google Hangouts account. What's more, he was still possibly using the chess app, though under a slightly altered username. HotBoy followed by a series of numbers. Miguel had decided to try the chess approach first, as it seemed more fun. He liked chess, and was partial to subtle openings.

Miguel had set up a chess account, and used a sweaty male model photo with his profile. Then he played two dozen games with other people, winning nineteen of them, before challenging HotBoy. He did that to establish a presence; if HotBoy examined his profile, it might put him on guard if it seemed too new.

Miguel could not be certain, at first, that this HotBoy was the same person who had been tormenting Jimmy. He needed to probe a little to determine that. But the prospects were good. The profile image was the same—a male model, naturally—and the player's opponent list included numerous common foes. Still, Miguel played it cool.

Angela called softly from the bedroom. "Oh, Mike. I am lonely."

Miguel smiled. "I'm sorry, my dear. I am working."

"I will wait," she said, in siren tones. "I am wearing the lingerie you bought me. Please do not make me wait long."

Miguel smiled again. "Oh, my temptress. I will make your wait worthwhile. Anticipation, my dear."

He was feeling anticipation himself, for the game he was about to play.

Miguel accepted a couple of open challenges left by others on the chess app. Several players were ready to start, so Miguel toggled from one game to the next and made his moves. He wanted HotBoy to see several games in progress if he checked.

Finally, the real game began.

HotBoy had accepted the challenge. Miguel had let HotBoy choose, and naturally the coward had chosen the advantage of playing the white pieces. "So be it," Miguel whispered. "I will beat you in chess, and I will beat you in life."

Miguel waited a few moves before starting the chat. "Hi," he typed. "Is that pic really U?"

He took a sip of cognac.

"Of course. Yours?"

Miguel smiled, took another sip, and responded. "U know it."

They played a couple more moves—HotBoy was already losing the initiative—before HotBoy replied with "nice pic!!!!!!"

"Yours, too," Miguel answered. The hacker was not the least bit surprised that things were already turning sexual in the chat. These bastards always wanted to get to the money as fast as possible. As far as they were concerned, foreplay was an obstacle. They always moved fast.

Then things moved faster. "U play other games?"

Miguel poured more cognac and typed again. "Like what?"

"SEXY GAMES!!!!"

That's subtle, Miguel thought, smiling. *As blunderingly transparent as your chess.* Then he typed: "Like, you mean 1 on 1 sexy talk, U and me?" There was no need to take it slow, he thought.

He got a winking emoji in reply.

Miguel decided to play dumb for a moment. "Here?????"

The chess game came to a grinding halt, but the chat continued as HotBoy suggested that a chess app chat wasn't optimum and that they might move the conversation elsewhere. *Another transparent tactic.*

Miguel sat back and took a sip, enjoying the warmth of the cognac in his throat.

HotBoy continued: "Google Hangouts is easy. We can even SEE each other!! Won't that be fun?"

"Oh, it will be fun," Miguel said aloud. He still wasn't certain this was Jimmy's tormentor, but he was damned sure he was dealing with a sextortionist. He'd take this bastard down just for fun and still go after Jimmy's guy.

Another sip of cognac, and then Miguel replied. "What's your hangout on Google?"

He got a reply right away. He checked his notes, and smiled.

It was the same Google account that had been used to target Jimmy.

"Gotcha, you smelly motherfucker!" Miguel smiled, then he typed: "Awesome. I've actually got some pics I think you will like. Go to Hangouts now?"

Another wink emoji.

"Oh, how you are going to regret this, motherfucker."

Miguel opened up his fake Google account. "I am going to have to buy more cognac."

CHAPTER FORTY-NINE

THERE WAS A knock on the doorjamb. "Ed? Detective Spears. How are you?"

I opened my eyes. "Feeling stiff, but no longer flying on pain meds."

"Good. Listen, I need to ask you some questions. Can I come in?"

"Sure. I'm not going anywhere. Dr. McLanan posted armed guards to stop me, I think."

He laughed. "Yeah, the nurses have been told to keep an eye on you." Spears walked in and pulled a chair up beside the bed. "Sure you're up to this?"

"Yeah. How is my truck?"

"Well. Big hole in the gas tank, bullet hole in the tailgate, dents up front, I hear. But it'll be OK, I guess, if you put some money into it."

"Bet you found a GPS tracker."

"Indeed, we did."

"Probably got placed on the truck when it was parked at that church," I said. "News reports, out-of-county plates, maybe I was seen driving slow past Suki's house, they pieced it together some way. Who knows?"

"Who knows? And the guy who chased you? He goes by Zip."

"Zip?"

"Yeah, these guys use code names, believe it or not. Real name is John Packwood, and he's associated with some names that Columbus PD has been looking into a long time, including the guy you killed on Indianola. You already know that guy was a drug salesman, right?"

"Yeah, cops told me that."

Spears continued. "We've been talking with Columbus, and they are pretty excited. We found Zip's phone—it did not get crunched by the rolling van like he did, just rolled around inside, so we recovered a lot of stuff—and he definitely had been tracking you. He called a certain number a lot of times, too, while he was following you, and so they're looking into that. Fellow named Poco, they tell me, kind of a ringleader and someone they really want to see wearing orange for the rest of his life. We probably are going to connect an awful lot of dots here, Ed, so I hope that makes you feel a little better about all the shit you've been through."

It kind of did, I had to admit.

"Packwood is dead, by the way," the cop continued. "Don't know if anyone told you."

"I watched the van roll down the bank with him hanging out of it," I said. "So, being a brilliant detective, I kind of put things together."

"Sure. OK. No loss there, right? Listen." He paused. "These are dangerous people, Ed."

"I don't doubt that."

"Their heads are down right now, and some are being rounded up as we speak. I know cops are moving on Poco. But we don't know how widespread this network is. There's probably others out there and, well, they are not going to just let this slide. Zip might have been chasing you because he thought you had whatever it was Charlie Boone stole, assuming that is what started this whole goddamned mess in the first place, but . . ."

"But what?"

"We think the guy you shot in Columbus is Poco's brother."

"Oh."

"Yeah," Spears said. "So, there may be a personal element to this. You need to watch your back."

"You may be right. I'll buy a couple more bowling balls, just in case."

"Now, don't be flippant, man. I'm serious."

I sighed. "I know you are, and I appreciate the warning. I'll keep my eyes open and my gun loaded. I do need another bowling ball, though."

"OK." He laughed. "You might consider a change of scenery, too."

"Why do people always want me to move?"

"You are kind of isolated, I hear. A trailer in the woods?"

"It's tiny, but quiet. And mornings by the pond are my favorite thing. I'm not moving."

"Have it your way, but be careful. Oh, by the way, Detective Gutierrez will be here soon, from Columbus PD. I'm not sure he likes you as much as I do."

"I'm not surprised."

"Gutierrez told me about an assault in a parking lot you reported? Jesus, you're a busy guy. Anyway, he said they scraped some blood off of a Toyota and we're comparing it to Packwood's blood. Jesus, we found plenty of that. Anyway, smart money says he's the perp from the hotel lot."

"Yeah, that makes sense. Tracked me with GPS, waited for me to leave the hotel."

"Probably. And it makes the personal angle more likely, if you ask me. Seems they went to a lot of trouble to track you down and try to kill you."

"Well, I didn't make that easy on them, did I?"

Spears shook his head. “Don’t joke. They might have more guys like that.”

“Maybe.”

We made small talk for a while, and then I told him I was getting sleepy and he departed.

I wasn’t really sleepy. I had a lot of things to think about. I also had to call a young lady named Marci, a young chess wizard who thought the world of Jimmy Zachman, and tell her the boy she adored was OK.

CHAPTER FIFTY

IT WAS BRAHMS tonight, the *Violin Concerto in D Major, Op. 77*. Miguel liked that one when he was feeling victorious, as he was tonight. This was an Itzhak Perlman performance, the best in Miguel's opinion.

He sipped his cognac and relished the moment.

He'd previously sent Jimmy's fool of an antagonist a video, just a short clip of gay amateur porn he'd used for similar purposes in the past. He'd embedded a link in it, and when the fool went to watch the video, he'd essentially opened the gates for Miguel.

"Mike," Angela said. She walked slowly across the carpet, silk hanging from her slender body, a vision in brunette beauty. "You are working again?"

"Yes, my dear, but not for long. I will be with you—all yours, in every way—in just a few short moments."

She bent to kiss him, and gave him a look that said he'd better not be long. Then she sauntered toward the bedroom, and he watched her. "Anticipation," he whispered to himself. Then he sighed and looked back at his screen.

Miguel had the target's IP address, and learned the fool was using an old laptop. After poking around for a while, Miguel had found an open port and a printer with a default password. "Oh, your security is shit," he whispered.

It had taken him very little time to break in. He shook his head. "John316. That's your password? Really?"

Soon, he'd created his own username on the idiot's home network and given himself complete admin privileges.

It was Miguel's network now.

The perpetrator was in Lagos, Nigeria. His name was Abeo Musa. Judging by his selfies, he was in his twenties. He had a girlfriend, and had a lot of pictures of her. Quite a beauty, but no Angela.

The criminal did not seem to have any sort of job, and didn't seem to be in school. He did have a lot of video and image files.

Jimmy had told him what to look for as far as his communications with this asshole, so it had taken Miguel almost no time to find the video of Jimmy and destroy it. Next, Miguel checked to see if there had been any USB or external drive connections, or whether the material had been shared via email or anything else. No signs of that.

Then, just for fun, Miguel accessed Abeo's chess app and made a few really bad moves on the fool's behalf. The idiot's rating was about to drop precipitously. Miguel smiled, then took another sip of cognac.

Exploring further, Miguel came to some conclusions. First, Abeo had many victims. Some were boys or men, like Jimmy, lured into traps. Others were men or women who thought they were having internet flings with U.S. soldiers or construction workers in foreign countries, who just needed a little loan to get through a rough patch of one kind or another. That was always followed by another rough patch, and then by blackmail threats once the target realized it all had been a fraud.

Miguel counted thirty-two victims altogether. That made life easier for Miguel, too. Multiple victims meant Abeo would not be able to tie the coming act of vengeance to Jimmy Zachman.

The second conclusion was that Abeo Musa was not part of a larger network. He was working alone, snatching up a few hundred dollars here, a couple thousand there. So much the better for Miguel's purposes. That meant he had only one device to destroy.

He turned up the music, closed his eyes, and listened to Perlman's masterful violin for twelve seconds. Then he returned to his work.

First, he sent a few emails from Abeo to the police in Nigeria. They were very insulting emails, expressly designed to make police officers very angry. Miguel hoped the officers would pay the son of a bitch a visit, very soon.

Then he sent some of Abeo's dirty pictures to the bastard's mom.

Next, Miguel deployed his own masterpiece, a little virus he called FuckYouAsshole. It was modeled after ransomware, but with his own personal touches. Once deployed, it would turn every file on Abeo's machine into an indecipherable mess. The cheap laptop would have only one function: When powered on, it would display a personal message from Miguel.

The message was customized, so Miguel spent a few minutes in thought deciding what he would say to Abeo Musa. Then, smiling, he typed:

"Your hold on all your victims is broken. Your machine is a brick. Your data is dust. You are a scourge on decency, a vile worm to be crushed beneath the heel of God. Repent, and pray for forgiveness. And never threaten anyone again. You are in my sights now, and I am always watching. This time, I have crushed your operation. Next time, I will crush you. —The Silver Demon."

Miguel sat back, closed his eyes, and wished he had a suit of comic book armor so he could fly to Abeo Musa's home right now and blast the bastard with laser beams. Alas, such power was not his. But he had done the next best thing.

He drained his cognac and turned up the music volume a bit more.

"Angela, my dear, I am coming for you."

CHAPTER FIFTY-ONE

My first stop after getting out of Ambletown General—several days later because Linda and nurses and cops were watching me like hawks—was the Zachman house. Jimmy and Suki were helping Bob shovel snow from the sidewalk.

"Ed! Hi!"

"How are you, Jimmy?"

He dropped his shovel, rushed forward, and gave me a high five. "Everything is good," he said. Then, in a whisper, he added: "Miguel says he turned the guy's computer into a brick. Anything on it is dead, he said, and it'll never boot again."

"Good," I whispered back. I decided to forward some of my pay for this case to Miguel. I hoped Lana could help me with that.

Suki gave me a high five, too. "Matt says I can live with him. Jimmy's parents say I can stay with them for a while, until cops are done asking me questions and all that. But then I am going to go to California and never, ever shovel snow again!"

"Great," I said. "Matt's not a druggie, right?"

"No," Suki said. "Matt is awesome."

"OK. I'm going to check on that, you know."

"Yeah. Knock yourself out."

Bob joined us by the car of my Uber driver, whom I'd left on standby. "Not sure it makes sense to shovel it, since we're going to get more," he said. "But . . ."

"But it's Ohio, and you can't bank on which way the weather is going to go," I said. "Probably good to do it now, though. Better to shovel a couple of inches twice than to shovel four inches once, maybe."

Bob shrugged. "Depends on how heavy and wet it is," he said. "Listen, Mr. Runyon . . ."

"Ed."

He smiled. "Listen, Ed, I can't tell you how much we appreciate all you did. And that you got shot and hurt and all that, well, it's just . . . we feel bad about that."

"I'll duck faster the next time someone aims a gun at me," I answered.

Bob laughed and shrugged. "Well, yes, please do that. Anyway, our church is putting together a fundraiser, nothing fancy, pancakes and sausage, but the proceeds are going to go to you, to help cover your medical bills."

"That's not necessary," I said.

"Yes, it is," he replied, staring me right in the eyes, and I decided not to argue with him.

"Thanks, Bob." I shook his hand.

I turned to Jimmy. "I want a chess game."

Suki laughed out loud. "You suck, Ed."

Jimmy grinned and shook his head. "I looked at the moves you made on the app," he said. "It's not going to be a game, but I'll give you a chess lesson."

"Probably a painful one," I said.

"Oh, yeah," Suki chimed in.

Jimmy nodded. "Yes. Learning hurts." He shrugged. "Don't I know it."

We nodded at one another, and did another high five.

"Jimmy, Suki, come here, please!" That was Jimmy's mom, calling from somewhere inside the house. Jimmy yelled, "Coming!" He took off, Suki in his wake.

Bob watched them go, and his lips quivered a bit. "I'm struggling," he said, barely getting the words out. "I just can't believe my kid stole from his mom, and spent it to buy a necklace for a girl he barely knew, and . . ."

"I'm sure it is a big adjustment," I said, while internally congratulating the young chess wizards for coming up with a cover story. I made a mental note to avoid saying anything that might blow it. I'd done my job. Reconciling all the Zachman family secrets was going to be up to them.

Bob blew out a gush of air. "Boy, is it! I don't know what's going on. I'm still not all sure what's happened—it's just all a big I don't know what."

"Talk to your kid, talk to your wife, keep praying," I said. "I think you guys will be fine."

The second place I went after getting out of the hospital was Tucker's Bar and Grill in Jodyville. I let the Uber driver go after that.

"Well, now," Tuck said, bright smile flashing. "Good to see you without tubes in your arms."

"Good to be here, but it feels like they left a few tubes or needles in my back. Give me one of those fancy IPAs like that last one you gave me. What was it? Dogfish Head? And a double cheeseburger. And fries. And another IPA."

"You got it. All on the house."

He went to arrange my order. I sat at the bar and looked around. There was a pair of longhorns stretched out across the top of the liquor shelf. That was new.

Tuck came back with my beer. "Like the new decor?" He aimed a thumb at the longhorns.

"I guess it fits in with the traffic signs and the buck's head and the trophy bass and all that. What the fuck is that?"

He grinned. "You don't recognize it?"

I looked at it. "No."

"Keep looking at it. It used to be on a shiny truck."

I took a sip of beer. It was as good as I remembered. Then I looked again at the longhorns. I had, in fact, seen them before.

"Son of a bitch," I said. "The deputy who smacked you around."

Tuck nodded. "Deputy Donnor Brogan, yep."

"That's from his truck."

"You know it." He poured himself a beer. "About all that is left of his truck."

I stared at him, as though seeing him for the very first time. "You don't say."

"Yeah. The way I hear it, somebody set the truck on fire."

"Really? Somebody?"

He just nodded and stared at me.

"And that somebody just happened to salvage the horns and drop them off here?"

He ignored me.

I emptied my glass and set it down. "Now wait a fucking minute. You didn't want me to go pound this idiot into pudding, but you went and set fire to his truck?"

He looked skyward, the way he does when he is about to get all philosophical, or write some poetry. "I admit to nothing, Ed. Still,

I feel that whoever burned up the truck is a kindred spirit, working toward a little karmic balance. I appreciate what they did."

"Whoever set the fire could have burned down his whole barn."

"Whoever started the fire must have noticed the truck was not in the barn. I hear it was parked by a field, with a bed full of fence posts. Away from the barn, away from the house." He smiled broadly. "That might have been what gave the truck arsonists the idea in the first place. A crime of opportunity, as they say."

"You are so full of shit, Tuck. You should have let me break his nose and tell him exactly why I did it."

He shook his head, sending his beads rattling. "No, no, no. A man is a living thing, Ed. Blood, flesh, and soul. One man should not harm another man. It just perpetuates violence, a dark cycle. We need to be bigger than that."

"Yeah, right. Bigger. As in truck arsonists. Pour me another beer."

He did. Then he continued. "A truck, on the other hand, is not a human being. It is an inanimate object. Just another arrangement of atoms. Soulless. In the grand scheme of things, it doesn't matter anymore what happens to a damned truck than what happens to a rock or a mud puddle."

"Gotcha. Did the Buddha tell you that?"

He winked. "I never claimed to be really good at Buddhism, you know that. You carrying a gun again?"

I lifted my Ohio State fleece to show him the shoulder holster. "You know it."

We clinked glasses. Then he brought me the best burger I'd ever had in my life.

I took a bite, chewed it thoroughly, and swallowed it. "When did you manage to do that? The arson, I mean, not the cheeseburger."

"Well," he said, "not stipulating that I did anything, mind you, but there was a window of opportunity after Linda and I dropped you off at your truck . . ."

"Linda helped you burn a fucking cop's truck?"

Tuck flashed a grin. "I plead the fifth."

"The same Linda who's always telling me to calm the fuck down and not beat the shit out of the guy who beat the shit out of you . . . you're telling me she helped you set his truck on fire?"

He shook his head. "Not saying anyone did anything, Ed. Just pointing out that, if I had decided to burn some racist asshole's truck, well, it could have happened then."

I took another bite of my burger. "Arson's a crime, you know," I said after swallowing.

"Yeah," Tuck said. "Ain't it, though. You're not a cop anymore, right? So not duty bound to report that someone, not stipulating who, mind you, burned the truck of a racist asshole you were going to beat up before you saw his angelic little girl?"

"Fuck you." I pointed at the longhorns. "Looks good up there. Adds a little class to the place."

"I thought so, too, man." He poured himself a shot of bourbon.

"Linda and Sam been back in here?"

He shook his head, swinging his beaded braids around. "This ain't really a second date kind of place, you know?"

"Tuck . . ."

He looked at me. "I think you ought to talk to her, man, not me. You know?"

"Yeah," I said. "I have a date with an atheist chick in Columbus, though."

"Yeah?"

"Yeah."

"But now that I know Linda is a vengeful arsonist, well, that's kind of hot."

Tuck laughed. "Damn, Ed, your love life . . ."

"Yeah," I said. "I know. Hey, listen, thanks for lending me the phone and the credit card and all. I really appreciate that. I'm going to need a ride to Columbus to get my phone and stuff."

"Sure. I got you," Tuck answered. "Tomorrow, OK?"

I nodded, and we settled on a time. Then things at the bar got busy and I didn't get to hear how Tuck and Linda pulled off their truck arson raid. I was sure it was going to be a hell of a story, and I was sure as hell going to ask them how they covered their tracks. Neither one of them is exactly a hardened criminal. Well, not before this, anyway.

I left before the bar closed. The streetlights of Jodyville made it easy to see until I turned down Big Black Dog Road. That was a tree-lined residential street, and most folks were asleep, so it was dark. Once I left the village limits, I had only moonlight to show the way. There was not much of that, but I had walked home from Tuck's in the dark plenty of times.

Headlights behind me made my own shadow stretch out like some wormy specter. I stepped as far off the road as I could to give the driver room to pass. Then I noticed the change in illumination and the sound of tires. The vehicle was slowing down.

It was slowing down a lot, and I suddenly remembered I had pissed off a lot of dangerous people.

It seemed to be a large vehicle, judging by the engine noise and the sound of the wheels on the cold, chip-and-tar-covered road.

I drew my gun, and ran for cover behind a tree.

The vehicle stopped. I couldn't see it, because I was shaking in my shoes behind a fat oak. But I could tell it had stopped.

Then a floodlight started questing in the woods around me, and I heard a familiar voice.

"Ed?"

I let out the huge breath I had not realized I'd been holding and stepped away from my cover. "Detective Scott Baxter, how the hell are you?"

"Fine as a pig with a new bike," the young man said, grinning. There was a blender somewhere between Baxter's brain and his mouth, and he was constantly tossing out phrases that sounded folksy but made no sense whatsoever. Actually, they made sense to him and they might even make sense to other people if he took time to explain, but nobody has time for that. All that aside, he was a good guy, and my departure from the Mifflin County Sheriff's Office had been his opportunity to move from road patrol to the detective team. It was only a team of two, but that's still a team.

I stepped toward his black Jeep Wrangler, and he turned off the floodlight and stepped out of the vehicle. "You out hunting?" He pointed toward the gun in my right hand. The look in his eyes said he knew that was not the case.

"No," I answered. "Just walking home from Tuck's. I'm not real popular in some circles and I am being extra cautious, you might say."

Baxter nodded. "That's kind of why I am here, Ed. Didn't mean to make alarms go off. I should've called you after Tuck told me you'd headed home."

"So, you're looking for me." I wondered if maybe Detective Gutierrez had decided to file some charges against me after all. Maybe Bax was here to take me in.

"Yeah, I came looking for you, Ed. Some of the stuff you've been through lately, well, that's some scary stuff, you know?"

"Yeah," I said. "I know."

"So, anyway—" he started looking around, everywhere but at my face—"I know you know that some of the guys at the SO aren't real happy with you. They feel like you screwed the pooch on Jeff Cotton, went off half-cocked, and put some fellows at risk."

"Yeah, I know. And they are right. I let that case get into my head too much, didn't handle things well. That's why I quit. So I could handle things well without involving others. If I get hurt, it's just me, not anyone else."

He looked at me. "I get that, and I respect it. And I wanted to tell you, well, there's others at the SO who respect that, too."

I wasn't sure where Bax was going with this. "You aren't trying to get me to come back to work, are you?"

He laughed. "Oh, hell no. Sheriff wouldn't have that, no way. To him, you're like eggs and wine."

"Huh?"

"A bad mix," Baxter said. "Eggs and booze don't go together, and you and the sheriff—

I waved a hand and stopped him. "Sorry, Bax. I get it. So, why are you here?"

He gulped. "Well, there's still guys at the SO who wish you well and don't want to see nothing happen to you, and we're all aware you have tangled with some rough characters and, well, they might decide to, I don't know, do something."

"I guess they might."

Bax looked at me. "Nobody wants to see you end up like that PI who got killed in a silo."

I scoffed. "Not all PIs get eaten by cats like Parker did, Bax. C'mon. I'll be OK." I was putting on a brave front, but I was keenly aware that I had just run to hide behind a tree and drawn my weapon because a car stopped on the road.

Bax nodded. "I hope so. I just want you to know we got your back, Ed. We're going to have patrols come by here, as often as we can. Some of the guys are going to be up and down Big Black Dog on their off hours, too. We'll have folks as close by as we can, as often as we can."

I nodded. Even if no one ever came to gun me down in my isolated country trailer, I figured folks in and around Jodyville wouldn't mind having a little extra law enforcement protection. If deputies were hanging close by to rush to my aid, they could rush to the aid of others just as well. "Thanks," I said. "Sheriff approve of this?"

Baxter winked. "We don't tell him everything. Anyway, you got my number, right? Anyone comes around that you don't like, call me. I'm the point man, and I'll get the cavalry coming, like dogs on biscuits."

I assumed he meant like dogs pouncing on biscuits, not dogs served on biscuits, but decided not to seek clarification. "I appreciate that, Bax. I really do." I shook his hand.

"I guess I'd better go. Got work to do," he said. "You know how that is."

"Sure do. Take care of yourself, Bax."

"You keep your eyes open, Ed. And call me if you need me."

I watched him climb into the Jeep. "Just a second, Bax."

He looked at me. "Yeah?"

My reaction to the approach of his Jeep, and the talk of dangerous people, and the dark woods surrounding us, had me thinking about how much luck I'd used up recently. Life is fucking short, and the only things of value you really have are the people you love and the time you have with them.

I looked at Bax. "Can you give me a ride?"

"Sure, but I ain't playing none of your shitty country music."

CHAPTER FIFTY-TWO

BAX DROPPED ME off, then kept going. I stood by Linda's mailbox, closed the door that kept falling open and remembered I'd promised her I'd fix that, and wished I'd made a backup plan with my chauffeur. This could end up being a very short visit, and it would be a long walk back to my trailer.

I walked across the yard and blew warm air through my chilled fingers. Smoke was curling from the chimney, so I knew she was awake. She never left a fire going while she slept.

I stood on the porch and gathered my thoughts for twenty seconds or so, then I knocked.

Next came a long wait. I started to wonder if maybe she'd peeked out the window when we'd rolled up. Maybe she knew it was me and didn't want to talk.

Maybe she had company. That would be awkward.

I had no ride and nowhere to go, though, so I just stood there waiting until she opened the door.

Finally, she did.

Linda seemed surprised, but happy, to see me, and took a little while before speaking. "What's going on?"

"Well, I came to tell you I need to break a date with a woman I met in Columbus." I looked steadily into her eyes. "And then I want to tell you why."

ACKNOWLEDGMENTS

Publishing a novel takes a considerable amount of time. I wrote a lot of this one during 2020, when most of us were staying out of public and away from the virus. Not knowing how COVID-19 was going to play out, I chose to set this novel in the Before Times, just before news of the pandemic broke.

As I write this note, the U.S. is seeing vaccines being ramped up in a major way. My wife and I and our kid have all had our second doses. We can't wait to get out and visit a bookstore.

I am hoping that the next Ed Runyon novel will be set in a post-COVID period, because everything is going to be better by the time any of you get to read it. That is my hope, anyway, as I write these words. We shall see.

So, while I take time here to thank my agent, Evan Marshall; and my publishers, Bob and Pat Gussin; and my eagle-eyed proofreader friend Tom Williams who made extremely valuable suggestions regarding this novel; and my beautiful and supportive wife, Gere; and my kid, Rowan, for all the support and help along the way, I also want to thank everyone who wore the masks without whining about it and who went to work every day because, damn it, society needed you to do that. I want to thank those who created and distributed the vaccines. I want to thank everyone who did what was needed to help us all get through that.

And by all means, let us all never forget those who did not make it through.

I also want to take a moment to thank the cops who do the job the right way. As I worked on this book about a fictional former cop in a fictional Ohio county, the nation was rocked by news of numerous deadly confrontations between police officers and citizens. I am not in the camp that sees every police officer in the worst light, and I am not in the camp that defends everything that cops do. I am in the camp that sees cops as humans with a tough, almost impossible, job, and I applaud those who do it the right way while hoping we can hold accountable the ones who should never have become cops in the first place. I am also in the camp that realizes people of color do not often see equal justice in this country, and I believe that has got to change.

I pray that someday we as a nation start to get this shit right.

PUBLISHER'S NOTE

We trust that you enjoyed *Wayward Son*, the second novel in the Ed Runyon Mystery Series.

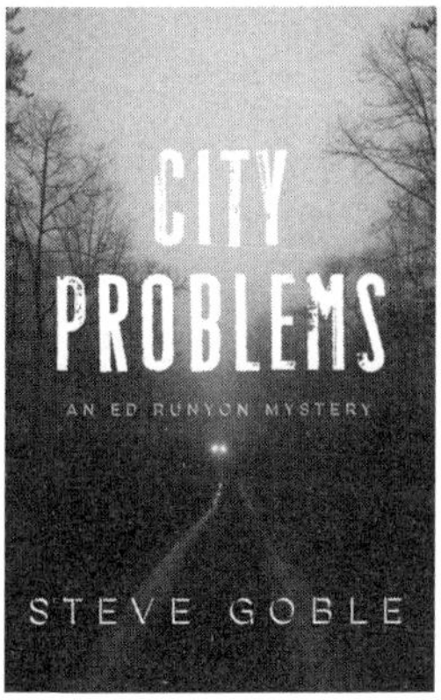

City Problems is the first book in the series and introduces Ed Runyon, a cop in rural Ohio, having relocated from New York City. A missing girl case sends his life into a dangerous downhill spiral. A moment of violence—a snap judgment—Ed's life changes to the core—leading to *Wayward Son*.

"Who would ever have thought that from the cornfields of Ohio a fresh voice in crime fiction would emerge? In this debut outing of a new series, Steve Goble delivers an authentic, compelling story of a rural cop with a haunted past. *City Problems* is both a dynamic procedural and an incisive portrait of a man at war with himself."

—William Kent Krueger,
New York Times best-selling author

We hope that you will read both the Ed Runyon mystery novels and will look forward to more to come.

If you liked Wayward Son, we would be very appreciative if you will consider leaving a review. As you probably already know, book reviews are very important to authors and Steve Goble would be very grateful.

For more information, please visit the author's website:

www.stevegoble.com

Happy Reading,
Oceanview Publishing